Long Way Home

by Ann Vaughn

This book is a work of fiction. Names, characters, places and incidents are the product of the author's imagination or are used fictitiously. Any resemblance to actual events, locales or persons, living or dead, is coincidental.

Text copyright @ 2013 Ann Vaughn

All rights reserved

Cover art by Carey Abbott
Ebookcoverdesignsbycarey.com
Spine and back cover art by Copper Rose Graphics
www.facebook.com/CRGphx

Also available by Ann Vaughn:

Finding Home

A Home for Christmas

Praise for Finding Home:

"This book was really good. I loved that it was steamier than the first. Also, characters that were in the first book were brought into this one. Be sure to read Long Way Home before this book. Ann Vaughn did an excellent job writing and has kept me wanting more from her series." ~Christine, Sinful Thoughts Book Blog

Praise for Long Way Home:

"This book will hook you from the beginning. I was laughing and crying. I was angry, and at one point I just wanted to hug Shane. Overall this is an amazing debut by author Ann Vaughn. Make sure you check it out!"
~Chelsea, Amazeballs Book Blog

For Shilpa, for all your hard work and help and texting and brainstorming and laughing and editing and all that other fun stuff!! Could not have done this without you! Good luck on your first year back to teaching after an 11-year break! You will do fine!!!!

For Cindy, who has always been the strongest person I know!

For Kym, for keeping me going and all the other great read recommendations, and a Baseball Mama shoulder to cry on!!

For Alex & Abby, never ever be afraid to go after your dreams! Love you both to the moon and back.

For Kristen Ashley, even though I've never met you…you have been an inspiration to me and it was because of you that I thought I might try my hand at the self-publishing end. Success or fail, you gave me the wind to support my wings and even though you may never see this, I just wanted to put this in writing. You are the Ultimate Rock Chick!! ROCK ON!!!!

And for Stanley, just for being you and letting me live my dreams! You have kept every promise you have ever made me and that means more to me than you will ever know. You are my rock and I love you!!!!

Table of Contents

Part One

Chapter One

Chapter Two

Chapter Three

Chapter Four

Chapter Five

Chapter Six

Chapter Seven

Chapter Eight

Part Two

Chapter Nine

Chapter Ten

Chapter Eleven

Chapter Twelve

Chapter Thirteen

Chapter Fourteen

Part Three

Chapter Fifteen

Chapter Sixteen

Chapter Seventeen

Chapter Eighteen

Chapter Nineteen

Chapter Twenty

Chapter Twenty-One

Epilogue

Part One

Chapter One

Going to Kindergarten was definitely not five-year old Shane McCanton's idea of a good time. It was summer after all; there was still fishing to do and baseball and swimming and all kinds of stuff. He knew his numbers and his letters already. He didn't see any point in having to sit in some dumb old classroom all day with a teacher and girls and books and...and girls.

He sent his mother a long-suffering glare when they found his name taped down at a table between two girls, one of whom was already sitting in her chair. He had two little sisters, didn't he get enough of girls at home? Sulking, he wondered if his teacher, Mrs. Uptmor, would let him move to where his best friend Steve Sinclair was sitting.

"Your daddy is Sheriff McCanton," the girl said to him. "I've seen you with him at Miss Nettie's."

Miss Nettie's was a restaurant in town that his great-aunt owned.

"Yeah," he said, not really looking at her.

"He is always nice to me. My mommy says she went

to school with him."

Shane shrugged. "He's the Sheriff. He's nice to everyone. 'Cept bad guys."

"He wears a gun and a star," she said.

Shane did look at her then. "He's the Sheriff," he repeated as if the wearing of a badge and a gun went right along with that explanation and she should have understood that.

"Do you ever get to shoot his gun?'

"Nah. He keeps it locked up when he gets home. But I have my own hunting rifle."

"It would be cool to shoot bad guys, don't you think?"

He gave her an odd look. She didn't talk like any girl he'd ever known.

"I don't think I'd like to shoot at people," he said after a moment, "but I think I'd like to be Sheriff one day when I'm big."

She nodded, her blonde hair swinging. "You will be...and you know what?"

"What?"

Her bright green eyes locked on his blue ones. "We're gonna get married one day. When we're big."

Now he looked at her like she'd suddenly sprouted two heads.

"You're nuts!" he exclaimed.

She shook her head. "No, I'm not. I'm Tessa. Tessa

Kelly."

"You're crazy."

"Am not."

"Oh, yes, you are!" he shouted.

"Shane Gabriel!" his mother admonished, turning her attention back to him. "What is wrong with you? Be nice."

"She's crazy, Mom. I don't want to sit by her."

"Stop it now. You be nice. I have to go, OK?"

"Just let me sit with Steve," he begged.

"Honey, just try to get along, OK?"

When she left, he scooted his chair as far from Tessa as he could and did his best to ignore her altogether. He could feel her watching him, though, and it creeped him out.

So began a pattern that held for the next several years. In their small hometown of Indian Springs, Texas, there was only one elementary school that fed into one middle school and one high school...and it usually always worked out that they were in the same class together.

Third grade was the worst. Shane did his best to keep away from her, but she constantly pestered him. She considered everything they did a competition; school work, games in PE...it drove him crazy. She criticized everything he did, too: what he wore, what he said, what he liked; nothing was off-limits.

One day, she'd been particularly hard on him. From the moment he got to school that day, she'd started in on him. His Nike baseball shirt said Bring the Heat; she said, why? so you can strike out? (he'd struck out twice in his Little League game the night before. She had been there and seen it). They'd had a spelling bee in class and as usual, it came down to the two of them. In the middle of spelling his last word, she "accidentally" stepped on his foot. He'd gotten flustered and misspelled his word. On the bus ride home she'd gloated about her victory and how easily distracted he was. He took and took her torment until finally, he'd had enough.

When they got off the bus at their stop, after the bus drove off, Shane intentionally tripped her. She fell but grabbed him as she was falling, pulling him down with her.

"You're not so tough, Shane McCanton," she taunted.

Pushed to his limit, Shane wrestled her down to the ground, pinning her arms with his knees. He glared down at her when all she did was laugh at him.

"Not so tough at all," she laughed, not the least bit intimidated by him.

Furious, he grabbed a handful of dirt, intending to grind it into her smug face. She was saved when his mother came running over to them, shouting at him.

"Shane Gabriel McCanton! Get off of her!" his mother cried, horrified. She grabbed his arm and jerked him up. "What has gotten into you? Tessa, are you all right?"

"Yes, ma'am, I'm fine."

"Shane, you apologize right this minute," his mother insisted.

"I'm not apologizing to her," he snapped. "I hate you, Tessa Kelly. You stay away from me!"

"Shane!" his mother gasped.

"I don't care if I get in trouble!" he shouted, shrugging out of his mother's hold. "I mean it, you stay away from me!"

"Go to your room right now!" his mother told him.

"Fine," he snapped, yanking his backpack off the ground and stormed off. His dad was likely to give him the whipping of his life, but just then he didn't care. He went into his room and flopped down on his bed, waiting for the worst.

Thirty minutes later, he heard his dad come into the house. Tears stung the backs of his eyes but he fought them back. He'd take whatever was coming to him. It had been worth it to finally shut Tessa Kelly up.

His door opened and both his parents stepped in. Shane sat up on his bed but didn't speak.

"You wanna tell me what happened, son?" Luke McCanton asked.

Shane shrugged. "I couldn't take any more. She's always on my case."

"Cordy says you tripped Tessa," his mother said, referring to one of his sisters.

"I just wanted her to shut up."

His parents exchanged a look. They knew of his

troubles with Tessa.

"Look, son, I know she pushes your buttons but no matter what, she's still a girl and you had no business getting physical with her," Luke admonished. "She could have been hurt, and it is never OK to hurt a girl. Do you understand?"

"Yes, sir," he replied, his eyes on his hands.

"We're going to go over to her house and you will apologize to her."

His head snapped up. "No, sir, I will not!" he exploded.

"Shane!" his mother gasped, truly appalled by his behavior.

He glanced briefly at her then back at his dad. "Whip me if you want, but I won't apologize to her. I won't," Shane insisted, "I'm not sorry. I'd be lying if I said I was."

His dad leveled him with a stern look. "I understand what you're saying, son, I do, and truth be told, if Tessa was a boy then you'd be justified, but she's not. It's never going to be all right that you lost your temper and got rough with her. How would you feel if someone did that to one of your sisters?"

Shane sighed and looked down at his hands. "Mad."

"Now do you see why I want you to apologize?"

"I guess...but Dad, she picks on me all the time! Am I supposed to just take it because she's a girl?"

Luke rubbed the back of his neck, quiet for a moment.

"Look, I'll talk to her mom. Mary and I grew up together so she'll listen to me. Maybe she can get Tessa to leave you alone from now on. How's that?"

"Do I have to apologize?"

"Don't push me, Son," Luke warned. "You're lucky I'm not gonna blister your backside over this. Push me too far and I will, understand?"

"Yes, sir."

After Shane apologized, Luke and Mary talked things over, and for the next few years they made sure that Shane and Tessa were never in the same class, which suited Shane just fine and dandy at first. But then a funny thing happened; he started realizing that he missed the drive of the competition with her. From Kindergarten through third grade, everything he'd done had revolved around beating Tessa. When she wasn't in his class to compete with every day, he found that he missed the competition.

They didn't have another class together until their senior year of high school. All through the rest of the years they would see each other in the halls but that was it. Shane got busy with school sports and cheerleaders. Tessa was busy with her sports and band. If he noticed how nicely she'd begun to fill out, he certainly didn't say. If she noticed how tall and muscular he'd gotten, she kept that to herself as well. What was the point? They were childhood enemies, forbidden to interact with each other, after all.

In high school, though, things began to change. Freshman, sophomore and junior years they would only see each other in passing. Senior year, they had three classes together and became lab partners in Biology. When the assignment of lab partners was read, a hush fell over the room, all eyes on them. Everyone knew their history, after all. In typical Tessa fashion, she ignored all the looks and began quietly gathering materials they would need for their dissection lab.

"Try not to trip her, bud," Steve teased Shane when he got up to join her.

Shane smiled but refrained from replying. When he stepped over to the lab space where Tessa was setting up, she met his gaze, direct as always.

"Are we going to have a problem, McCanton?" she asked. "Because I don't need you screwing up my GPA."

He shrugged. "I don't know. Are we? And same goes."

She regarded him a moment. "Can you handle this dissection?"

"I hunt. We process what we kill. This frog's been pumped full of formaldehyde, it's not gonna bother me."

A slight smile tugged at her lips. "A simple Yes or No would have sufficed," she teased, "but, hey, at least you're talking to me. That's an improvement."

To his consternation, he could feel heat creeping up

his neck and he rubbed the back of it to mask the blush he knew was there.

"You want to do the cutting or you want me to?" he asked.

"Knock yourself out," she replied, "I'll keep the lab sheet...look, about all that happened back then, I -"

"Let's just leave it in the past, Tess, OK?"

She nodded. "OK, sure, but I just want you to know I never meant to upset you."

He met her gaze a moment, studying her, then sighed. "I know. I'm sorry I over-reacted and I'm sorry I tripped you that day."

Tessa laughed then. "Well, I can't say I didn't deserve it. I'd been particularly brutal to you that day."

"Yeah, you were," he agreed with a smile.

"What do you say to a truce now? I've only ever wanted to be your friend."

"Yeah, OK. Truce," he agreed, offering his hand for her to shake. She took his hand then they got on with their dissection.

Chapter Two

Over the next days and weeks, Shane allowed himself to relax around Tessa and finally let a friendship begin to develop between them. Tessa was included amongst his circle of friends and he found they had a lot in common, from sports to movies and music to books and an interest in law enforcement, which he had to admit was pretty cool.

He also found himself watching her when she wasn't looking. He liked that she was sporty and not just a girly girl like his sisters, though not to say she wasn't feminine. She had really pretty long blonde hair and eyes so green at times they bordered on turquoise. He thought she smelled good, too...truth be told, he thought about her all the time. It jolted him.

At the annual town street dance to celebrate the county fair, Shane became aware the minute Tessa and her mother came into the square. He'd been dancing with Natalie Peters and looked up when he heard Tessa's laugh, causing him to miss a step and step on Natalie's foot. He'd apologized and forced himself not to look around for Tessa any more, concentrating on finishing the dance with Natalie. As soon as the song ended, however, he excused himself from the crowd. He had a feeling things with Tessa were about to change...at least he thought he might want them to, and that confused him even more. He ended up heading toward his dad's office for an escape.

"Hey, Shane," Bob, one of the deputies, greeted him.

"Hey...just need to use the restroom. Is my dad here?"

"You just missed him. He's out at the square now."

He headed back to the restroom then went into his dad's office for a bit, just to collect his thoughts. He thought maybe he should just head home. Being around Tessa like that, in a social environment maybe wasn't the smartest thing for him right now, not with the thoughts and feelings he had going on for her lately. But then he realized that he couldn't hide out here forever and decided he might as well head back out.

Shane stepped outside his dad's office to head back to the dance when something in the shadows just to the right of the front entrance caught his attention. He wasn't quite sure what it was at first, but as he turned in that direction he could tell it was the sound of someone quietly crying. When he got closer, he was stunned to see it was Tessa. She was sitting on the bench in front of Mr. Jeffries' travel agency, arms wrapped around her knees that were drawn to her chest, forehead resting on her knees. For a moment, he debated about whether he should just walk away, but as her whole body began to shake from her effort to keep her sobs quiet, he knew he couldn't.

"Tess?" he called out to her in a low, cautious tone.

Her head snapped up and a soft gasp escaped her lips. He took a couple of steps toward her before she shook her head.

"Go away, Shane," she said softly, stopping him in his tracks.

"What's wrong?"

"Nothing."

He snorted. "Yeah, no offense, but that doesn't look like nothing. What's wrong?"

"What do you care?" she snapped back.

He shook his head. "Whoa! What is it with you?" he asked, truly puzzled. "I thought we were friends now. I heard you crying. I'm just trying to be nice, but you bite my head off. That time in third grade when I tripped you aside, what have I ever done to you that has made you treat me the way you have? Because I pushed you away when we were five? I was a little butt to you, I get it. You've made me pay a thousand times for it, every day since…but I thought we were past all that."

She sighed. "I know."

"Wanna tell me why?" he asked, shoving his hands in his pockets.

"You are Shane McCanton. Even in Kindergarten, all the girls wanted to be yours; your friend, your girlfriend. Yours. I was no different."

"Yeah, you told me we were going to get married one day, when we were big. Way to freak out a five-year old boy, by the way," he chuckled, and felt a strange little fluttering in his stomach when she actually smiled slightly back at him.

"I learned my lesson. I've never brought up any of my dreams again after that day."

He cut his eyes sharply over at her. "You dreamed about me? In Kindergarten?"

She sighed. "I've always had…interesting dreams about people I know."

Not quite sure how he should reply to that, Shane chose to change the subject.

"So, why are you sitting here alone in the dark, crying?"

She raked her fingers through her long blonde hair, sweeping it away from her face to push over one shoulder.

"Steve and Stacy and some of the others were talking about me earlier. They didn't know I was there. What they said…well, I don't blame them, really. I mean, I have made a habit out of beating up on one of the town's favorite sons."

"They were saying something about you and me?" She shrugged. "Well…what did they say?"

"It's nothing. Don't worry about it."

"It's not just nothing if it made you come over here and cry. You've been a lot of things over the years, but a crier has never been one of them."

"I really don't want to talk about it," she said, standing and trying to walk past him. He reached out and placed his hand on her arm, stopping her.

"Talk to me, Tess, don't walk away."

"Shane, please," she said softly, her voice breaking slightly.

"You're always walking away. What would it hurt to stay and see what happens?"

For a moment they stood silent, each staring at the other, trying to convey in a look what the other was feeling. When the band began the opening chords of "I Cross My Heart" by George Strait, Shane's hand shifted from her arm to her hand.

"Dance with me?" he asked softly.

She sucked in a harsh breath and closed her eyes, as if his words physically hurt her. He saw a tear slip down her cheek and used that moment to pull her closer and began slowly swaying to the music with her. Tessa held herself rigid right at first, then allowed him to pull her closer, one arm around the small of her back, the other hand laced with hers, held against his chest, right over his heart.

"Stop thinking," he whispered to her, his lips close to her ear.

Tessa shivered and tried to pull away but he tightened his hold on her.

"Come on, Shane," she said, pulling her head back enough to look up into his eyes, "I'm the enemy, remember? We aren't supposed to even talk to each other, much less dance together."

He chuckled. "That was for when we were kids. I think we're both mature enough now to handle being friends, don't you?"

"Hey, so long as you don't try to rub dirt in my face again, I'm good," she said after a moment, a smile touching her lips.

Shane laughed. "You gotta admit, you would have deserved it."

"Ha!" she laughed up at him. "Never!"

He gave her hand a light squeeze. "See? This is nice. We can dance and have a conversation and even be nice to each other."

"Guess that means we've grown up, huh?" she said, and he couldn't help but notice the way her eyes were shining up at him.

"Guess so…so, what do you say we really shock the heck outta every body, and you come back to the dance with me?"

At that, Tessa missed a step in their dance. "Oh, well, I don't –"

"What's the matter, Tess? Chicken?"

She frowned at him. "I'm not chicken."

"Oh yeah? Prove it. Put your arm thru mine, walk back down there at my side and dance with me out in the open in front of everyone."

"All right. Who are you and what have you done with Shane McCanton?"

"I'm serious. Come dance with me. Out in front of everyone. Lets really give them a show and keep them guessing. What d'ya say?"

After a couple moments of silence, Tessa sighed and shrugged her shoulder. "Why the hell not?"

He winked at her. "Let's go rock everybody's world."

Tessa slipped her arm through his and together they walked back to the main square to rejoin the street dance. Shane led her directly out onto the dance floor and expertly spun her into his arms, causing her to squeal and laugh, drawing all sorts of eyes to them. Shane smiled and found that she was an easy dance partner, super light on her feet and easy to stunt with. He knew that all eyes were on them but at that point, he really didn't care. He hadn't been enjoying the dance prior to excusing himself to use the restroom at his dad's office. Now, he couldn't remember ever having such a good time at a dance.

When the band began another slow song, Shane pulled her close and led her in a two-step, squeezing her hand when she looked up into his eyes.

"Now, aren't you glad you came back with me?" he asked, keeping his voice low so she had to lean into him to hear him.

"This has been fun, I gotta admit. And I gotta give you Props…you got some serious moves, McCanton."

"Amazing what six years of cotillion will do for a guy, huh?"

"This is more than just dance lessons, my friend. I'd say you're a natural."

Before he could respond, they were bumped from the side. They each looked up to see Shane's best friend Steve Sinclair and his girlfriend Stacy Bennett dancing beside them.

"Did Hell freeze over and we missed it?" Stacy asked, eyeing Shane and Tessa skeptically.

"Yeah, man, what the hell?" Steve said.

Shane felt Tessa stiffen in his arms and wanted to curse at his best friend for putting a damper on their mood.

"We're just enjoying the dance, man," Shane replied.

"Be sure you keep your hands above her waist, there, Bud. She's got a mean left hook," Lane Reynolds laughed.

Tessa stopped dancing and flashed a bright but completely false smile at Lane, putting Shane instantly on alert.

"Would you like another demonstration, Lane?" she asked sweetly. She'd punched him their Freshman year when he'd taken one liberty too many at the Back-to-School dance.

"Relax, Tess," Shane told her, twirling her away from them, "it's just you and me out here, OK? Look at me," he coaxed when she was still glaring over at the group they'd just left. He waited until she complied and then gave her hand a squeeze, "just you and me here."

She closed her eyes a moment then nodded and looked back up into his deep blue eyes. It was a jolt, seeing them this close to her after all these years of them pretending the other didn't exist.

"Why are you being so nice to me, Shane?" she asked, genuinely puzzled. "I've certainly never deserved your kindness."

"Not when we were kids, no, but that was a long time ago. People change. I know I'm not the same person as I was back then."

She watched him cradle their joined hands close to his heart again, still extremely puzzled by his actions.

"So…are we friends now, Shane? Is that what you're saying here."

He squeezed her hand. "I thought we already were, after being lab partners and hanging out with the group all this time. I know I'd like to be. What about you?"

She tossed her head in such a way that her long blonde hair slung back over her shoulder, then cringed at the obvious flirtatious nature of the move. It was habit, but it could be misconstrued by those watching.

"Tess?" he prompted. "Do you want to be friends now?"

She smiled at him. "It's what I wanted from the very beginning. I just didn't go about it the right way."

He chuckled. "Yeah, I'd say that's the understatement of the decade. So, my study group meets tomorrow night at Miss Nettie's to go over notes for the

English Lit test. Want to come? You're the best in that class anyway. "

She bit her lip. "Will Lane be there?"

"Yeah, but I'll talk to him. He won't bother you. We could all benefit from you being there. You know that stuff inside and out."

"I'll think about it," she hedged.

"Don't wimp on me. I need to ace that test."

"Oh, please. You always do good on your tests."

"Yeah, but not without a lot of studying. Why do you think we have the study group?"

She snorted. "So you guys can hit on all the girls."

He acted wounded. "Please! When is the last time you saw me flirt with anyone?"

"Seriously? You flirt with everyone…well, except me, but we haven't exactly been on speaking terms the last ten years."

"Guess we need to make up for lost time, then," he said with a wink.

Tessa shook her head and frowned at him, missing a step in their dance.

"What's wrong?" he asked.

"I just keep waiting for the punch line."

He stopped dancing and shocked the heck out of her by cupping her face in his hands. In that moment she was acutely aware of how tall he was, how much bigger he was than her.

"I'm not pulling a prank on you, Tess. I promise."

She looked up into his eyes, her breath catching when he lightly skimmed his thumbs over her cheeks. Just when she thought he might lean in to kiss her, his mother walked up, turning his attention.

"I need you to take your sisters home, Shane," Susie McCanton said, her voice breaking the mood completely.

"Yes, ma'am, I'll be there in just a minute."

"Now, Shane Gabriel."

Shane sighed. "Yeah, OK. Do you need a ride home, Tess? I don't really want to leave you here alone."

"Um, yeah, actually, if you don't mind."

"Not at all. Let's go round up my sisters before my mom has a cow."

"I heard that, Shane Gabriel!" Susie called over her shoulder.

He shook his head as he took Tessa's hand and led her over to where he'd spotted his youngest sister, Gracie. After collecting her, he skimmed his eyes over the dance floor, finding his sister Cordy dancing with Pat Baker and felt his blood boil. He led Tessa and Gracie through the dancing couples and inserted an arm between his sister and his classmate.

"Hands off my sister, Baker," he growled. "She's a Freshman."

"Shane! Back off," Cordy snapped.

"Can't. Mom said it's time for us to head home."

Cordy glanced at her watch then scowled at her brother and Tessa. "Great. Because you had to hook up with her, I get penalized."

Tessa's brows raised. "What?"

"Hey, come on, McCanton, cut a guy a break," Pat groaned.

Shane released Tessa's hand and took a menacing step toward Pat, growling at him.

"You keep your hands off my sister and eyes in their sockets and you and I won't have any problems."

"Shane!" Cordy protested.

"Let's go."

"Fine," Cordy huffed. Gracie, having spotted the scene with Shane and Cordy had already made her way to their side. Shane nodded to his sisters to follow him, then to Tessa's shock, he laced his fingers with hers as he led them to his truck. He had a single cab truck so they all squeezed in the bench seat, Tessa beside him. She wanted badly to ask Cordy what she'd meant when she said they had to leave early because of her but Cordy was nursing a bad mood so Tessa wasn't interested in stirring her up.

When they pulled up to her house, Tessa watched Shane get out and motion for her to slide out on his side.

"Be right back," he told his sisters, then shut the door and turned to walk Tessa to her door.

"Thanks for dancing with me tonight, Tess. It was fun."

She nodded as they stood just outside the reach of her front porch light. "It was fun."

"Will you need a ride to Miss Nettie's tomorrow?"

"Um, I'm not sure."

"I don't mind picking you up if you do."

"I'll let you know.'

"OK. Don't wimp on me, all right? I expect you to be there."

"OK. Thanks for the ride."

"Any time," he answered with a wink, then turned to go.

"Good night, Shane."

He turned back to her and flashed a smile that had her heart pounding. "Night, Tess."

He watched her go inside then jogged back to his truck.

"What are you doing, Shane?" Cordy asked when he got in.

"What?" he asked, backing out of Tessa's drive.

"Are you seriously falling for Tessa Kelly?"

"You need to stay away from Pat Baker. He's got a big mouth. I wasn't trying to just be a jerk brother. I've heard him bragging in the locker room. I don't want his next story to be about you."

"Nothing happened, Shane. We were just dancing."

"Nothing does have to happen; you just have to be seen with him. Then his mouth gets the better of him and he starts telling lies. Trust me. He's no good."

"Fine, duly noted. But what about Tessa? Mom'll have a cow if you start dating her."

"I'll cross that bridge when I get to it, OK?"

Gracie spoke up for the first time. "Well, I think you and Tessa would make a great couple."

Shane and Cordy exchanged a look at their younger sister's junior high romanticism but both refrained from teasing her.

The next day in the study group at Miss Nettie's, Shane found it hard to concentrate on anything but Tessa. Her hair, her eyes...her lips. She was so pretty she took his breath away.

"What?" she asked self-consciously when she felt him staring at her.

He shook his head and looked down at his notes, embarrassed to be caught staring. "Nothing," he mumbled. "What number are we on?"

Steve elbowed him but Shane ignored him. Tessa gave him an odd look but didn't say anything. At the end of the night everyone left, but Tessa hung back to talk to Shane. She helped him clean up their tables for Miss Nettie and together they loaded the dishwasher, keeping conversation light since Miss Nettie was around.

"Oh, Tessa, honey, your mother called," Miss Nettie said as they were finishing up. "She said your dad was there and for you to call her before coming home. You can use the phone over there."

"Thank you," Tessa said, her voice small. Shane noticed that she was pale and that her hands were shaking as she reached for the phone. "Mama? Are you OK?" He heard her ask, thinking that was an odd thing for her to ask.

"Shane, will you take the trash out for me?" Miss Nettie asked, interrupting his thoughts. He gathered the bags and carried them to the dumpster. When he got back, only Miss Nettie was left in the restaurant. He said good night to her and walked out to find Tessa leaning against his truck.

"Hey, you OK?"

She raked her fingers through her hair. "Not really. My dad popping in is never a good thing."

Shane shoved his hands in his pockets to keep from reaching out to see if her hair was as silky as it looked.

"Your folks are divorced?"

"Separated and heading to divorce," she corrected. "He hasn't lived with us for a while, ever since your dad booted him out one night when he was drunk."

That brought Shane up short. "What?"

Tessa shrugged. "I guess I thought everyone knew. My dad is an alcoholic. He used to beat my mom. She took it and took it until that night when he started hitting me. She called your dad and he came in and saved us. I'm surprised he didn't tell you."

"He doesn't talk about his work much to all of us. Just my mom. Is he still there? Is your mom safe with your dad over there? Should I call my dad?"

"She called him when my dad showed up. Deputies are sitting across the street. Your dad takes care of us. They used to date. My mom and your dad. Did you know that?"

He shook his head. "No. When? In high school?"

She nodded. "They got into a fight Christmas of their freshman year at college. Your dad was off at UT and my mom was at the community college. Mom said she was insecure about him being in Austin away from her. He wasn't coming home every weekend like he'd promised and she got mad. Said it was the biggest mistake of her life. He met your mom not long after they broke up and the rest is history. I don't think she ever really got over him. Kind of pathetic, huh?"

"Your folks must have loved each other, though, right?"

"I suppose. She said he was different before he was in an accident at work when we were in the first grade. I remember he wasn't always drunk and mean. Seems like a lifetime ago, though."

"God," he managed, "you were going through all that kind of stuff when we were having our little spats at school?"

She smiled. "Don't look to excuse me, Shane. I picked on you pretty good back then."

He chuckled. "Yeah, ya did. Made my life Hell."

"Well, they don't call me Tornado Tess for nothing," she giggled. "I'm glad we can put all that behind us now. These last few weeks have been nice."

"Guess Ms. Sheldon knew what she was doing, making us lab partners."

"Guess so."

"Come on, we'll drive by your place and see if he's gone yet."

He held his hand out to her to help stand straight. She hesitated for just a brief moment then placed her hand in his. Shane gave her hand a light squeeze and stood still a moment, looking down into her eyes.

"If I never said before, your eyes are really pretty," he said softly.

She was quiet a moment, looking up into his. "So are yours," she replied.

He stood a moment longer, aching to kiss her but afraid to act. Finally, he released her hand and walked around to open the door for her.

The ride to her house was quiet but oddly comfortable. Shane realized he liked having her beside him.

"Looks like he's gone," Tessa said when they approached her house. "I don't see the Deputies, either."

"They're here," he said, pulling into her driveway, "they're in the van across the street. Stay here while I talk to them, OK?"

"That's OK, Shane, you don't -"

"Humor me. Just stay put while I make sure it's OK."

"OK."

He jogged across the street and went to the driver's side window.

"Hey, Shane," Scott, one of his dad's deputies greeted him.

"Hey. Did Mr. Kelly leave?"

"Yeah, about thirty minutes ago. You got Tessa with you?"

He nodded. "Is it safe for her to go in?"

"Yeah, he's gone. I'm here until midnight and then Brandon'll be here until Tessa leaves for school. The Sheriff doesn't like to take any chances, you know?"

"Cool. I'll let Tessa know. Thanks, Scott."

He went back to his truck and opened the door for her.

"He left about thirty minutes ago and they will have someone watching your house all night."

"OK," she said, taking a deep breath. "Thank you for finding out for me...and for bringing me home."

"Yeah, sure, no problem. Call me if he shows up again, OK? I can have my dad here in five minutes."

"I will."

They stood awkwardly in silence for a moment, neither wanting to walk away.

"You want to maybe go to a movie with me tomorrow?" he asked, surprising them both.

"OK. Sure. Why not?"

He smiled. "OK. I'll pick you up around five thirty. We can go eat first. How's that?"

"Sounds good. I'll see you in the morning."

"Yeah, OK. Good night, Tessa."

"Good night, Shane," she echoed.

He watched her walk inside then got in his truck and drove off, waving to Scott as he left. Glancing at the clock on the dash he knew he'd have to fast-talk his way out of trouble for being late but was sure they'd understand once he explained what happened.

Sure enough, both parents were waiting on the front porch when he pulled into the driveway.

"Sorry, I'm late," he said as soon as he got out. He quickly explained the situation and watched them both relax.

"Tessa and her mom have had a rough few years," his dad said.

"She said you saved her a few years ago, when her dad was beating her."

Luke shrugged. "I did my job. He'd been beating Mary for years but she would never press charges. Not until he turned on Tessa."

His mother remained quiet up until that point. She touched his cheek in a light caress but he could see in her eyes that she was upset.

"I'm glad you took her home and made sure she was safe but I don't want you to make a habit of it, OK? You don't need to get involved in the Kelly's troubles."

"Susie," Luke warned but she ignored him.

"Harrison Kelly is trouble, Luke. Shane doesn't need to get pulled into that."

"I'm taking Tessa to a movie tomorrow night," he told his mother.

"No, you're not," she countered firmly.

"I've already asked her."

"Tell her something came up. I mean it, Shane, I do not want you getting involved with that girl."

"You're being unreasonable, Susie," Luke intervened. "I talked to Mary earlier. We're filing a restraining order against Harrison. Their divorce should finally go through in another few weeks. Shane will be fine."

"I don't want my son going out with that woman's daughter!" Susie exploded. "It's bad enough I had to watch them dancing together last night, starting all the tongues wagging."

Both Shane and his father gaped at her in stunned silence. Shane thought about what Tessa said, that her mom and his dad used to date. Did his mom think his dad still cared for Mary Kelly?

"Go on in to bed, son," Luke said quietly. "Don't worry about your date. Everything will be fine."

"Luke!" Susie gasped. "Everything is not fine! I do not want Shane seeing that girl. Look at all the misery she's caused him over the years already!"

"We're not like that any more, Mom. We've both grown up. I like Tessa. She's really nice."

"So is Lauren Jenkins. Or Ivy Sinclair."

"Ivy is Gracie's age!" he countered, incredulous that she'd even bring up Steve's little sister. "And it's just a date. It's not like we're getting married."

"That's right," Luke agreed. "This is Shane and

Tessa, not me and Mary...and I married you, not her."

"But you sure do drop everything and run to her side whenever she calls."

"That's my job. You know that."

She ignored him, turning to Shane.

"Please don't do this."

"That's enough, Susie. Leave him alone. Go on to bed now, son, I mean it."

"Yes, sir. Good night."

He left them on the porch, feeling shell-shocked and two inches tall. He hated that his mom was upset with him but he didn't think it was fair for her to say he couldn't see Tessa.

"You know this really isn't about you, right?" His sister Cordelia said, surprising him. She and Gracie were sitting at the base of the stairs in the dark, having obviously been eavesdropping.

"It's because of what Miss Nettie and Mrs. Pendleton said," Gracie confirmed.

"What did they say?"

"They were talking about how you and Tessa are finally friends now and Miss Nettie said you two were a good match," Gracie, four years younger than him said.

"And Mrs. Pendleton said if the two of you started dating it would be God's way of righting the wrong Daddy and Mrs. Kelly did by not marrying each other," Cordy said.

She was just one year behind him.

"That's just stupid," Shane spit out.

His sisters nodded.

"Mom's been really edgy ever since," Gracie said.

Shane met Cordy's gaze. "I asked Tessa out for tomorrow. What do you think? Should I cancel?"

Cordy shrugged. "I can't make that call for you...but I do know that you like her and she likes you...you're only seventeen. It's not like you're getting married."

He looked to Gracie. "What do you think?"

"I think Tessa was right."

"About what?" he asked.

Her eyes twinkled as she leaned in a little closer to him. "You are going to marry her someday!"

Shane thought about the conversation with his parents and his sisters when he was on his way to pick Tessa up for their date the next night. His mother spoke very little to him that morning before he left for school and she wasn't home when he got home that afternoon. His dad stopped by as he was getting ready and told him not to worry about his mom, that she'd calm down about it soon enough. Shane felt torn, though. His mother was upset and he hated that it was because of something he was doing. Truth was he'd thought about canceling a hundred times today, but every time he saw Tessa he couldn't do it. He wanted to spend time with her, just the two of them, away from school and their friends. He wanted to know if they were just good friends or if there really was something more between them.

Tessa was sitting on her front porch swing when he pulled up. She was wearing a yellow sundress that showed off her tan and her long blonde hair hung loose over her shoulders. He sat for a moment just taking her in, and telling his heart to calm down. He couldn't help it, though; he thought she was the prettiest girl he'd ever seen.

He got out when she stood, smiling at her.

"You're late, McCanton," she admonished with a smile.

"You're beautiful," he countered.

Her smile was radiant. "You're forgiven."

He opened the truck door for her. "I'm only three minutes late, anyway," he defended. "The Miller's' cows got loose. I stopped to help Mark herd up the last two."

"Their cows always get loose. I've nearly hit one a few times out on Thistle Road."

"My dad told them they'd better get the fence fixed before someone gets killed. Any sign of your dad?"

"Not that I know of, thankfully. Was something wrong at school today? You seemed quiet."

He shook his head but kept his eyes on the road. "Just worried about that Lit test."

"Boy, are you a lousy liar! C'mon, out with it, McCanton. You were having second thoughts about tonight, admit it."

"No, I wasn't," he argued, but even to him it sounded forced.

"It's OK if you were. I would understand."

He sighed. "Look, it wasn't about you, OK? I mean, well, it was, but not like you think."

"Uh huh," she said, her green eyes locked on his profile.

"Ah Hell," he cursed, pulling over to the side of the road so he could face her. "Look, before I say anything else, I asked you out last night because I want to spend time with you. You're beautiful and smart and funny and while I'm being honest, I've probably had a thing for you since the day we met in Kindergarten."

She blinked at his honesty. Admired it.

"OK."

"Yeah. So, I want you to know that."

"But?"

He sighed and raked a frustrated hand through his dark hair.

"Not a but per se," he began.

"But?" she led with a half smile.

"OK...but...when I got home last night my parents were waiting for me."

She nodded. "I made you late. I'm sorry."

"They were fine when I explained what

happened...but then my mom was upset. She said she was glad I took you home and made sure you were safe but then she said she didn't want me spending time with you."

Tessa's eyes widened. "Oh. Wow."

He shook his head. "It isn't about you, personally. It's that you're Mary Douglas' daughter. See, Cordy and Gracie told me that Miss Nettie and Mrs. Pendleton were talking and said how if we got together it would be God fixing the mistake your mom and my dad made when they broke up. That naturally made my mom uncomfortable."

"Wow...OK, well, you should take me home."

"What? No, that's crazy."

"No, it's not. I don't want to cause problems for you with your mom. Just turn around and take me home."

"I will if that's what you really want, but it's not what I want."

"Shane...she's your mother."

"Yeah, and I love her and she loves me, but we're three months from graduation, then we're off to college and my days of living at home are numbered...my days of living in Indian Springs are numbered. I want to go into DPS and try to make Ranger. And my mom, while well meaning, has very little to say about the choices I make in my adult life. And beside all that, Tess, you're one of my best friends now. I asked you out because I want to see if we can be more. If we can, great. If we can't, that's fine, too, but I want to at least try, don't you?"

She was quiet a moment. She turned her head to gaze out the window, watching other cars fly by. When she looked back at him there were tears shining in her eyes.

"I'd like that, Shane, but your mom..."

He raised her hand to his lips, kissing her knuckles. "You let me worry about her, OK?" She nodded. "Good...now, you hungry? I thought we could go into Sorghum Mills, to one of the places there instead of staying in town. That OK with you?"

She wiped an errant tear from her cheek. "That sounds wonderful."

"Hey, there's no crying," he teased, reaching up to softly swipe his thumb across her cheek. "Everything's cool."

"I hope you're right," she replied.

"I'm always right," he countered with a wink and a laugh, putting the truck in gear and merging back onto the road.

Tessa laughed. He loved the sound of it. The rest of the drive they talked more about his plans for college and his hope to one day become a Texas Ranger.

"I thought you wanted to grow up to be Sheriff of Indian Springs like your dad. You know what everyone says. Everyone feels better with a McCanton in charge," she said when they were seated at the restaurant. It was a town saying that had been around ever since Shane's great-great-great grandfather became the first McCanton to be Sheriff of Indian Springs.

"I don't know. Maybe someday after my dad retires...but he's a long ways from that."

"Would you really want to come back?"

"Guess it would depend on what's going on in my life at that time. My dad's only 42 right now. He'll be in office another twenty-five years at least."

"My mom wants me to stay and help her run Dreams Come True and one day take it over," she said, referring to her mother's wedding service.

"Is that what you want?"

"I'm not sure. Part of me does. I enjoy planning weddings and parties and doing the decorating. But I'd like to get out of town, too. Maybe go to Austin or the DFW area. Somewhere exciting."

"What do you want to go to school for? Still journalism?"

She laughed. "No, I think I outgrew that finally. I've actually gotten interested in criminology. I don't want to be a cop like you, but a profiler maybe. Or forensics," she shrugged. "I don't know. It's a big jump from Wedding Planner to Criminal Profiler."

"You'd really like to study Criminal Justice?"

"I've thought about it. Ever since your dad saved me

that day when I was little. I've also toyed with going into the military." She could tell that she had shocked him with that statement with the way his eyes widened.

"Really? Why?"

"Well, I don't know if my mom can really afford to send me to college. I could pay my own way, though, through the G. I. Bill."

"What branch?"

"I've looked into all of them. I kinda like the idea of being a Marine, but I'm open to all of it. I guess I would need to research it all more if that's the route I chose to go."

His jaw nearly scraped the floor. "You're joking."

"No, I'm dead serious."

"Wow. That's kinda...sexy."

"Don't laugh at me!" she scolded though she was smiling.

"Who's laughing?" he asked, holding his hands up in a gesture of innocence.

"That's right, keep a straight face, McCanton," she said, shaking her finger at him. "I'm sure I will end up staying with Mama at Dreams Come True."

"You think so? You might get a scholarship, you never know."

"Maybe, but I'm not going to hold my breath. I haven't really talked things over with her. I'm just assuming she won't have the money because of the divorce."

"My dad said she filed a restraining order against your dad this morning."

Tessa nodded. "For all the good it will do."

Shane reached out and took her hand, playing with her fingers.

"I'm sorry you had to live like that for so long. I wish I would have known. Maybe I'd have gotten over myself and we could have been friends before this year."

"I'm glad you didn't know. It's all been embarrassing enough."

"You have nothing to be embarrassed about."

"I know, but still. Can't help how I feel."

The rest of the night went smoothly. They talked non-stop through dinner, decided on a comedy movie and walked hand-in-hand through the park afterward, conversation just as full and lively as before.

"We'd better be heading back home," he said when they made the complete circuit of the park. "I don't want your mom to get mad at me because I kept you out too late."

"I don't think we have to worry too much about my mom," she said, though she was smiling.

"Probably not but I don't want to give her any reason to get mad," he said, tucking a lock of her hair behind her ear, just for an excuse to touch her.

"This has been fun. I'm glad you didn't take me home."

"Me, too. Got plans for tomorrow?"

Her smile brightened. "I'm helping set up a wedding. That will tie me up from 8:00 am until noon, then tear down is around 5:00, but it shouldn't take too long."

"It takes up your whole day like that?"

"Decorations don't put themselves up."

"Guess not...can I help? I want to spend time with you."

"I'm sure we can find something for you to do, but are you sure? Wedding stuff?"

"Why not?"

"Well...OK. When we get to my house I'll ask Mama if she can use you."

"Cool," he offered her his arm to head back to his truck.

She held on to him with both hands, holding his arm so close to her that he felt her breast touch the back of his arm every few steps. He opened the door for her and helped her inside then went around to his side. When he got in she reached out to take his hand. He liked the feel of her hand in his, and he liked having her next to him in his truck.

She was quiet on the drive home and that was fine with him. He enjoyed stealing glances at her.

"Let me run in and see what she says about tomorrow," she said when he pulled into her driveway.

"Want me to come with you?"

"Just wait here in case she's already in bed."

He nodded but knew she wouldn't be. Mom's tended to stay up until their kids were home. She'd barely been inside five minutes before she came back out and got back in his truck.

"She said she'd love to have you. First Baptist at 8 am."

"I'll be there."

"Good! Now I'm excited!" she said on a giggle.

"It'll be fun."

"OK then. Thank you, again, for tonight. It was -"

He stopped her with a kiss. It was brief contact, over before she could fully process it.

"I've been wanting to do that all night," he confessed.

"Really?" she asked, a smug smile on her face, "because I've been wanting to do this."

She put her hand on the back of his neck and pulled him closer, kissing him until all coherent thought flew from his brain. When she finally pulled back he knew he was doing good to remember his own name.

"See you in the morning, McCanton," she said, leaving him breathless and alone in his truck.

He watched her walk up to her house and wave to him when she got to the door.

"Oh, yeah, I'm a goner," he said to himself.

Chapter Three

The next morning, Shane got up early, trying to be quiet and not wake anyone else. When he went downstairs, though, his mother was already up, sitting at the breakfast nook with her morning coffee.

"You're up early," she said.

"I'm going to help Tessa and her mom set up for a wedding at the church."

Susie sat her mug down. "I really wish you wouldn't," she said, though without much conviction.

"I'll probably be gone most of the day. Gotta help with take down, too."

She drew a deep breath and released it slowly. "Honey, just...keep in mind that you're going to be going off to college soon."

"I know that," he said, grabbing an apple from the fridge. "Gotta go."

He left before she could protest further. Her words hadn't been completely lost on him, however. He understood that it was probably foolish on his part to start a relationship with Tessa right now. He was going to be four hours away in Austin.

Pulling up to the church he pushed the thought of

school aside for now. He'd had a good time last night and he intended to enjoy today.

"Well, he's on time at least," Mary said to Tessa as she pulled her van up to the church.

"Yes, he is," Tessa agreed. And, she added to herself, he was looking particularly gorgeous and adorable in his faded jeans, Texas Rangers T-Shirt and scarred work boots.

"Good morning, ladies," he greeted them when they got out.

"Good morning," Mary echoed. "Ready to get to work?"

"Yes, ma'am," he replied with a smile and a wink.

"Good. You can start by bringing in the pieces to the arch and then I'll show you how to put it together."

"Yes, ma'am," he repeated, going to the back of the van.

Tessa met him at the rear doors while her mother went to make sure the church was open.

"Good morning," she said, standing on her toes to give him a quick kiss. "I'm glad you're here."

"Me, too," he replied, sneaking another quick kiss.

She watched him gather the first two pieces of the white arch, test their weight, then gathered the rest of the pieces. What normally took her and her mother two trips each, he easily handled all in one trip.

"You sure you got that?" she asked, watching his muscles bunch.

"Yeah, I'm good. Take this to the sanctuary?"

"Um, yeah, up on the stage."

She watched him go up the steps to the front doors that her mother had propped open, admiring his butt as he went. Giving herself a mental shake, she set about collecting pew bows and flowers.

"With Shane helping we may finish ahead of schedule," Mary stated when she came back outside. "He's already got the arch in and started putting it together."

"Wouldn't that be..."

"Looks like you lost your police escort," Harrison Kelly said from behind them.

Tessa and Mary both jumped, startled. Neither had even heard him approach.

"You go on now," Tessa said to him. Her mother might be afraid of him but she wasn't. "The Restraining Order says you can't come near us."

Harrison backhanded her, sending her sprawling without even sparing her a glance.

"Stop it, Harrison!" Mary screamed. "Tessa, go call 911," she ordered even as Harrison grabbed her.

"You think some piece of paper is going to keep me from you? I own you! Both of you! And you're going to pay!"

He drew back his hand to strike Mary but before he could he was violently tackled, his head cracking against the concrete and a fist landed against his nose. Shane landed two more blows to the lowlife's face before Harrison finally managed to get his bearings and clocked Shane on the jaw. To Tessa's amazement, the shot barely shook Shane and after they both landed a few more blows, Shane, being younger and faster managed to flip Harrison face down on the pavement, and in a move reflective of a veteran cop, pinned Harrison's arms behind his back, holding his wrists down with a knee.

"Get me something to tie his wrists," he said to Tessa.

"Get off me! I'll kill you!!"

"You're welcome to try," Shane bit out.

Tessa brought a roll of floral tape. Shane wasn't crazy about it but figured it would hold until his dad or his deputies got there. After he was satisfied the tape was secure, he looked over at Tessa and her mother. Mary looked shaken, but fine. Tessa had a darkening bruise forming on her cheek and right eye. Apparently, Kelly had gotten at least one blow in before Shane made it outside.

"You OK?" he asked Tessa.

"Yes. Are you?"

"Yeah," he said, looking toward the street when he heard siren's approaching. His dad's truck screeched to a halt just behind Mary's van where Shane still held Kelly pinned to the ground.

Luke took in his son's battered face and the fact that he had secured the SOB responsible, then looked to Mary and her daughter.

"Did your father hit you, Tessa?" he asked.

She nodded. "Before Shane came outside."

"Are you all right?" She nodded again. Luke shifted his gaze to his son, his eyes again roaming over his son's facial injuries. "Good job, son," he said, laying a hand on Shane's shoulder and giving him a squeeze. "Let me have him now, OK?"

"You can have him, but you gotta help me up. I busted my knee pretty hard when I took him down. I don't think I can stand on it."

Tessa gasped when she shifted her gaze to his knee as Luke helped him to stand. His jeans were soaked with blood and even she could see that it had begun to swell.

"Let me cut the jeans away from his knee," Mary said, reaching in her van for a pair of scissors. Luke helped Shane to sit on the back of the van while Mary split his pant leg up to his knee. "This is bad, Luke. He needs to go to the hospital."

In the background, Harrison was spitting out insults as Scott and another deputy arrived to take him into custody. Tessa barely spared him a glance, her concern on Shane. Her cheek was throbbing now that the adrenaline was wearing off. She could only imagine how he was feeling.

Luke walked over to speak to his deputies while they loaded Harrison into their squad car, then came back to Shane.

"We need to have them both checked out, just to be safe," he said to Mary. "You can both ride with us," he said as he scooped Shane into his arms to carry him to his truck.

Tessa didn't wait for her mother to respond. She climbed into the backseat once Luke settled Shane back there, so her mother followed wordlessly. On the short drive from the church to Doctor Curtis' office, Luke radioed for dispatch to call his wife and let her know what happened, that he was taking Shane to be checked out and to bring Shane a change of clothes.

Tessa watched Shane's profile as he turned to look out the window. She knew he was worried about his mother's reaction since she hadn't wanted him associating with Tessa in the first place, because of her father. At this point, Tessa couldn't blame her. Shane had been hurt because of her.

At the clinic, she winced when Shane groaned as his dad helped him from the truck. His knee was swollen to nearly twice its normal size and there were bits of gravel embedded in his skin, making her feel even worse. If his knee was messed up he wouldn't be able to play baseball, which she knew he loved.

They were taken immediately to an examination room. Nurses took their vitals. Concussion was ruled out for both of them. Tessa was given an ice pack for her face while Dr. Curtis and the nurses got to work on Shane. A cut under his eye required stitches and his nose was broken but the knee was of the most concern.

"Ladies, we need you to wait in the lobby, now. His jeans have to come off," Dr. Curtis told them.

Tessa caught Shane's eye briefly before she left; knew he was in pain. A lump sat tight in her throat, robbing her of breath. As soon as they were safely out of the room, she let her tears fall free.

"Oh, baby," Mary cried, embracing her. "I'm so sorry."

"He was hurt because of me," she whispered.

"Don't think about it, sweetie."

"His knee..."

"What about his knee?" Susie McCanton asked, her harsh voice interrupting them.

"He's in room four," Mary told her. "Dr. Curtis was just beginning to look at it."

Susie puffed up as if she was about to say something but thought better of it and rushed past them. Tessa held her breath until Susie was out of sight then released it slowly, wiping tears from her cheeks.

"What are we going to do about the wedding?" she asked her mother, in an effort to take her mind off of Shane.

"I'm going to call Linda and see if she will come get me and help me finish and see if Lauren will take you home."

Tessa shook her head. "No, I'm fine and four of us will get done faster."

Shane looked up when his mother came in, bracing himself for her reaction. Thankfully, though there were tears in her eyes, she merely kissed his brow and stepped back to let Dr. Curtis continue cleansing his knees. He knew she had to have passed Tessa and her mother on the way in, he just hoped she hadn't said anything to them.

"The left one needs stitching and I want to get an x-ray and an MRI to make sure nothing is fractured. Give me just a minute to get everything set up."

"Thanks, Doc," Luke said, shaking his hand.

"All-in-all, I'd say Shane's an extremely lucky young man, considering."

When they were alone, Luke again squeezed Shane's shoulder.

"I'm proud of you, boy," Luke told him.

"Thanks," Shane murmured, but he didn't feel proud. He was angry...and ashamed, because he kept seeing that bastard hit Tessa and he wanted to kill him.

"Are you hurting?" Susie asked, lightly stroking his hair.

"The doc gave me a shot of...something. I'm not feeling much right now."

"Doc said it would make him groggy," Luke told her.

"What happened?" she asked.

"I was inside the church and they were getting supplies from the van. I'd just finished putting the arch together so I went out to see what they wanted me to do next. I was in the vestibule when he hit Tessa. He had hold of Mary and was about to punch her when I tackled him. We fought for a few minutes and then I subdued him, taped his wrists. Bet that hurt like he...heck to get off," he chuckled.

"You probably saved their lives, son," Luke told him.

Shane closed his eyes knowing his dad was likely right but still not happy about all that happened.

"This is exactly why I didn't want him associating with that girl," Susie said to Luke, thinking he was asleep.

"Now, Susie, they couldn't have known that Harrison would violate the restraining order, but beyond that, what Shane did today is exactly what he will do when he becomes a cop. You know this...and he's damn good at it already."

"But he isn't a cop yet, Luke. He's just a boy."

"He is eighteen, Susie. The US Government says he is old enough to vote and go to war. He is an adult now."

"He's my child!" she cried.

"I'm right here, Mom," Shane said sleepily.

She wiped tears from her eyes. "I'm sorry, honey."

Dr. Curtis came back in with a nurse and they wheeled him down to an x-ray room. He was asleep before they got there but not before he caught a glimpse of Tessa and her mother in the hallway.

Thirty minutes after they took Shane in to be x-rayed, his dad came out to talk to them.

"Dr. Curtis wants to transport Shane to the hospital. He says his knee is going to need surgery. He apparently twisted it at some point, tore the cartilage pretty good."

"Oh, no!" Tessa gasped. "Baseball?"

Luke shook his head. "He's likely done for the season."

"I'm so sorry, Sheriff McCanton," Tessa cried.

"Hey, it's all right," he said, hugging her. "Shane's going to be fine. There is nothing for you to apologize for. I'm just glad he was there to stand up for both of you."

"He saved our lives, Luke. I have no doubt about that," Mary said.

"Harrison has a concussion," he told her, "and he's lost a few teeth."

Tessa managed a smile through her tears. "Shane got him pretty good. It was kinda satisfying to see him get a taste of his own medicine."

"Yes, it was," Mary agreed. "Linda is coming to get us. We have to get the church finished; but will you page me and let me know his room number? We'd like to come see him."

"Of course. And I would appreciate it if, after you

finish the church, you stop by the station and give Scott your statements."

"Certainly," Mary agreed.

"Will you tell Shane I'll be there as soon as I can?" Tessa asked.

"I sure will...and put that ice pack back on your cheek. You're swelling again."

When Shane woke up he was disoriented and in more pain than he'd ever been in his life. He glanced to his right and saw a pretty nurse sitting near the foot of his bed. She got up and moved closer to him when she saw he was awake.

"Hey, there, cutie," she smiled at him.

He turned to watch her check an IV bag then realized it was attached to his arm.

"Where am I?" he asked, puzzled by the hoarseness of his voice.

She took his wrist to check his pulse. "You're at Sinclair County Hospital. Dr. Curtis referred you to Dr. Kinsley. He operated on your knee to repair a tear in your cartilage."

"Surgery?"

She smiled again. "It's OK. It will all come back to you in a bit. The anesthesia makes you a little foggy right at first. Are you cold?"

"Um...yeah, a little."

"OK, I'll bring you a warm blanket, then I'll go get your folks, all right?"

He nodded and scrubbed a weary hand over his face. Surgery? He knew his knee hurt but he hadn't realized he'd messed it up that bad.

"Here ya go," she said, tucking a warm blanket around him. It felt really good, he thought as he drifted back to sleep. The next time he opened his eyes, both his parents were beside him.

"There you are," his mother said, brushing her hand gently through his hair. "How do you feel?"

"Whole body hurts," he replied, more awake now than he'd been earlier.

"Can he have anything for pain?" he heard his dad ask someone.

"Shane?" the pretty nurse called out. "On a scale of one to ten with ten being the worst pain you've ever felt in your life, tell me how you feel."

"Ten," he said without hesitation, "definitely a ten."

"All over, just the knee, what?"

"All over. Head is throbbing. Face hurts. Knee is throbbing. Other knee is burning. Throat hurts."

"Throat?" Susie asked, alarmed.

"From the tube," the nurse explained, "we weren't sure if he had food on his stomach or not. Just hang tight,

Shane. Let me get Dr. Kinsley in here."

He closed his eyes with a scowl. "What's the deal with my knee?" he asked when the nurse left.

"You must have twisted it in the fight," Luke said. "Do you remember?"

"I didn't feel anything at the time. Adrenaline. How is Tessa?" "She's fine. She will be here as soon as she can. They had to get the church done for that wedding."

"How long is this gonna bench me?"

"Most likely for the season, son, I'm sorry."

He met his dad's direct gaze, knowing he wouldn't lie to him.

"Will this keep me from DPS?"

"Doctor says you'll be good as new so long as you don't push your recovery too soon."

"Are you sure?"

"I asked. I knew you would want to know."

"What about Harrison Kelly? He violated the restraining order. Will he be put away now?"

"For at least five years. I'm going to try to press for more. He's a threat to Mary and Tessa. That'll carry some weight."

Dr. Kinsley came in, examined him and approved more pain medication for him. The next time he awoke, he was in a different room and Tessa was sitting next to him.

"Hey, Tess," he said, making her smile.

"Look who's awake! How are you feeling?"

"Like I got the crap kicked outta me."

She hugged her arms closer to herself as if fighting off a sudden chill.

"I'm so sorry about all of this, Shane."

He shook his head. "Not your fault and if you apologize to me one more time you'll piss me off."

She giggled in spite of being upset. "All right, no apologies. But I will say thank you. I'm glad you were there today. I don't even want to think about what would have happened if you hadn't been."

He reached for her hand and brought her fingers to his lips.

"Dad says he'll go away for at least five years. More if Dad has his way."

She nodded. "Yes. That would be a good thing."

"He'll never hurt you again, Tess, I promise."

"Don't make promises you can't keep, Shane. He hurts me all the time. He's my father."

"Don't let him. He's not a father. He's nothing more than a sperm donor. Don't let him mess you up."

"He already has, but you're right. It's time I put him behind me."

"There you go. Don't let him break you."

Chapter Four

Shane's words stayed with Tessa. She was determined to stick to them; she would not allow Harrison Kelly to break her spirit. She enrolled in self-defense classes. She spent a lot of time at the Sheriff's office, volunteering to do filing and whatever paperwork Sheriff McCanton and the dispatcher, Kim, thought she could handle. She and Shane continued dating and while they remained close friends, she held back from him, not allowing herself to become too close.

Shane knew she held back. He could feel it in her kisses; they weren't quite as passionate as those first few had been. Any time he tried to advance things between them, she held him off. He told himself she was just being smart, preparing for when he left for college, but in the back of his mind he knew it was something else.

But he couldn't stand it, so today he wanted to try to do something about it. He hated the distance and that she was keeping him at arms length.

"Where are we?" Tessa asked when he parked his truck.

"This is part of the original McCanton homestead," he said after he helped her out of the truck. He grabbed a blanket and a picnic basket from the back and then laced his fingers with hers.

"I didn't realize y'all had this much land," she said.

"Twelve hundred and fifty acres," he replied, "but this is my favorite. I told my dad this is where I want to build a house someday."

She looked at him, surprised. "I thought you wanted to be a Ranger."

"I do...but I want to come back here someday."

They rounded a thick growth of trees and brush and he heard Tessa gasp. He smiled, seeing his favorite spot through her eyes. It was really breathtaking. A waterfall roared over the limestone cliff and pooled into a large opening of the lake.

"Shane," she breathed, "this is beautiful! How did I not know this was here?"

"Not many people do outside my family," he said, spreading the blanket on the shore.

Tessa smiled down at him when he sat on the blanket, a wicked gleam in her eyes. "Let's go swimming," she said.

"Swimming? Tess...we don't have suits," he said but froze when she lifted her shirt over her head, revealing her white, lacy bra. She tossed her shirt at him and then her hands went to her shorts.

"Come on, McCanton, don't tell me you're chicken."

He cleared his throat and caught her shorts when she tossed those to him as well. It wasn't that he was chicken exactly, it was that he'd gone so hard at the sight of her bra, he didn't want to freak her out.

"Come on, Shane, come swim with me," she coaxed.

"In a minute," he said, and cringed when she stepped closer to him. She leaned down until mere inches separated their faces, her hand reaching down to caress him through his shorts.

"Like what you see, baby?" she asked, leaning in to kiss him.

"Tess," he groaned.

She laughed, squeezing him. "Come swim with me."

He cursed under his breath and kissed her, then stood and stripped down to his underwear.

"Let's go," he said, lacing his fingers with hers.

Together they went into the water and splashed and played until Shane swam up and snagged her around the waist and pulled her to him. Tessa was laughing and wrapped her arms and legs around him, combing her fingers through the hair at the nape of her neck.

"You are so beautiful, Tess," he whispered, his free hand skimming her face.

"Shane," she breathed, her legs tightening around him so that he could feel her core pressed against him.

"Graduation is right around the corner," he said.

"Don't remind me," she groaned.

"We won't have much more time together."

"You're right. We won't."

"I want you, Tess."

She smiled. "I can feel that," she said, wiggling against him.

"Babe," he groaned, pressing his forehead to hers.

She licked at his bottom lip then caught it between her teeth.

"Make love to me, Shane."

He crushed her to him, sealing his lips over hers, holding her tight while he walked to the shore. He wasn't sure what had changed, but at this point, he wasn't going to question it or push his luck. Still holding her in his arms, he carried her to his truck, pulled a blanket from the behind the seat and carried her back to the shore by the waterfall. He placed her on her feet, spread the blanket and then took her down.

"Tessa, look at me," he said, smoothing her hair back from her face. She looked up into his eyes, cupping his face in her hands. "You with me, baby?"

She licked at his lips. "I am so with you,"

"I don't have protection with me."

She smiled up at him. "Lucky for you, I'm on the pill."

His eyes widened. "What?"

"Regulates my period, and I really don't want to be

talking about this right now."

"Right, yeah, I'll just..."

She wrapped her legs around his waist and kissed him as he took her signal and thrust into her. She gasped and he absorbed her cry as he felt the thin barrier of her innocence give way. In that moment, she was finally, really and truly his.

Later, they snuggled together on the blanket, watching the waterfall. Tessa turned on her side and traced her finger over his lower lip.

"This spot would be a perfect place to build a house. Can't you just see it? Large, wrap around porch, rocking chairs and porch swings all over. Swimming pool. And inside...lots of fireplaces."

Shane laughed. "Fireplaces? This is Texas, babe, how often does it really get cold enough for a fire?"

She shrugged. "Well, not often, but I don't care. I like fireplaces. I want one in the kitchen and in the living room and definitely one in the master bed and bathroom."

"So, at least four?"

"The one in the master suite could be a pass-through from the bedroom to the bathroom."

"OK, so three."

"Oh, but I want one on the porch or by the pool, too."

"Duly noted. Anything else?"

"Let's see...oh, I want a sitting area in the master

bedroom...and a balcony."

"Master sitting area, balcony. Check."

She rolled so that her upper body rested on his. "What about you, what do you want?"

"A really big bed," he said, making her laugh.

"A big bed, OK. How big?"

"Big, big. Bigger than a King size."

"We'd have to have linens custom made for it."

"So, you can sew, right?"

"Shane!" she gasped, playfully slapping at him.

"Of course, all this depends on whether you stay here and wait for me," he said, sobering.

"Why do I have to stay here? You're going off to college, why can't I leave?" she asked, sitting up.

He sat up, too. "Are you leaving, Tess? You haven't said what your plans are for after graduation."

She raked her hands through her hair. "Ugh. That's because I don't know, Shane. I don't know what I'm going to do. Like I said before, Mama can't really afford to send me to college. She'd try, but it would be extremely hard on her. I can't ask her to do that."

"Are you still considering the military?"

She got up and paced to the shore, her back to him. Shane watched her for a moment then got up and wrapped his arms around her from behind, kissing her shoulder.

"Talk to me, Tess," he urged.

"I wish I had a clear vision of what my future held. I just don't know anymore."

"What happened to the little girl who told me we were going to be married one day?" he teased.

"Life got in the way," she replied.

"What was that all about, anyway? Your dream? You never did explain that to me."

She hugged her arms over his, making him tighten his hold on her, one arm just under her breasts, one around her waist.

"I had a dream about you, just before school started. I didn't exactly know it was you. I knew it was Sheriff McCanton's son. In the dream, we were married and we had a baby."

His arms tightened and she felt him smile against her neck. "A baby?"

She nodded. "A boy. We named him Gabriel Shane."

"Well, yeah, that's kind of a given."

She looked over her shoulder at him. "What?"

"The first McCanton who was Sheriff of Indian Springs was named Gabriel Shane. He named his son Shane Gabriel. Ever since then, the oldest son is given the name either Gabriel Shane or Shane Gabriel, depending on what the father's name is."

"But...your dad's name is Luke."

"He's a second son. My Uncle Gabe was killed in

action in Vietnam before having any kids. So, since he was Gabriel Shane, I was given Shane Gabriel...and one day, my son will be Gabriel Shane...but how would you have known that when we were five?"

Tessa shrugged. "I probably just thought reversing the name was cool. Who knows."

He kissed the side of her head and for a few more moments, they stared at the waterfall, each lost in their own thoughts. Shane knew she was holding back something. He knew that finally having sex with her wasn't a fix-all, but he'd hoped it would have her opening up more.

"Tess...baby, please, talk to me," he pleaded.

"I don't want to get into it all now, Shane, please."

"Don't shut me out."

She sighed. "I'm not, I just...the world and all its problems can crash in on us tomorrow. Let's just have this time now, just you and me."

"I'm going to be leaving for Austin in a few weeks. I just...I want to know what you'll be doing, where you'll be."

She closed her eyes a moment, then turned in his arms, rocking up on her toes to kiss him. It was a rotten trick, distracting him with sex, but she just couldn't get into her future plans with him now.

Frustration with her grew as the days melted into weeks. Tessa dodged him at every turn when he tried to press her about her plans while he was at UT. And even though they were intimate nearly every time they were together, he could feel her pulling farther and farther away from him. Confirmation came on the eve of him leaving for UT.

On their last night together, he'd driven her two hours away to a hotel. They soaked together in the en suite whirlpool tub and made love like it was what it was: the last night they would be together for a while. Neither wanted to address the elephant in the room but as the time wore on, Shane knew the sands were running out.

"Baby...you have to talk to me," he said when they were back at her house, sitting in her driveway.

She took a deep breath and turned to face him.

"I know...these last few weeks have been...amazing, Shane. I've loved every single minute of it. And it's going to hurt when you're gone."

"So, you're staying here?"

She met his gaze and shook her head. "No...I enlisted in the Army. I'll be leaving next week for Basics."

"What?" he breathed.

"I told you I was considering the military."

"Yeah, you did, but I assumed you would discuss it with me."

"It hasn't been an easy decision...but it's been mine. I had to be able to make it on my own, Shane, can't you understand that?"

"I do understand, but that doesn't mean you should have shut me out...where will you..."

She shook her head, "It doesn't matter. I don't want to hold you back. I want you to go to UT and I want you to have the full college experience, and you can't do that if you have your mind on a girlfriend who may end up on the other side of the world in her deployment."

"Tessa-"

"You'll see I'm right when you get on campus and are surrounded by all those hot college girls."

"Stop it," he said, his voice low.

She placed her hand on his cheek and looked deep into his eyes.

"I love you, Shane, I always will...but our lives are going in different directions now. Maybe, someday, when you're done with college and I'm...wherever I'm going to be at that point, we can re-visit this and see if there's something here to salvage, but deep down, you know I'm right. We have to move on with our lives."

Shane felt like his heart had been ripped from his chest but he let her go. He knew it had more to do with her issues with her so-called father but it didn't make her leaving hurt any less. A part of him even knew in the long-run that she was right; their lives were moving in different directions and it would be difficult, if not impossible, to maintain a long-distance romance. But he couldn't help feeling that when he left town to head to Austin, he was leaving his heart in her hands.

When he was settled in his dorm, he fired up his computer to send her an email, only to find one from her in his inbox. Taking a deep breath, he opened it.

Dear Shane,

I'm so sorry I wasn't able to tell you about my plans. Every time I tried to talk to you about it, I couldn't get the words out. You know this hasn't been a decision I came to lightly. I suppose I never really told you my reasons behind the decision, however. As I sit here typing this, I realize I still have a hard time putting into words why I chose this. I guess the easiest answer would be, I want the challenge of it. I want to see if I can do it. And I want a chance to see the world beyond Indian Springs.

I know if it had been up to you, we would still be considering ourselves together. In a perfect world, I would stay with you forever, but that isn't our reality. You're at UT and I want you to have every ounce of the college experience while you are there. After Basics, I have no clue where I'll be, if I'll even be in the States or not. I just didn't think it was fair to ask you to wait.

I love you, Shane. I always will. I don't know where our roads will take us.

Someday, I hope we find each other again. I meant what I said when I we were five: we're going to get married, someday, when we're big...it just may be that we have to take the long way home to get there.

  Forever yours,

  Tessa

He stared at the screen a long time. He wasn't quite sure what to make of what she'd written. How was he supposed to take that? His heart was still reeling from her cutting him loose yesterday.

Taking a deep breath, he decided for the first time in his life to lay his heart open and bare all in an email.

Tessa:

I'm not really sure how to respond. I'm sitting here in my dorm room and I feel like there is a huge hole in my chest. You ripped my heart out last night. I don't understand why you couldn't talk to me about the Army. I thought we could talk to each other about anything. That's what you do when you love someone. You talk things over and work things out.

That being said, I guess I understand why you let me go. I don't agree
with your reasoning, but I do understand...a little. Neither of

us really know life outside of Indian Springs. We don't know what the world holds for us, and you're right, holding on to each other may be a mistake. Doesn't mean I don't love you.

Can't shut off my feelings like that. So, from this point on, we can be friends.

Your vision, not mine. I gave you my heart. It's yours to keep. If you don't want to be mine any longer, I get it; but I ask that you don't shut me out of your life. I want to know what is happening with you. Ever since we called our truce, we've always been able to talk to one another. I still want that. You're my best friend and I don't want to lose you. So, please, as pathetic as my begging
sounds, just promise you will stay in touch. Email me. Text me. Call me.

I'll do the same. I love you.

Always,

Shane

Chapter Five

Over the next years, they stayed in contact via email, texts and instant messaging but he'd had to work hard at guarding his heart. In the years since graduation he'd dated here and there, but no one could replace Tessa in his heart, and he was afraid no one ever would.

Every time he went home for the holidays or to visit his family, he found himself aching to see her, but she was never there when he was. It got to be too painful to be back home in their old haunts so he began coming back less and less.

The last time he saw her, was again at the street dance to open the county fair. It was right after he graduated college, when he'd just finished training to be in DPS. He hadn't really wanted to come, but Gracie was dating a new guy and he wanted to be able to read him the Big Brother Riot Act and see if he was worthy of his baby sister.

He was sitting at a table on the outskirts of the dance floor, watching his sisters dance with their boyfriends and feeling a bit at loose ends himself. He had gone out with girls through college, but never had an exclusive relationship with anyone. He'd enjoyed his college years, had plenty of female companionship, but since losing Tessa, he hadn't really wanted to attach himself to anyone else.

Lifting his beer bottle to his lips, he started to feel a current running through the crowd. Something was happening on the other side of the dance floor area from him. He watched with mild interest until he saw the crowd shift, and then it was like in a movie…time literally stood still.

Coming through the crowd, looking better than he ever remembered, was none other than Tessa Kelly. His heart began thumping hard in his chest. Blonde hair, eyes so green they were almost turquoise, so bright he could see them from across the dance floor, even with the dim illumination from the party lights and tiki torches. She wore a white tank top with a rhinestone cross on the front, jeans that hugged her hips and showed off curves that she hadn't had the last time he'd seen her and boots that were heeled and sexy as hell on her.

He stood and the movement drew her gaze to him. When her eyes met his, she laughed and took off at a run toward him, dodging the couples dancing. He met her half way and she leapt into his arms, wrapping her legs around his waist and her arms around his neck, squealing with laughter when he spun her around.

"How the hell are you?" he asked, laughing.

Before answering, she cupped his face in her hands

and leaned down to plant a scalding kiss on him. Shane tightened his hold on her and kissed her like there was no tomorrow. She tasted even better than he remembered.

"Get a room, McCanton!" someone called, causing Tessa to pull back. She pressed her forehead to his and slid her hands from his cheeks to his hair.

"Oh, my God, I've missed you!" she breathed.

"Why didn't you tell me you were coming? I would have picked you up at the airport.."

"It was a last minute thing, and I'm only here until Monday morning."

As if on cue, the band began to play "I Cross My Heart" by George Strait. Tessa pulled her head back and Shane let her slowly slide down to her feet, then pulled her close and they began to dance, just as they'd done at the street dance all those years ago when they first got together.

"You look amazing," he told her, his hand running up and down her back as they danced.

"You aren't so bad yourself, handsome," she said, smiling at him. "So, do we consider this our song?" she teased. "It was the first song we ever danced to."

"I remember," he said, bringing her hand that was clasped in his to his lips, kissing her fingertips. "I can't believe it's been so long since I've seen you. You're even more beautiful than I remembered."

She curled her other hand around the back of his

neck and pulled his head down so that her lips were near his ear, her fingers teasing the hair at his nape.

"Let's go by the waterfall on your land," she whispered to him. "I want to be alone with you."

Shane pulled back to look into her eyes, "Yeah?"

"Oh, yeah, baby."

He gave her hand a squeeze, shifted his hold on it, then pulled her off the dance floor. "Let's go."

As they were walking away, he heard his mother calling him but decided he wasn't going to let her sidetrack him like he did all those years ago when he first danced with Tessa. He wasn't going to let anyone come between them now, especially not if she had less than forty-eight hours to be here.

"How long are you home for?" she asked.

"Gotta leave late Sunday."

"Even sooner than me."

"Low man on the totem pole. I got lucky just being able to get off for this weekend."

"We have a short window to come home before we ship out."

He stopped walking and glanced at her, feeling a shot of fear shoot down his spine.

"Where?"

"Afghanistan."

"God," he breathed, pulling her back into his arms,

holding her as if she might disappear at any moment.

She clung to him for several moments before turning her head and kissing his throat.

"Come on, Shane. Take me to the falls."

He took a deep breath. "Yeah. Let's go."

He took her to his truck and held her hand while they drove to his land and the waterfall where they first made love.

"It's so beautiful here," she sighed when he parked and she jumped out of the truck. It was dark but there was a full moon that gave off just enough light so she could see where she was going. "Never thought I'd say this, but I've missed being home."

"There's something to be said for this place," he agreed. "I can see why my dad walked away from DPS to come back here when he did."

Meanwhile, his career had taken off with flying colors. He was on the fast track to becoming a Ranger. The only thing holding him back was the required eight years of high level criminal investigation; he had a year to go. He'd been a member of the Governor's security detail, which led to him being placed in command of a SWAT task force, and now he was in the role of Special Crimes Investigator. The next step was Ranger and everyone felt he was a lock to make it on his first try.

He and Tessa were still emailing and texting on a regular basis, but they hadn't seen each other in years; in fact the last time they saw each other was the night she ripped his heart out of his chest. He'd tried to set up a meet with her a few times he knew she was stateside, but she'd always had some reason why she couldn't, and eventually he'd gotten the hint and stopped asking. They spoke on the phone at least every other month, but their conversations were always short and light. In essence, she'd become that friend that you stayed in contact with via social media and those light meaningless conversations but had no real relationship with.

"Hey, Mac," one of his fellow investigator's called, pulling Shane's attention from his computer; he'd been hoping for an email from Tessa. It had been a few weeks since he'd heard from her; he was getting worried. "Captain's called a briefing."

"Now?"

"Yep. Getcha butt in gear, kid."

He shut his computer down and followed the older officer to the briefing room. He took his usual table in the back left of the room, noting that there were four Fed-type suits occupying the front center table, three men and a woman. For the Captain to be running the briefing meant that whatever the Fed's were here for, it had to be high profile.

Captain Martin called the meeting to order and began his Power Point presentation. Everyone groaned when the group in question was highlighted.

"That's right, boys and girls. This is in reference to the Heltons and the Naturalists. We've tangled with them before. Well, now they've managed to lure a Senator's daughter into their ranks and he wants her out. We've been asked, due to our experience with them, to work with the Feds on this one. They are prepared to send an agent in to infiltrate, locate the Senator's daughter, and get her out while collecting as much evidence as possible. McCanton, since your team has had dealings with the Heltons before, I'd like you to work with them, bring them up to speed on everything you know of the group."

"Yes, sir."

"This is Special Agent in charge Glen Gibson. He'll introduce the rest of his team."

Gibson stood and faced the room. Shane guessed him to be in his late 40s, early 50s. He introduced two other men, both in their 30s and then gestured to the female agent.

"This is Special Agent Tessa Kelly, who we will be sending in undercover."

The rest of the room literally disappeared as Shane watched Tessa stand and face the room. Shane knew he was in trouble the instant their gazes collided. He muttered a foul curse under his breath, causing the guy beside him to nod.

"She is hot," one said.

"I'd surrender to her any time," another spoke.

"Cuff me, Agent Hotness," yet another joked.

"Can it, guys," Shane snapped.

They all looked at him in stunned silence. He'd never spoken to any of them like that, but he couldn't help it; that was Tessa they were speaking so disrespectfully about.

"Is there a problem, Sergeant McCanton?" Tessa asked, her voice detached and professional.

"No problem, Agent Kelly," he replied, his tone just as neutral.

"Our plan," Gibson interrupted, "is to put Agent Kelly in the path of the Naturalists, get her noticed and recruited."

"Look, sir, no offense to Agent Kelly, but she's not exactly the kind of female they would consider," one of Shane's guys, Crownover, spoke up. Shane agreed but he wasn't about to give voice to that just yet.

"And why is that?" Gibson queried.

"She's too hard for one, and I'm not just referring to her physical fitness, which, yeah, OK, that's a problem, too...I'm talking about her eyes."

"What's wrong with my eyes?" Tessa asked.

"You've got Cop's Eyes, sugar," Pete Dooley, another of Shane's guys said. "Hard, assessing, missing nothing.

Shrewd. Again, no offense, but you're the kind of woman these pu-, um, excuse me, pansies are afraid of."

She walked down the aisle to stop before their table, dangerously close to Shane. She wore a black pant suit with a cream colored shirt and sensible yet stylish boots Shane knew were chosen for ease of running. Up close the changes to her face were striking. Gone was the rounded innocence of youth he remembered. The woman before him was every inch as Pete described: a hardened, seasoned cop.

"Call me Sugar one more time, Officer. I dare you."

Pete held up his hands in supplication.

"Hey, my bad. But what we're saying is true. The girls, and I do mean girls, they recruit are your stereotypical Girls Next Door. They're sweet to the point of naivety. They're gullible. Most have been abuse victims or have been so sheltered their BS meter doesn't pick up on much. That's not you."

She smiled then. "Thank you. I consider that a huge compliment. That's not me...now. But as your Sergeant McCanton can testify, that was me, not so very long ago."

All eyes turned to Shane. He rubbed the back of his neck.

"Agent Kelly and I grew up together," he said simply.

He cringed as he watched realization dawn upon his guys.

"Holy shit! TK," Pete said, looking over at Tessa with wide eyes.

"Yeah," Shane confirmed, hoping they wouldn't reveal too much.

Tessa's gaze shifted to him. "TK?"

"Long story," he murmured.

"OK, well, my point, gentlemen, is that by the time I'm set to come in contact with the Naturalists, I'll be ready and the perfect candidate for them. Count on it."

She walked off and the briefing continued. Shane did his best to pay attention but just being in the same room with Tessa after all those years had shot his concentration.

He absently rubbed the heel of his hand over his left pec. For his SWAT Task Force, he and his men got a tattoo of a tribal dragon. Among the elaborate swirls of the design, Shane added Tessa's initials. He'd been drunk at the time but in the years since, knowing he carried her initials on his body was a comfort to him.

As he watched the woman at the front of the room move, he realized he was looking at a stranger. His Tessa was never shy, but there had been an innocence about her that this woman didn't posses. Quite frankly, the woman before him now terrified him. She looked like the type who chewed men up and spit them out on a regular basis.

When the briefing ended, Shane addressed his team, assigning each a task to help brief the Feds on their knowledge of the Naturalists. After his guys left, Captain Martin approached.

"With me," the Captain said and Shane fell in step beside him. "SSA Gibson mentioned that one of his agents knew you. He didn't tell me which one. Is there anything I should be aware of?"

An image of Tessa on a blanket by the natural waterfall where the river fed the lake near his house popped into his mind, but he didn't think the Captain needed to know about that.

"We grew up together. She was my high school girlfriend. We've barely seen each other since graduation."

They entered the Captain's office and he shut the door behind them.

"How did the relationship end? Friendly or bitter?"

"Friendly. I went off to college; she joined the Army."

"She joined the Army?"

"Yeah. She was battalion support for the Rangers. Probably how she ended up with the Feds. I didn't know she left the Army."

"What was she referring to with Pete that you could testify to?"

"She grew up with an abusive father."

"I see. Do you think she can pull this off? I'm inclined to agree with your guys. She looks too hard to be the type the Helton's will go for."

Shane took a deep breath. "Honestly, I don't know. The girl I knew before would be the perfect candidate. I know she hasn't forgotten how she was; but after the last run-in with her dad she changed. She took self-defense classes and became a black belt...I don't know how the woman I saw in there will pull it off."

The Captain, Bruce, was quiet a moment. "I want you to report directly to me, one-on-one like this about the progress of the preparations. I trust your judgment. If you don't think she can pull this off when the time comes I want to know."

"Yes, sir...I will tell you this...if she was still like I used to know her there's no way in Hell I'd send her undercover with them. They'd break her. Now, though, I just don't know."

"She's changed that much?"

"It's been ten years, sir."

"Just let me know."

"I will."

He opened the door and wasn't at all surprised to see Tessa leaning against the wall waiting for him. He felt his heart accelerate when their gazes collided and locked on one another. Would she always have this effect on him, he wondered.

"Can we talk?" she asked.

He glanced at his watch. "I've got PT exercises for

the next two hours," he said, heading off down the hall.

"You're the C.O., you can be late."

"Not really."

She grabbed his upper arm, stopping him.

"Come on, Shane. Talk to me."

"Why? So you can pull rank on me?"

"That comment is beneath you, McCanton."

He rounded on her, stepping right into her personal space. "You knew you were coming here. I didn't even know you weren't in the Army any more. You couldn't be bothered to tell me in one of your emails or texts? You couldn't tell me you would be coming to work here?"

"I wasn't allowed to tell you."

"Bullshit!" he roared.

Captain Martin stepped out into the hall. "Is there a problem, children?"

"No, sir, heading to the gym," Shane replied, walking away.

"Dammit, Shane!" Tessa seethed.

"Right back at you, sweetheart," Shane tossed over his shoulder.

The Captain chuckled, extending his hand to Tessa.

"Bruce Martin," he said, once again introducing himself to her. "and that, my dear Agent Kelly, was my Godson."

Tessa turned speculative eyes to the Captain. Shane

was his God-son, huh? This might just work to her advantage.

Chapter Six

Shane got stopped several times on his way to the gym. Reports needed his signature. Phone calls needed his attention. By the time he rounded the corner to the gym, he was wound so tight he felt sorry for whoever was fool enough to step into the ring with him first.

"Son of a bitch," he groaned when he stepped out of the locker room, seeing Tessa in the ring as he stepped through the gym doors.

"You're late, Sergeant," she chided.

"I'm not fighting you, Tess. Forget it."

"I trained with the best of the Army Rangers. I can hold my own."

"I don't doubt that for a minute but I'm not fighting you."

"Come on, McCanton."

"I will not fight you."

Turning on his heel, he went back toward the locker room. Tessa was out of the ring and blocking the door before he reached it. He stopped in his tracks and glared at her.

"Look, I get it, you don't want to hit me. I just want to show you that I know what I'm doing. I can handle this."

"I know you can. In a fair fight you could probably kick my ass, but these guys won't fight fair. I outweigh you by a hundred pounds at least. You might get a few good shots in but at some point I will over power you. You may fight like a man but you're still a woman."

"Yes, I am. I don't have to win the fight. I just have to incapacitate you long enough to get away. Don't underestimate me."

"Fine. You wanna out macho the boys go right ahead. Doesn't mean I have to watch."

For a moment they stood glaring at each other. Each knew from past experience that they wouldn't make the other back down.

"I recommended you over a Ranger battalion for this because I thought you'd be the best person for this job," Bruce said from behind him. "Are you going to be able to put your personal issues aside?"

Shane shifted his gaze from her to his Captain. "How would you feel sending Patricia into something like this?" he asked, referring to Bruce's wife. He watched the horror flash across the Captain's face and nodded. "Exactly."

"Shane, I can do this," Tessa insisted.

"Fine...but if I don't feel you're ready when the time comes, we pull the plug."

"You aren't the one to make that call," Tessa dismissed.

"SSA Gibson has given us that authority," Bruce clarified, "and I agree with Shane. When the time comes, if he doesn't green light this, it will be a no-go...now, the two of you are old friends. I want you to figure out how to get along so this case has a chance for success. Am I clear?"

"Yes, sir," Shane replied.

"Absolutely," Tessa agreed.

Bruce left them then and for a moment Shane considered walking out, too, but he thought better of it.

"You drive me insane," he seethed, "I feel like we're back in grade school."

"Don't stand in my way on this, Shane."

His eyes raked over her, from her pony tail to her FBI grey T-Shirt to her black Nike shorts and long, tanned, muscular legs.

"Hey, Serg, we doing this or what?" Joe called out from the mats on the far side of the gym.

"In a minute," he called. "You wanna train with us, fine. We're practicing take-downs. But don't you ever ask to get into the ring with me again. I got no problem dropping you on your ass but I will never hit you, not even with full gear on, you get me?"

"Lead the way, Serg," she smirked.

He bit back a retort and turned to cross the gym, knowing she was behind him. As the exercises got underway, he had to admit he was impressed with her skills.

She was quick; it took his guys a few tries to get her and so far they'd all managed to get hands on her but none had succeeded in taking her down.

"Your turn, McCanton," she said after she finished with Pete.

"Yeah, come on, Serg, this has to be an equal opportunity smack down," Crownover panted.

Shane took a deep breath and let it out slowly.

"Fine."

Tessa smiled when he stepped up to her. "Can your ego handle this?" she asked.

"Can yours?" he countered, making her laugh. He knew he was going to win; she was too confident and he'd spent the time she was taking on his guys to assess her weakness. They circled each other a few times and when she lunged for him, he easily side-stepped, shot his leg out and just like the third grade, planted her on her smart ass. The guys whistled and laughed. Tessa glared up at him but accepted his hand to help her to her feet.

"Class dismissed, boys and girls," Shane said, heading to the locker room.

"Walking away, just like that, McCanton?" she called after him.

"Looks like," he tossed over his shoulder.

His guys chuckled as they each shook hands with her.

"Just what exactly is the history between the two of you?" Joe asked, "I've never seen him like this. We've trained with women before."

"We dated in high school," she supplied.

"Ended badly?" Pete asked.

"No, we were just headed in different directions at the time. He's actually my best friend."

"Well, no offense, ma'am, but if he's your best friend, he sure seemed blind-sided by your arrival today," Crownover said, "and the Sergeant? He don't like surprises."

She sighed. "I wasn't at liberty to tell him. Look, I really need to talk to him one-on-one. Can y'all help delay him while I change?"

The guys exchanged an uncomfortable look. She didn't think they wanted to tick Shane off, so she was surprised when Crownover spoke up.

"I'll keep him talking while these two change. When I come out you can go in. How's that?"

"Bless you," she replied.

"Are you nuts?" Joe asked when they were walking away from her. "He'll kill us."

"Won't be the first time," Crownover shot back.

Shane knew his guys were up to something the minute they walked into the locker room. He had no doubt it involved Tessa since they'd stayed behind to talk to her. They'd all come in singing her praises, impressed that he'd been the only one to drop her. He also saw right through their whole ploy of each one coming to talk to him one-on-one while the others showered and changed. They were stalling him. His suspicions were confirmed when Crownover abruptly ended their conversation the minute Joe and Pete left. When the locker room door opened two minutes after Crownover left and he saw Tessa walk in he could only shake his head.

"Why am I not surprised," he mumbled, buttoning the cuff of his sleeve.

"We need to talk, Shane."

"I really don't have time right now."

"Make time. Don't shut me out like this."

He sent her a pointed look. "Just returning the favor."

"You're being petty and that's not like you."

"Isn't it?" he countered. "How would you know? I've been little more than a pen pal to you these last ten years."

"That's not fair."

"It is what it is."

She watched him pack his gym bag, aching to touch him. Throwing caution to the wind, she stepped closer to him, invading his space.

"I think you've gotten taller," she mused, placing a bold hand on his chest, right over his heart. "I know you've put on more muscle."

"So have you," he said, his eyes on her body...but he

kept his hands at his sides.

She trailed her hand up his neck to let her fingers tangle in the hair at his nape.

"I've missed you," she said, brushing her lips lightly, quickly, over his.

"Have you?" he asked dryly.

"Stop being such a cynic, McCanton. I can feel how much you missed me," she said, pressing against his arousal.

"You're beautiful. I got eyes," he said simply.

She smiled and caught his bottom lip between her teeth, running her tongue over it before releasing it.

"My hotel is just down the street."

His gaze locked on hers. She could tell he was tempted.

"How do you know I'm not seeing someone?"

She laughed. "Because I know you, McCanton. If you were serious about someone else you wouldn't have still been keeping in touch with me all this time and you damn sure wouldn't be letting me touch you now."

Nailed him and he knew it. "You wanna walk or drive?" he asked.

"I rode with the others so either you drive or we walk."

"Let's go," he said, slamming his locker door shut.

They didn't speak on the walk through the station. He stopped briefly at his desk to shut his computer down then they continued on to the parking garage.

"Nice," she said as he opened the door to his black Ford truck for her.

"Which hotel?" he asked when he got in.

"Marriott."

He didn't speak again so she remained quiet, too. He pulled into the valet parking station and they got out and went into the elevator still not speaking. When the doors shut and they were alone, she stepped closer to him, looking up into his deep blue eyes. Again, nothing was said. The elevator stopped. She stepped back and led the way to her room. She put her card key in the reader and opened the door. When it shut behind him, she turned to face him, intending to ask what his problem was but she never got a chance. Shane's arm snaked around her waist and pulled her roughly to him. She gasped but clung to him when he claimed her mouth in a kiss that left her breathless and lightheaded.

He lifted her with his hands under her butt and slammed her back against the wall, being sure to keep her head from hitting. She blinked when he pulled back abruptly, pressing his forehead to hers.

"God, Tess," he breathed.

She wiggled her hips, grinding his arousal against her core. He groaned, kissing her again. It started out intense and aggressive, but halfway through, she felt him gentle, melting into her.

"Shane," she whispered when his lips dropped to her neck.

"Tell me you're still on the pill," he said, his lips to her ear.

"Absolutely," she confirmed.

He lifted his head and looked into her eyes, studying her.

"You want this?"

Her hips again ground against him. "More than anything."

"You aren't seeing anyone?"

"Shane, seriously, shut up and take me."

He studied her a moment more, then nodded once. He placed her back on her feet and tried to step away but she wanted no part of that. She grabbed his shirt and yanked it from his pants, then sent buttons flying when she ripped it open, pushing it off his shoulders, eager to get her hands on his skin, frustrated when she realized he wore an undershirt.

Shane pulled back to shrug out of his shirt, undoing the buttons at his wrists to free them, then made quick work of peeling her out of her clothes. When she was nude, he lifted her into his arms and carried her to the bed, lips locked together.

"God, I've missed you," he breathed, his hands going

on a journey of exploration. Her body had changed so much since he'd last seen and felt her. Gone was the soft hometown girl he remembered. In her place, he felt cut muscles, still soft in all the right...

"Tessa!" he cried, shaking fingers tracing a long, jagged scar that began by her navel and ended at her hip. "Baby, what happened?"

"Shrapnel from an IED," she explained, fascinated by his change in behavior.

"You never told me you'd been wounded," he said, tenderly caressing her scar.

She shrugged. "I didn't want you to be upset."

"Is this why you left the Army?"

"Partly…you're over dressed for this party, McCanton," she said, tugging at his undershirt.

"In a minute," he said, brushing her hand away. "What's this?" His fingers brushed some ink just above her bikini line on her hip.

"Oh. Uh, yeah, um…that's a tattoo."

"I can see that. What does it say?"

"You have suddenly lost the ability to read?" she asked dryly.

"No, but I want to hear you say it."

A smile tugged her lips. "It says, 'Shane's'."

He rewarded her admission by placing a lingering kiss over the ink. "Bet that made for some interesting conversation with your other boyfriends."

She didn't reply. Her silence alerted him and he looked up from the tat to meet her direct gaze.

"There haven't been any other boyfriends, Shane."

He went completely still. "What?"

"There hasn't been anyone since you."

"It's been ten years."

She nodded. "I've been busy building my career."

"No one? None of those Army Rangers you were around?"

"Fraternization is against regs, and I wanted them to see me as a soldier, not a potential bedmate."

He stroked his thumb over the tattoo. It was small, maybe the length of his middle finger, black ink in beautiful script.

"When did you do this?"

"For my 21st birthday. I wore a bikini sometimes at parties. I wanted the guys to think there was someone back home waiting for me, so they'd leave me alone."

"You wore a bikini low enough for this to be seen?" he asked incredulously.

She smiled. "Hey, ya got it, flaunt it."

"Hence your need for the tattoo of a semi-imaginary boyfriend."

She looked up into his eyes and stroked her hand over his cheek. "You look pretty real to me. Besides, they'd heard us on the phone together before."

"Must have worked."

"Well, that and the fact that they were all intimidated by me."

He shook his head. "I'm sure they placated themselves by saying you were a lesbian."

"Yeah, there was some of that talk, too."

"Got some ink of my own," he said, pulling his shirt over his head.

Tessa came up on her knees to inspect the tribal dragon on his left pectoral. It was black ink, intricately done, and within the swirl and points of the design, where the heart of the dragon was, were the initials T.K. in red, right over his heart.

"T.K.," she said, touching the letters.

He rubbed the heel of his hand over the ink, catching her fingers under his hand. "You've never been far from my heart, Tess," he confessed.

"Aww, you can be sweet. My hometown golden boy," she teased.

She kissed the tattoo then pulled his head down to kiss her lips. That they both marked their bodies with the other's name said worlds about their feelings. Shane smoothed his hands over her hair and face, pushing her back to the mattress. Tessa looked up into his blue eyes and what he saw in her eyes took his breath away. Absolute trust. It was as if they were back on that blanket by the waterfalls. She looked at him in that moment like he was everything in her whole world.

"I've missed you so damn much, Tess," he whispered.

"I've missed you, too, Shane," she admitted.

She wrapped her legs around his waist and when he slid inside her, they both took a deep, calming breath, both realizing they'd just come home. They made love tenderly, rediscovering and reclaiming each other. He found other battle scars on her body; she kissed the scar under his eye and on his knee from his fight with her father all those years ago, found other battle scars on him as well.

In the afterglow, she lay nestled against his side, her ear over his pounding heart. For several long moments they lay silent, each lost in their own thoughts, still stroking each other.

"You've seriously not been with anyone since me?" he asked, stroking her hair.

She looked up at him, her eyes serious. "No," she confessed softly. "What about you? I'm not naïve enough to think you've been celibate all these years."

He was idly stroking her hair, loving the feel of its silky strands between his fingers. "No, I haven't…but there've only been a few and nothing serious. No real relationships since you."

She smiled then laid her head back on his chest,

letting her fingers lightly explore his six-pack abs. "Why do you think that is? Are we too career minded? Or is it really that we are perfectly matched like Miss Nettie and her friends said?"

"Probably both…talk to me about this assignment, Tess. I gotta be honest, it scares the living daylights outta me to think about sending you into that. Have you really done your research on them? I've had run-ins with them over the last few years. I know what they are capable of."

She got up and grabbed his shirt to cover herself while she paced. "I've read up on them. I spoke with Laura Burney, the one woman who did manage to get out."

"I know Laura well. She and I have talked extensively about her time there. We could arrest them on her testimony alone but she's too terrified of the Heltons to press charges."

"I know. She's willing to help as much as she can behind the scenes but her fear of them is too strong for much else."

He sat up, leaning back against the headboard, sheet draped over his midsection. "Then you know what she says they do to women. They aren't just some religious cult, Tess. It's all a front for their sexual perversions."

"I know that…but if there's a way I can help those women then I've got to try."

"Why you? How did you go from the Army to the FBI anyway?"

She raked her hands through her hair and reached for the room service menu.

"I'm starving, you want anything?"

"In a minute. Talk to me, Tess."

With a sigh she put the menu down and resumed pacing. "Gibson was CO of the Ranger battalion I was assigned to. I'd been with him ever since leaving Basics. His secretary retired a few months after I was assigned to his office. She liked me, thought I had a good work ethic and would be suited to his personality. We clicked. He took me under his wing and led me safely through nearly 8 years of service. It was a little over a month after he left to join the FBI that my convoy was hit by an IED. He came to see me in the hospital and offered me the position once I recovered from my injuries. He said he always thought my talents were wasted just doing technical support. That was two years ago."

"Two years? Why didn't you tell me? All this time I thought you were still in the Army."

She shrugged. "I honestly don't know. I just…we never really talked about our careers. Whenever I talked to you I just wanted to hear your voice and hear about you…and it's not like you ever really talked about your job."

"No, but you knew what my job was, where I was living. I wasn't off being a fireman when you thought I was a cop."

She stopped pacing and leaned against the credenza across from him. "I just….I didn't want to get into deep dark discussions with you the few times we got to talk. Those precious few conversations carried me through all the crap I was dealing with. Can you understand that?"

He got to his feet, uncaring of his nudity and came to her. He took her hands into his and raised hers to his lips.

"Yeah, I do understand…and I know you aren't the same person you were ten years ago, but that doesn't mean I don't still feel protective of you. The thought of you going undercover and putting yourself in the path of those psychopaths terrifies me."

She closed her eyes when his arms enveloped her, allowing herself to feel soft and feminine for the first time in a long, long time.

"Is there anything I can say to talk you out of this?" he asked, his voice thick with emotion.

"Not really. Those women, girls really…they need help."

"Have you done undercover work before? Deep cover like this?"

"Not this deep, no, but I have done short undercover stints."

"Damn," he breathed, kissing her brow. "This kind of work, going in that deep and living a lie…it changes you, Tess…please, don't do it. Let someone else go."

She drew back and looked up into his eyes, touched at his concern for her.

"I'll be all right. I can do this, Shane, you have to trust me."

"I do trust you…I just don't want to see you get hurt any more than you already have been…and it's not like you're going to bust a drug ring or something. The Heltons are smooth, master manipulators. They can tell you the sky is purple and by the time they're done with you, you believe them."

"I'm not so easily manipulated these days. Trust me."

He kissed her brow again and pulled her back tightly into his arms.

"How about we get dressed and I take you to dinner?" he suggested, dropping the subject for now.

"That sounds perfect...except you have no buttons left on this shirt," she said, holding the edges out to remind him she'd ripped them off.

"Got one in the truck. Let's go."

Chapter Seven

Over the next few weeks, Shane and Tessa continued to grow closer. Every day they trained, planned and prepared for her eventual entry to the Naturalists' compound. He'd gotten her to give up her extended stay suite and move into his condo so that they were together every night. It was during the first couple of days of staying with him that Shane discovered she was having nightmares about the IED explosion. She fluffed it off, but he couldn't quite dismiss it. He was concerned about how subjecting her to the Naturalists would affect her psyche down the road but the kicker was that he couldn't mention the nightmares to Bruce or Gibson because if they weren't sleeping together he'd never know about them.

He had to admit she was good at what she did. She was an excellent shot, excelled at hand-to-hand, and did an amazing job at softening the hard Cop's Eyes his men had questioned her on that first day. As D-Day approached, though, he couldn't help but wish that he could somehow convince her not to go.

The Wednesday before they planned for Tessa to attend a Naturalists Revival, Shane requested a meeting with Bruce and Gibson just before lunch. They met in

Bruce's office, just the three of them.

"What's on your mind, Shane?" Bruce asked.

"Everything is ready for Saturday night. There isn't anything more we can do. I'd like to take Tessa away until Saturday, just give us both a chance to breathe…and to say good-bye."

Gibson shook his head. "That's not a good idea. This assignment is unlike anything Tessa's ever done before. I need her fully focused and ready."

"With all due respect, sir, she's as ready as she's ever going to be. We're about to send her in under deep cover. Who knows how long it will be before she can return to her own life. Give us this time."

"I agree with Shane," Bruce said, "This case could take months. Let her have this last bit of freedom."

Gibson stood and stared out Bruce's window to the bullpen where Tessa sat with the rest of the joint team going over the layout of the compound.

"That girl is like a daughter to me," Gibson confessed. "Do you have any idea what she went through in Iraq?"

"I know her convoy was hit by an IED. I know that her uterus was so damaged by shrapnel that she was told she may never be able to have children…and I know that the first thirteen years of her life were Hell on Earth because her father beat her mother and constantly berated her. Don't think for one minute that I don't know what Tessa has suffered through. Don't think that it's not killing me to know we're about to drop her right back in to that type of environment. It is. I know what it will do to her, what it will cost her…but I know that she wants this, and as much as it hurts me, I won't stand in her way. I want to. I want to take her away from all of this and protect her, but she'd hate me for it…please…just give us this time together."

The room fell silent while the two older men contemplated what he said. He was fully prepared to take her without their permission if it came to it. Bruce knew it, he was sure.

Finally, Gibson took a deep breath, released it. "Have her back here first thing Saturday morning."

"Thank you," Shane said, leaving the office.

Gibson leveled Bruce with a look. "You said he wouldn't let his feelings for her interfere with this investigation."

"They haven't."

"He's taking my lead asset away two days before the start of the operation."

"It's the right thing to do and you know it.":

"Is it?" Gibson asked, watching Shane approach Tessa. "In all the years I've known her, she's never dated. Some of the guys thought she was a lesbian…she told me about McCanton one time. We were in Afghanistan. She said he lost a baseball scholarship because of her, that he'd injured his knee in a fight with that POS who fathered her. She said she would never love anyone but him. I asked why she wasn't with him and she told me she wasn't good enough for him." He turned back to face Bruce. "Truth is, he isn't good enough for her. No one is."

Bruce smiled. "On that point, my friend, you are wrong. There's no one more honorable than Shane McCanton."

Tessa had seen Shane enter Bruce's office with Gibson and watched an animated discussion unfold. It looked heated between him and Gibson for a few moments, but when Shane emerged his features seemed relaxed.

"C'mon," he said, offering Tessa his hand, "we're outta here."

"What? But -"

"Guys, see you here Saturday, 10 am."

"Later, Boss, Tessa," Joe said.

"What are you doing?" she asked, following him out of the office.

"We're checking out for a couple of days. How's San Antonio sound?"

She gaped at him. "Shane! We have to prepare for-"

He stopped her in the elevator with a quick but heated kiss. "You are ready, Tess. It's time to focus just on you for a couple of days."

She allowed herself to smile then. "San Antonio sounds perfect."

When they got home, he was on her the minute the door closed. Tessa laughed and eagerly welcomed him. She met him with equal passion, kiss for kiss, stroke for stroke. He took her hard up against the wall and she loved it, screaming his name when her climax came.

"Uh uh," he said, slowing, "more. Give me more."

He brought her to a second peak before carrying her to the bathroom and starting all over again in the shower. By the time they finally landed on the bed, Tessa wasn't sure she'd ever be able to walk again…and she loved it.

Shane held her tight in his arms, afraid to let her go. The past few months had been the best of his life. He couldn't stand the thought of her leaving in a few days. The condo would seem empty without her; he didn't know how he'd make it.

"Shh," she soothed, kissing the scowl from his forehead. "Don't think about it."

"I can't help it," he admitted on a hoarse whisper. "I only just got you back."

"It's only temporary. I'll come back to you."

"But we have no clue as to when…and…"

"Let's not talk about it now, OK? We're together now…are we going to San Antonio?"

He stroked her hair. "Do you want to?"

"I just want to be with you."

He kissed her. "Get packed then. Let's go."

In San Antonio they did their best to enjoy each other's company and the city. They walked hand-in-hand on the river walk and took a riverboat cruise. They shopped and got massages at their hotel spa, and made love as if they would never see each other again. Tears streamed from her eyes each time and Shane wordlessly kissed them away. It was the most perfect time of her life. She loved Shane with all her heart and she knew he felt the same for her…and it was why she knew she would have to let him go, though just the thought of it broke her heart.

She knew he planned to ask her to marry him. She'd seen the box in his bag when they'd arrived. On one level, she was thrilled; Shane was all she ever wanted; but it was foolish of her to dream of a life with him. He deserved someone who wasn't damaged and who would give him a family.

Feeling her heart break into a million tiny pieces, she hugged his arms closer to her and couldn't stop the sobs that took over her entire body.

"Tess…hey, what's wrong?" he asked, trying to sit up. She kept a death grip on his arms which kept him on his side. "Baby, talk to me." She shook her head, still sobbing.

Shane placed tender kisses along her brow, smoothing her hair back, whispering soothing words to her.

When nothing worked, he used his strength to pull his arms free, then proceeded to make love to her once again.

"Tessa…look at me," he demanded while they were still joined. "I mean it, Tess. Look at me!" he said forcefully.

She slowly opened her teary eyes and focused in the dark on his deep blue ones.

"I love you, baby. I always have and I always will. No matter what."

"Shane," she cried, knowing what he would say next, "please, don't."

He flexed his hips, moving deep inside her, making her gasp. "Marry me, Tessa," he said on a thrust, "Say yes. Say yes."

"Oh, God…Shane," she sobbed, pushing on his chest.

"I love you so much, Tess. No one will ever love you more."

"Let me up," she panted, pushing on his shoulders, panic setting in. "Oh, God, Shane, let me up."

Stunned, he rolled away. She scrambled off the bed but her knees gave out and she crumbled on the floor, sobbing. He sat for a moment just watching her, trying to understand what was happening. He knew she loved him; knew she wasn't flat out rejecting him but still, it hurt. It hurt to ask and to have her turn away from him. Finally, he got up and gathered her into his arms, sitting and cradling her in his lap, letting her cry it out, just stroking her hair.

"I'm sorry," she whispered after several long moments.

"Wanna tell me what you're thinking?" he asked quietly.

She drew a deep, ragged breath. "You deserve so much more."

"Than you?" he asked. She nodded. "Why would you think that?" Her hand automatically covered the jagged scar on her abdomen. "Because of that?"

"I can't give you children," she whispered.

He kissed her brow. "Do you really think I care about that?"

"You should."

"Don't tell me what I should care about," he admonished gently.

"You may not care right now but you will."

"Who told you that you couldn't have children? An Army doctor?" She nodded. "We can go see a specialist, baby. Don't turn away from what we have because of this."

"Shane,"

"Do you love me?" he asked, cutting her off.

"You know I do."

He reached over to the side table and pulled the ring box from the drawer. Opening it, he took the diamond out and slipped it onto the third finger of her left hand.

"Wear this until Saturday morning and then I'll keep it for you."

"You can't give up a possibility of a family because of me."

He wiped tears from her cheeks with his thumbs, cradling her face in his hands. "I can't live without you. Not now."

More tears fell down her cheeks. "This assignment-"

"Is temporary, like you said. Don't you want to be with me?"

"I just don't want you to miss out on…"

He stopped her with a tender kiss. "I love you. If you want kids, we can adopt."

"But you could have-"

"You. I want you, Tess. If we can't have our own child, I'm fine with it just being us or adopting. Whatever you want."

She stroked his face and kissed him. "I love you," she whispered against her lips.

"You wanna get dressed and hit the river walk again?"

She shook her head. "I just want to stay here in your arms as long as I can."

"I can do that. Wanna soak in the Jacuzzi?"

Later that night when Shane had fallen asleep, Tessa went back into the bathroom to soak in the tub by herself and to try to sort through everything. She stared at his ring on her finger. It was beautiful, a large round diamond that she guessed to be two karats bordered on each side by two more diamonds, so five in all, set in platinum. It showed off her tan to perfection. She already loved it and hated that she'd have to give it up to him tomorrow…but if she allowed herself to be honest, it terrified her too.

She did love Shane. She'd known, even that first day of Kindergarten that they were meant to be together. There was a niggling fear, though, buried deep in her mind, that told her she didn't need any man; that her mother had completely lost herself to a man and she vowed that would never be her. Even though she knew beyond a shadow of a doubt that Shane was nothing like Harrison Kelly, it was hard to shake that fear.

Her mind shifted to her upcoming assignment. The Texas Mountain Naturalists were a separatist group who believed Texas should once again be it's own nation. They were also a pseudo-religious group who believed their Supreme Leader, Nathaniel Helton and his younger brother, Paul, were direct descendants of Jesus, a la the DaVinci Code. She really even hesitated to put them in the religious cult category, though, because they were basically anarchists using their own twisted interpretations of the Bible to cover their subjugation of women, both physically and emotionally.

She looked up when the door opened and Shane

came in. He was still nude from their last round and not a bit bashful.

"You OK?" he asked, massaging her shoulders.

"Mm, that feels good," she moaned. "I'm fine…just getting my thoughts organized for tomorrow."

He kissed the top of her head and continued the massage. "I just checked my messages. Gibson's got your condo and bank account ready to go. Closet is stocked so you won't be taking any of your own stuff."

She nodded. "How long do you think it will take them to recruit me?"

"Not long once they run a check on your financials, which I believe they will somehow do tomorrow while you're in their tent."

"Think so?"

"You'll present just enough class for them to notice you. Just remember to act like Missy Andrews and you'll be all set," he chuckled, referring to an old classmate of theirs.

"Noticed I was imitating her, did you?"

"You nailed her. 'Why, Pete, whatever do you mean?'" he singsonged.

Tessa smiled. "She always did have that perfect Southern Belle thing going for her."

"I'm surprised she didn't end up in a group like the Naturalists. She was so naïve."

"Maybe she has more brains than you give her credit

for. Didn't she end up marrying a doctor from Dallas?"

"A plastic surgeon at that," he laughed. "Come on, come to bed. You need to sleep."

"I'll be there in a bit. I just need some time to myself."

He nodded and kissed her. "Don't take too long, OK?"

"OK. Shane?"

"Yeah?" he said, stopping at the door.

"I love you."

He came back to her and lifted her left hand, placing a lingering kiss over the engagement ring. For a moment, he stayed, gazing into her eyes, then winked at her and left.

She almost called him back but her body was too deliciously sore for another round with him, and honestly, she didn't know how much time she would have to herself in the weeks to come.

Chapter Eight

The ride back to Austin and the offices went much too quickly for them both. In spite of their best efforts, neither slept much the night before. They lay wrapped in each other's arms, dozing periodically, but always waking at the other's touch.

She made him stop by his condo before going to the office; there were a couple of things she needed to take care of before she left. Last night she'd written two letters on hotel stationary, one to him and one to her mother, just in case anything were to go wrong. She placed them under his pillow then retrieved her Army dog tags.

Shane was standing out on the balcony when she emerged from the bedroom. She went to him, took his hand, and placed the dog tags in it.

"Hang on to these for me?" she asked.

He looked at his hand, saw that she had placed his ring on the chain with the tags.

"It's a beautiful ring," she said, smiling, "I don't think I told you that last night."

He was solemn as he slipped the chain over his head and tucked it beneath his shirt.

"Promise me you'll come back to claim these."

"I'll do my best," she offered.

He pressed his forehead to hers a moment, running his hands up and down her arms, just needing to touch her. It was killing him, knowing what she was walking into, knowing he couldn't stop her.

"We're going to be late," she said softly, "Gib'll have a cow."

He kissed her forehead. "I know. Bruce has already called and texted several times."

She cupped his face in her hands and kissed him with every ounce of passion she possessed. "I love you, Shane McCanton."

"I love you, too. You take care of my Tessa, Maddie Parker," he said, using her undercover name.

She kissed him once again and then stepped back. It was the hardest step she'd ever taken.

"Let's get this show on the road, Serg."

Everyone was waiting for them in the Briefing Room when they arrived just ten minutes late. Gibson gave them a stern glare but wisely kept silent. They went over last minute details, quizzed her and Ian, the other agent going undercover, on their personas, then implanted each with a GPS tracker under their skin and a listening device attached to their scalps.

"We will be able to monitor everything whenever you press it to activate it," Crownover explained, "but the only time you'll hear us is when you insert the ear piece."

"It stays fairly well concealed but don't press your luck with it," Shane told her, "try only to use it when you're checking in."

"The glasses are of course, a camera," Crownover continued, "wear them as often as you can when you first arrive at the compound. Look at everything and everyone. They may not allow you to keep these and insist on giving you some of their own so the first few hours are crucial."

She nodded. "Are you ever going to tell me your first name, Crownover?" she asked, making them all laugh.

"Not likely," he said.

"OK, well, I should go. It's going to take nearly an hour to get to their revival tent from here."

"Be careful, Tessa," Gibson told her.

"Always."

"I'll walk you down to your car," Shane said when she turned to him. She nodded and together they headed for the elevator. "If things get too rough, if you need me, you work San Antonio into a conversation and I'll be there in a heartbeat, you hear me?" She nodded. "I mean it, Tess. I'll tell the others too in case I'm not monitoring. If things go south, you say San Antonio and we're there."

"I will." She placed her hand on his heart, over her

initials in his tattoo. "I love you."

"I love you, too. You come back to me, Tessa Kelly."

"Always."

The instant she was out of his sight, Shane felt a cold emptiness settle in his chest. He rubbed the heel of his hand over the tattoo, over his heart and prayed God would help them both through the coming days.

Part Two

Chapter Nine

Getting recruited by the Naturalists turned out to be easier than Tessa had expected. She went to their so-called "revival" meeting Saturday evening, which turned out to be little more than a cattle call in her opinion. The "sermon" lasted just over 45 minutes and was followed by a mixer. She was amused to see that the "Supreme Leader", Nathaniel Helton, had stepped off the stage and walked directly to her. Shane and his guys had a good chuckle over it.

"Make a bee line to the hot blonde in designer clothes," Pete had teased.

It had been the perfect thing to say to put a smile on her face as Nathaniel approached. She had to admit he was handsome. He had dark blonde hair and golden eyes. She knew he was in his mid-forties but looked much younger.

"Welcome to our meeting," he greeted, a warm smile pasted on his face. A smile, Tessa noted, that didn't quite reach his eyes.

"Why, thank you," she said, adding a bit of a breathless tone to her voice. "It was most enlightening."

"I am Nathaniel Helton," he said, taking her hand into

his. "And you are?"

"Madalyn Parker," she replied.

"Ah, Maddie, there you are," Ian said, coming up to join them. "Nathaniel, I see you've met Maddie. She is the friend I was telling you about."

"You failed to mention how absolutely stunning she is, Ian," Nathaniel said, raising her hand to his lips and placing a lingering kiss to her knuckles.

"Aren't you sweet," Tessa purred to him, smiling brightly.

"Just stating the obvious," he said, giving her hand a squeeze before releasing it. She noted that his hands were smooth, no working man's callouses. It was probably a good bet that the man had never done any physical labor in his life.

"Maddie was saying that she was interested in exploring new experiences and so I thought she may enjoy your little group," Ian told Nathaniel, "excuse me, won't you? I want a word with Paul."

"Nathaniel," a man across the way called out to him.

"Yes, John, give me just a moment," he replied, then turned his attention back to Tessa. "Forgive me, Ms. Parker, I'm afraid duty calls. "Of course," she replied.

"I would like to speak more with you on our group. How about lunch tomorrow?"

"That would be wonderful."

"How about I pick you up?"

"All right," she agreed. She gave him her address and phone number then watched as he again raised her hand to his lips.

"Until tomorrow then," he said.

"Until tomorrow," she echoed.

She watched him cross the room to join the men who had called out to him. She wandered the tent for a few more moments then decided to call it a night. Making eye contact with Ian, she nodded to him then began walking out of the tent.

"Leaving already?" she heard Gib question.

"It's OK," Shane spoke up, "she secured a meeting for tomorrow, Helton has her address and number now. There really isn't more she can accomplish tonight."

"Fine," Gib relented, "but Tessa, go straight to the condo. You and Shane can have no contact in case they are monitoring."

"I know that, Gib," she spoke when she was safely in her car.

"Come on, man," Pete spoke, "chances that they will already have someone on her condo are slim to none, and transmissions…"

"It's OK, Pete," Shane broke in, "I wasn't planning on going over there. I don't need to be seen by anyone in the building. It's all good."

"All right, guys, I'm unplugging until the morning. You're all going to be living in my life soon enough. I'm taking every last second of privacy I can get."

"No worries, Tess. We'll talk more in the morning," Gib assured her.

When she got to her condo, Tessa powered up her personal phone and sent a text to Shane.

I'm back now. That meeting was really weird. I'm still not clear on exactly
what their appeal is, but it is clear to see Nathaniel's appeal. He is much
more handsome in person than in pictures.

She hit send and poured herself a glass of wine while waiting for his reply. She didn't have to wait long.

Should I be worried?

She laughed. He's handsome but he gives me the creeps. His eyes are cold.

He's a bastard, Tess. Don't lose sight of that, he replied.

Yes, dear.

I'm serious. The man is a master manipulator.

I know. I'll be fine, I promise. I'd better get in bed so I can be fresh for tomorrow.

I wish I was there with you, he sent.

Me, too. I love you. Good night.

Tessa dressed carefully for her lunch date the next day. He didn't specify what type of restaurant they would be going to, but she was banking on him wanting to impress her so she wore a Valentino form-fitting dress in a pale pink that showed off her tan and hit at a respectably conservative two-inches above her knee. She kept her legs bare and paired it with Louboutin pumps in a matching color. Her hair she wore in a sleek braided knot at the nape of her neck, but allowed a few flirtatious wisps to remain free to fall on her left cheek. She kept her jewelry elegant but simple. Diamond stud earrings, no necklace, a simple cocktail ring on her right hand and a diamond tennis bracelet to complete the ensemble.

Her doorbell rang and she noticed he was precisely on time.

"Show time," she said, checking her hair in the hallway mirror.

"You look perfect, Blondie," Shane encouraged.

"Of course I do."

His laughter filled her ear as she opened the door to greet Nathaniel.

"Don't you look stunning," he greeted her. "These are for you," he said, handing her a dozen long-stemmed white roses.

"They're beautiful," she said, opening the door wider. "Come in while I put these in a vase."

"Bottom right cabinet in the kitchen," Crownover advised her.

"Would you like a drink, Nathaniel?" she asked when she went into the kitchen.

"I'm good, but thanks."

"They're running your financials right now," Shane told her.

"What did you think of our little service last night, Madelyn?" Nathaniel asked her as she arranged the roses in a vase. "I didn't get a chance to ask you last night."

"You know, it wasn't so bad. I've always been skeptical of revivals, but yours wasn't like I've always heard about them."

He flashed her a smile, showing perfectly straight and whitened teeth. "No fire and brimstone threats?"

Tessa laughed. "Exactly. My friend Ian has visited several times and told me I would find your services enjoyable."

"How do you know Ian?" he asked.

"We went to college together. He dated my friend for a while, that's how we met."

"Nothing romantic between the two of you? Ian is a handsome fellow."

"Ian's more like a brother to me."

"Careful," Gibson cautioned, "No close associations."

"Like a bossy big brother," she added. "If you know

Ian at all you know how…domineering he can be. We get along, though."

Nathaniel nodded. "Ian has visited our retreat several times. Has he spoken of it?"

"Just that he thought your group might be good for me."

"Why would he think that?"

"He said your group seemed like a family. I've never really had much family to speak of. It appeals to me."

Nathaniel smiled and looked around her condo with an appraising eye.

"Your home is nice," he said, changing the subject. "What do you do for a living again?"

"Oh, well, I live off my trust fund. My parents were killed in a plane crash just after I graduated college. Although, I went to school to be a teacher."

His face brightened at that. "Really? We are always looking for teachers at the Retreat. Do you think you would be interested?"

"Possibly," she hedged.

"Well, if you're ready, lets discuss it over lunch."

"I am ready," she agreed, following him out the door. He led her down to a black Cadillac Escalade with a driver waiting to open the door for them.

"Seriously trying to impress the lady," Joe's voice sounded in her ear. "Fancy car, uniformed driver. Pull out all the stops."

She tapped the mike to get him to cut the chatter so she could concentrate. Their drive into town was short. They stopped at a small bistro that she knew was hard to get reservations for. When they walked in, she wasn't surprised to see that the hostess was one of Nathaniel's starry-eyed admirers who led them directly back to an intimate table in a quiet corner near a serene water feature. Nathaniel ordered for them both, without even asking her which irritated Tessa but she decided to let Maddie just go with the flow about it.

To her surprise, conversation flowed freely between them. She found herself oddly relaxed in his presence and began to see even more of his appeal. He had a way about him that put her at ease in spite of the fact that she knew she had to keep on her toes with him. Conversation ran so smoothly that at one point, Shane actually growled in her ear to remember who he was, which made her inadvertently laugh out so that she had to offer a hasty explanation for it. Other than that, she felt everything was moving along well.

"I would love to show you around The Retreat," he said as they were finishing their meal. "You could see how we live and see whether you would want to take on teaching the children who live on the grounds."

"I'd like that, Nathaniel."

"Yeah?" he asked, smiling. He took her hand in his and once more brought it to her lips, this time kissing her fingertips and then her knuckles. Had Shane ever done this, kiss her hand like this? She tried to recall but didn't believe he had...they were kids when they got together, he hadn't needed this type of courting, and since she hadn't really dated anyone but him, she really didn't have anything to compare this to. She found that, while pleasant, she didn't really think she'd like someone who was overly demonstrative like that. It wasn't real affection and it felt that way, and she wouldn't want Shane to be any way other than he was with her.

"I could come pick you up tomorrow," Nathaniel offered, pulling her from her thoughts.

"That's OK, I can drive myself," she said, not wanting to surrender that little bit of freedom.

"Are you sure? It's no trouble for me to come get you, and The Retreat is a bit of a drive from here."

"I don't mind driving. Just give me the address and I'll plug it into my GPS. What time would you like me to come?"

Chapter Ten

She arrived at the compound at noon on Monday, was waved through the checkpoint and directed to the Main House where Nathaniel and his brother, Paul waited to greet her. Paul was in his late thirties, similar in height and build to his brother but she found his eyes to be a bit colder than Nathaniel's. Here was the nasty side of the operation, she thought. Paul definitely reminded her of Harrison Kelly.

"So glad you could make it, Madelyn," Nathaniel greeted her when she got out of her Lexus. "Paul, this is the lovely young lady I had the pleasure of spending the afternoon with yesterday, Madelyn Parker. Madelyn, this is my brother and Associate Leader, Paul."

"Pleased to meet you, Paul," she beamed at him.

"Miss Parker," Paul replied coolly, his eyes assessing her.

Tessa had to fight the urge to shudder under his scrutiny and kept a bright smile on her face. Nathaniel kissed her cheek and placed his hand on the small of her back to lead her up the steps of the Main House. The satellite images hadn't really conveyed the opulence of the buildings. This was definitely no Branch Davidian compound.

"This is your home?" she asked Nathaniel, taking his arm when he offered it.

"This is it," he confirmed. "We live here in the Main House with a few select others."

"Look around at everything, Tess," Shane reminded her. Just the sound of his voice in her ear sent a shiver down her spine.

"Are you all right?" Nathaniel asked, feeling her shiver.

"Just got a chill," she said, smiling when he rubbed her arm.

Nathaniel stopped walking and turned to face her fully. "You are absolutely stunning, Madelyn. Your smile is brighter than the sun."

"Thank you," she said, ignoring the gagging noises she was hearing from the guys in her ear.

"Nathaniel?" Paul said from behind them, "May I have a word with you, please?"

"Not just now, Paul. I'm giving Madelyn a tour of the grounds."

"Oo, tension amongst the brothers," Joe said.

"Use that, Tess. Play them against each other," Gibson advised.

"Thank you, Captain Obvious," Pete replied.

Tessa cleared her throat, hoping they would get the

message to shut up. It was hard enough to concentrate without them carrying on all the time.

"If you'd like to talk, I could make a quick trip to the ladies room," she offered.

"Certainly," Nathaniel said, "Just around the corner, first door on the right. I'll be right here."

"Then if you'll excuse me, I'll leave you to talk." She walked off, acutely aware that both men's eyes followed her as she went.

"Do not under any circumstances speak to us when you get in there," Gibson ordered. "Chances are they have the restroom monitored."

"Again, Captain Obvious? You've known her for years, I've known her for weeks but I know she's not that dumb. C'mon," Pete said.

Tessa tapped the mike twice to let them know she was turning it off and removing the glasses briefly while she used the restroom. When she put them back on and tapped the mike she was standing before the mirror.

"Hey, babe," Shane's voice sounded, "Just me for a few. I sent everyone else out for a minute. Look directly in the mirror and give a slow blink if you can hear me." She did.
"Look, it's obvious Nathaniel is attracted to you. Are you OK with encouraging him? One for yes, two for no." She blinked once, slowly, an apologetic look on her face. "You don't worry about me. I'm a big boy, I can handle it. I know you

love me. You'd best head back out. You're doing great, babe. I love you."

She gave him a wink then headed out. When she rounded the corner, Nathaniel was talking to two women, one older, one younger. The older woman, who looked to be in her fifties, had salt and peppered hair pulled back into a braided bun at the nape of her neck and wore a white shirt with black slacks. The younger woman appeared to be in her early twenties, wore her brunette hair long and flowing and wore a long white shift dress with sandals. From all she knew from their research, she knew that the older women acted like "Dorm Mothers" to the younger women.

There was a stern look on Nathaniel's face as he spoke to the women but it was completely masked when he spotted Tessa.

"Joyce, take Olivia to see Paul in his office," he instructed the older woman.

At his declaration, Olivia paled and grasped his hand. "Please, Nathaniel," she cried in a soft whisper.

"Our rules are in place to assure your safety, Olivia," he said in a fatherly tone. "Now, go with Joyce."

Olivia dropped her hand from his and slowly followed Joyce from the room.

"That girl was terrified, Nathaniel," Tessa said when he approached her.

He offered her an indulgent smile. "Not to worry. Just

a small matter."

"But why would she be scared?"

"Don't push too hard right now, Tess," Shane cautioned.

"One of the reasons for our success in maintaining a peaceful, harmonious atmosphere with so many people living together is our adherence to structure. Rules are set to maintain everyone's happiness and safety. Those who choose to live within our walls do so of their own free will and with the knowledge that rules are set, maintained and enforced for the greater good of the community. Everyone works together and it runs smoothly; however, there are times that rules are broken. Consequences are severe in order to keep violations to a minimum."

"Consequences? You sound as if you are speaking of children. Olivia can't be much younger than me, but it seems as if you were sending her off to be punished like a child."

He once again raised her hand to his lips, something she supposed he was fond of doing.

"Not like a child, Madelyn. Like a beloved woman of the Naturalists fold who just needs a reminder of why she chose to be here."

"I'm afraid I don't follow."

"You're supposed to be buying into the lifestyle, Tess," Gibson reminded her.

Nathaniel smiled indulgently, tucked her hand in his arm and began walking.

"Think back to when you were in grade school. With a few exceptions, you generally loved and respected your teachers, did you not?"

"Yes."

"No one would dare sass a teacher back then because the consequences were more severe than they are now. Discipline was key. Here within the walls of the Retreat, we have brought discipline back and our members are happier because of it." He took her into a building to the back left of the Main House. "This is our single women's dormitory, where Olivia lives. There are three floors, with the Main Floor being the common areas and study rooms. As you can see, this is where we allow our men to visit the ladies, supervised of course. The upper floors are dorms and Paul and I are the only men allowed on those floors. The safety of our cherished females is our top priority."

"Look at as many people as possible, Tess," Shane reminded her.

He led her to the elevator and they took it to the top floor. As soon as he stepped out of the doors, dozens of young, beautiful women surrounded him, calling out his name and smiling like star-struck teens. They all wore the same long, flowing white shift Olivia had worn, all with long hair, all thin, none larger than a size 8 she would guess, and all pretty; not a fat, ugly duckling among them.

"Holy David Koresh, Batman," Joe said and Tessa had to fight hard not to laugh.

A stern woman dressed as Joyce had been emerged and firmly clapped her hands. "Ladies, step back, let Nathaniel breathe for pity's sake," she scolded them.

The women all took a step back and instantly hushed.

"Thank you, Deborah," Nathaniel addressed the older woman.

"I'm not seeing the Senator's daughter," Crownover said.

"Me, either. Are you looking at everyone in the room, Tessa?" Gibson inquired.

Tessa wished she could tell them all to be quiet. They were very distracting.

"Have you brought us a new sister, Nathaniel?" a starry-eyed petite blonde asked.

"Well, Tina, I'm not quite sure. Ladies, this is Madelyn Parker. She is my Very Special Guest."

A unison feminine gasp sounded from the room and as one they all bowed their heads and curtsied as if she were the Queen of England or something.

"What the hell?" the men in her ear all gasped at once.

"Oh, um, OK," Tessa said, taken aback by their gesture. "Nathaniel? Am I missing something here?"

He chuckled. "Not at all. They are merely showing deference to you as my Very Special Guest."

"Welcome, Madelyn," Deborah said.

"Um, it's Maddie, actually, and thanks."

"Madelyn is such a distinguished name," Nathaniel said, stroking a lock of Tessa's hair. "I prefer it."

"Um, OK, well-"

"Relax, Tess," Shane's soothing voice sounded, calming her. She was thankful for his voice; she was beginning to be weirded out by their behavior.

"Come, let's resume our tour," he said, again kissing her hand. She was beginning to feel like she'd need to disinfect her hand as soon as she got back to her condo. As it was, she had to fight the urge to jerk her hand away. He led her through the dormitory, showing her where the women slept. She noticed that the rooms were plain, with very little personal items or decorations, and exceedingly neat. The clinical feel saddened her. These women were being programmed, stripped of their personalities to become like brainless Stepford Wives.

One door they came to was closed. Nathaniel immediately demanded an explanation from Deborah. Tessa took that to mean closed doors were not common.

"It is Stephanie. She's just returned from the Arena," Deborah explained.

"The Senator's daughter's name is Stephanie,"

Gibson said, "that could be her."

Tessa tuned out the Captain Obvious remarks from the men and watched when Nathaniel opened the door. Tessa saw a dark haired girl lying on her stomach on the bed, her dress pushed down to her waist and a poultice of some sort on her back.

"Excuse me just a moment, Madelyn," he said, going to the girl on the bed. She watched him sit on the edge of the bed and gently place his hand on Stephanie's head. "Stephanie?" Tessa watched the girl slowly turn her head toward Nathaniel.

"That's her," Gibson confirmed.

Tessa's breath caught in her throat when Nathaniel carefully removed the poultice. There were bloody, criss-crossing stripes on the girl's back. Tessa thought she was going to be sick. Nathaniel was talking in soothing tones to the sobbing girl but she couldn't make out their words.

"Tess?" Shane's voice sounded in her hair. "Keep it together. I know you're pissed. You can't show that to him. Not yet." She closed her eyes a moment, listening to his voice. He knew her so well. She wanted to rush in and pummel Nathaniel, pull Stephanie away from this awful place. She gasped when Nathaniel's hand touched her cheek, her eyes flying open.

"I'm sorry you had to see that on your first visit," he said softly. "Stephanie is one of our newer members and is having a bit of a hard time adjusting."

"Why not just let her leave?" Tessa asked, unable to keep the shock from her tone.

"She was given the option. She chose to stay and accept the consequences of her actions."

He led Tessa from the building, casually strolling with her in the sunshine.

"What could she have possibly done to warrant that, and what's this Arena you speak of?" she asked. "I take it that is where that was done to Stephanie."

"It's nothing you need ever to be concerned with," he said, stopping in a flower strewn gazebo that very much reminded her of the one back home in Indian Springs. "What do you think? Beautiful here, isn't it?"

"Very much so. But, Nathaniel, what was done to that girl-"

"You know, I couldn't help but notice how much you outshone all those beautiful women back there," he said, dodging her remark. "You are truly stunning, Madelyn. You take my breath away."

She felt a blush rising on her cheeks that had nothing to do with Nathaniel's flowery words and everything to do with all the gagging and kissing noises she was hearing in her ear from the guys.

"Thank you, Nathaniel, but you didn't let me finish. That girl had been whipped…as in, with a whip. Again, what could she possibly have done to warrant that?"

"Back off, Tessa," Gibson again warned her.

"Just relax, babe," Shane cut in.

"I'm not aware of the specific infraction," Nathaniel told her. "But be assured, Stephanie chose this, and she will be a better member for it. Think of it as a purification of sorts."

Tessa was afraid she wouldn't be able to keep the horror she felt from her face so she turned from him to gaze out over the grounds. He came to stand behind her and placed his hands on her shoulders, gently massaging them.

"Nathaniel-" she began but he cut her off.

"When she is feeling better in a couple of days, you can talk to her. See that this is indeed her choice. Would that make you feel better?"

"It would, yes."

"Would you consider coming to stay here at the Retreat? Getting to know me and our lifestyle a little better?"

"Oh. Wow, um…I don't…wow."

"I know we just met," he said in a rush, "but I feel such a connection to you. Not just your beauty but your intelligence."

"Not to mention your bank account," Joe said dryly.

She turned back to face him. "I feel a connection to you as well, Nathaniel, but I have to be honest, what I saw back there, I'm not 100% comfortable with. I don't think I could live the way those women back there are."

"Tessa!" Gibson admonished.

"I wouldn't dream of putting you in the dorms, Madelyn. You would stay in the Main House. I meant what I told them; you are my Very Special Guest."

"And what does that mean to them, Nathaniel? Why did they treat me the way they did?"

"Just a sign of respect."

"Yes, but why to me? What are you telling them when you say I'm your Very Special Guest?"

He smiled, "Can't slip anything past you…I was telling them that I'd like for you to be mine."

"Nathaniel," she gasped with a smile.

"Too fast for you?"

She stepped closer to him. "Well, now, I don't know. You haven't even kissed me yet."

He stroked his finger down her cheek then touched her lower lip. "I don't usually move this quickly, but ever since you walked into my tent I haven't been able to get you out of my mind."

The guys all groaned when he leaned in to touch his lips to hers. Shane clenched his teeth and cut the mike so nothing they said would distract her. He drew a deep breath and let it out slowly, getting up to pace.

"You all right?" Bruce asked him.

"I'm fine," he said in a clipped tone. He glanced at the

monitor, saw that Helton had removed her glasses so at least they weren't looking at a close up of the creep's face.

"How is it that someone as beautiful as you isn't taken?" Helton asked her.

"I was in a relationship," she said. "It ended badly."

"I'm sorry…but then I'm grateful, since it has allowed you to be here with me."

Their conversation died again and Shane knew he'd probably kissed her once more. He thought of his time with her in San Antonio and touched his hand over her ring and dog tags. He knew as hard as this was for him to watch and listen to, it was worse for her.

"Pictures's back," Joe said.

He looked back at the monitor, taking in Helton's smug face. He wanted to knock that look off the SOB so bad he couldn't stand it, especially when Tessa's hand appeared on screen, wiping her lipstick from his face.

"Want to see the classrooms? Meet some of the children?"

"Absolutely," she replied. While they began walking, she tapped the mike.

"We're here, Tess," Gibson replied. She tapped it three times, her signal for Shane.

He closed his eyes his eyes for a moment then turned his mike back on.

"I'm here, babe. Everything's cool," he assured her,

keeping his voice level.

"How many children live here?" they heard her ask, letting them know she was satisfied with his reply.

"Thirty two in all, but only eleven are school age as of now. We have a couple of women who home school them but we'd much rather have an actual teacher."

"What are their ages?"

"Five thru eleven. We go ahead and allow the older students to attend public schools. Less red tape that way."

Thankfully from all of Shane's investigations they knew that the children were not subject to the abuse the women were. He didn't know if she would be able to stand it if the children were being abused.

He ignored the chatter between them concerning school matters, wondering off hand how she knew so much about curriculums. He couldn't wait for her to get out of there tonight. He needed to see her. He thought he could handle knowing she was kissing someone else but he'd been fooling himself. It hurt. It brought out a vicious, Neanderthal side of him he never knew existed.

"She'll be fine for the time being," Bruce said, clamping a hand on Shane's shoulder. "Come on, let's take a walk."

Shane nodded, allowing Bruce to escort him out of the control room and into the kitchen of their temporary command house, just over a mile up the road from the

Naturalists compound.

"That was hard for you to see," Bruce stated.

Shane rubbed the back of his neck. "Yeah…it was."

"I was worried about you in there."

"I'll handle it…somehow."

"If this is going to tear you up, maybe you should-"

"Don't, Bruce, OK? I'll be fine. I'd rather be here watching than not knowing what's going on."

"I understand. Just don't let it eat you up inside."

Shane pulled the dog tag chain from his neck. "I gave her this the other day," he said, showing Bruce the ring. "Haven't even told my folks yet. Hell, they don't even know Tessa's back in my life."

"Well…your dad knows. Sorry," Bruce smiled.

Shane smiled, opening the fridge and taking out a Coke. "That's OK. My dad likes Tessa. My mom? Not so much."

"Susie'll come around."

"Maybe…I don't really care. Tessa has always been it for me."

"Hey, Mac, she's asking for you again," Crownover said, stepping out of the Control Room. "He's trying to get her to stay the night."

Tessa was getting worried about Shane. She hadn't heard from him ever since they left the gazebo. She'd tapped the mike and Joe told her they'd get him but that had been several minutes ago. After seeing the children and the school she needed to hear his voice, was desperate to hear him, actually.

"Hey, Tess, I'm back. The guys said you saw the kids and they all look healthy and happy. That's good news at least."

Tessa took a deep breath, taking comfort in the sound of Shane's voice.

"I really would like for you to stay tonight," Nathaniel pressed again when they arrived back at the Main House.

"I can't tonight, Nathaniel. I have an appointment in the morning."

"You can't reschedule?"

"I'm afraid not…but I can come back when it's over, and plan to stay tomorrow night. How's that?"

"I suppose it will have to do…you do promise to return, though, right? I'm afraid I've already gotten spoiled by your presence."

She laughed. "I absolutely promise."

He cupped her face tenderly in his hands and kissed her in full view of everyone gathering for evening chapel.

"Be careful going home and hurry back to me," he said against her lips.

"I will. Good night, Nathaniel."

He kissed her once more then opened her car door for her. She got in and took a deep breath.

"Do not say anything yet," Shane cautioned her. "There's a diner on the way out of here, about twenty miles down the road. Ed's Café. Stop there and we'll talk."

She smiled and waved to Nathaniel as she drove off. He was an extremely charming man, she thought. It was easy to see why so many women had fallen under his spell. He was handsome and charming and honestly, he was a really good kisser. Not quite on Shane's level, she admitted, but close. But then, she recalled the coldness that had passed over his face when he'd sent Olivia off to Paul's office, she assumed to receive the same "punishment" Stephanie had. That coldness totally contradicted the tenderness he'd shown to Stephanie when he talked to her. It was a contradiction Tessa didn't fully understand at this point.

About a mile up the road, a horn honking caught her attention. She looked up to see Shane and the others in a van beside her.

"Hey, sexy, going my way?" Shane said, making her laugh. "Just follow me, baby."

They couldn't get to that diner fast enough. When they arrived, Shane flashed his badge and asked for the use of the manager's office. He led her inside and as soon as the door shut, he was on her, determined to wipe the taste of Helton from her lips and her thoughts…and from his as well.

"Are you OK?" he asked, stroking her hair.

"Yes…but could you just hold me for a minute? I need to feel your arms around me."

He crushed her to him, holding her tight. "I'm so sorry, babe."

She drew a deep breath. "Stephanie Quinn was beaten this morning. If we went in now, she'd have fresh cuts on her back for evidence."

"But she signed the consent forms so there isn't enough to shut them down."

"Nathaniel is charismatic and charming. Those girls in the dorms…did you see their faces, Shane? They were so enraptured of him…like the pictures you see of all those fans with Elvis."

""He's just a man, Tess."

She looked up at him. "I know that, Shane…but the others. They're all so weak-minded. He can manipulate them so easily."

"He took a lot of liberties with you today. Touching you, kissing you at the end for all to see…he's claimed you, Tess…how are you going to hold him off? Especially with you moving in tomorrow?"

"I'll think of something…how long do you think I'll have to stay there?"

"I don't know. I guess that's up to Gibson and Bruce."

"I hope not long…the children are all so sweet. They actually have an innocence about them you don't see in other children because they don't watch TV or play video games…how can people who so obviously cherish their children turn around and treat women the way they do?"

"Sex does strange things to people."

"Yes, but-" she stopped when a knock sounded on the door.

"It's Gib. I'm coming in."

"Door's open," Shane called.

"Everything OK?" he asked, stepping inside.

"Just fine," Shane answered, his arm still around Tessa's waist, anchoring her to his side.

"We need to come up with a game plan to get Stephanie out of there…it would be easier if you were to be staying in the dorms. Why would you tell him you wouldn't?"

"He'd already made a move on me, Gib. I just thought I may be able to collect more evidence if he regarded me as above the girls in the dorms."

"But when you questioned him about the Arena he said it was a place you would never have to worry about."

"It wouldn't matter if she got eyes in there anyway," Shane said, "Those consent forms block us from doing anything. They only way we could go after them is if they send a minor in there."

"Look, I have a feeling that once I'm there tomorrow Nathaniel will figure out a way to keep me there. Things are moving much faster than we anticipated."

"And if those woman are made to feel you are above them as his mate, they may be intimidated by you."

"Just trust me, Gib, OK?"

He sighed. "I do, kid. I'm just concerned for your safety."

"I know."

"You'd better get back on the road. If they are monitoring you then you don't need to linger too long."

"Just give us a few more minutes, then I'll send her on her way," Shane told him.

"Fine, but not too long. Stop at the counter when you come out, Tess. We ordered a dinner for you to help with your cover."

She nodded. "Thanks, Gib."

After he left, she turned back into the comfort of Shane's arms, snuggling to his chest.

"I know you can't be there all the time, but I really will need to hear your voice every day."

"I know…but you can't wear the earpiece all the time like you did today. Especially not with Helton trying to get intimate with you."

She sighed. "I know."

He tilted her head up and claimed her lips in a kiss that left them both breathless and clinging to each other.

"I'm sorry you had to sit through him kissing me," she said softly.

"You don't worry about me," he repeated, "I'm just sorry you had to endure it."

"If it means helping those girls I'll do whatever it takes."

He tightened his hold on her. "I know you will, baby. You just be damn sure you take care of Tessa in the process."

"I will."

"I know you will…we'd better get out of here so you can get on the road. I love you, Tess. Don't you ever forget that."

"I love you, too. No matter what you see or what you hear, know that, Shane Gabriel. Know that I love you."

Chapter Eleven

The drive back out to the compound the next day didn't take nearly as long as Tessa needed it to. She was painfully aware that this was likely the last time she would be outside of its walls and have time to herself for a long time. She'd packed carefully last night, all the fancy designer clothes that went along with her rich girl persona. This morning she'd dressed with calculated precision, Prada, Chanel, the telltale red soled Louboutin heels…everything that would convey wealth and confidence to Nathaniel and remind him that she wasn't just the average girl off the street.

The guard waved her through the gate with a bow that made her uncomfortable. She drove up to the Main House where a valet took her bags, another took her car, and Paul Helton stood waiting for her.

"Nathaniel is currently unavailable," Paul told her, his cold brown eyes sweeping over her from head to toe. "James will take your bags to your room. Nathaniel has asked that you wait in his office with me and then he'll show you to your room himself."

"Sounds good."

He led her to Nathaniel's office, a huge room of deep dark wood tones that reminded her of classic Lord of the Manor type spaces. She decided it suited Nathaniel perfectly.

"We really didn't a chance to speak to one another yesterday," she said when Paul shut the door. "You are Nathaniel's brother?"

Without warning, Paul grabbed her shoulders and roughly forced her back against the wall, causing her to cry out when her head slammed against it.

"Let's get something straight here, bitch," Paul bit out, his fingers digging painfully into her upper arms. "My brother may be enamored with you but I assure you I am not. To me you are no different than those whores in the dormitories. Nathaniel sees something in you and has claimed you before witnesses. That gives you a measure of freedom not afforded to the others, but know this, if you test him he will not hesitate to educate you and I'll be right there to aid in the lesson."

"You'd like that, wouldn't you, Paul?" she threw back at him.

His eyes narrowed, "Don't test me, either, Madelyn."

She actually laughed. "Or what? You'll take me to the Arena? Nathaniel already promised that as a place I'd never go."

"Promises made to a woman are meaningless," he

shot back at her.

"Careful, Paul, you're sounding like a petulant little boy afraid of his Mama."

His temper exploded and he backhanded her, knocking her to the floor. She scrambled to retrieve her glasses before he could step on them, then began laughing.

"Really? Is that all you got?" she taunted him, thankful that she wasn't wearing the earpiece to hear Shane and the others telling her to back off. "I fought girls in summer Camp when I was growing up who hit harder than you.'

He grabbed a handful of her hair and yanked her up off the floor just as Nathaniel walked in.

"Let her go, Paul," he said in a mild tone, as if he was used to diffusing his brother.

"She's not the docile thing you think her to be, Brother. She's oozing with disrespect."

"I never said she was docile, Brother," Nathaniel countered. "On the contrary, I said she had spirit."

"Nathaniel," she said, calling attention to the fact that she was trying to pry Paul's hands from her hair.

"Paul. I said release her. Now."

Paul growled and pushed her roughly back to the ground, sending her sprawling. Nathaniel stepped to help her up with surprisingly gentle hands, but his eyes never left his brother.

"Do not ever touch her again, Paul, do you hear me? Madelyn isn't one of the dorm girls, nor will she ever be."

"You're going to side with that bitch over your own flesh and blood?"

"Go attend to your ladies in the Arena, Paul. Leave Madelyn alone."

With a final glare at her, Paul left, slamming the door behind him. Nathaniel gently brushed her hair away from her face and examined her cheek.

"I should have known better than to leave you alone with him. I apologize."

She offered him a weak smile. "He hits like a puny girl."

Nathaniel laughed and drew her into his embrace. "You are a delight. You aren't even intimidated by him, are you?"

She shrugged. "He's weak. I'm not."

"He truly didn't frighten you. He can be…volatile at times. I try to indulge him with women who give consent but I'm afraid he oversteps himself at times."

"He doesn't scare me, but I will watch my back from now on."

"That would be wise. I'm afraid he gets jealous of anyone who tries to get close to me."

"He's your brother. Surely I'm no threat to him."

"It's just been the two of us for so long…but enough

about him. Are you OK? He didn't hurt you too bad? I don't see a bruise forming."

"Nothing I can't handle. I've definitely had worse."

He lightly stroked a finger over her reddened cheek. "You've been hurt before?"

"Let's just say my father wasn't exactly a Prince. He liked to pick on anyone weaker than himself."

"I'm so sorry, Madelyn. What monsters you must think we are here," he said, catching her off-guard. "What you saw yesterday with Olivia and Stephanie…I assure you it's all an act. It's part of the service we provide our clients."

In the control room, the men all exchanged puzzled glances. Clients? Services? How stupid did he think Tessa was, Shane wondered. He was still shaking with rage at seeing Paul Helton strike her. And now Nathaniel was telling her that everything she saw yesterday was an act?

"You all right, kid?" Gibson asked Shane.

"I'll be better once I can get my hands on Paul Helton."

"You and me both. She handled it well, though."

"Yeah. Real well," he murmured, clutching her ring and dog tags. He looked up at the monitor just in time to see Helton lean in to kiss her. Perfect. Exactly what he didn't need to see just now.

"We created quite a bit of a stir last night, you and I. Everyone can't wait to meet you," Nathaniel told her. "I'll formally introduce you at Sunset Chapel tonight."

She reached up to stroke his golden hair, smiling when he was at first startled.

"You aren't used to having someone freely touch you, are you?"

"Honestly, no. I've run this place for so long with such rigid rules that I've forgotten what having someone with free will around is like…it's quite refreshing."

Tessa laughed, she couldn't help it. When he was like this it was hard for her to remember that she was supposed to be wary of him.

"You mean all those wide-eyed girls in the dorms who look ready to fall at your feet aren't cutting it for you anymore?"

"I don't think they ever did hold an appeal for me. That's all for Paul."

"They why do you do all of this?"

He shrugged. "The money's good and it gives me the freedom to pursue my true interests, Texas Independence."

"And preaching?"

"Well, I wouldn't call what I do preaching, per se. More like teaching. I could take or leave it but the clients expect it."

"He's downplaying everything," Joe said, "why would he do that? And he's setting Paul up as the Gung Ho one."

"Does he suspect her?" Bruce wondered.

The thought made the room fall silent for several minutes and voiced a small suspicion that had been bothering Shane. Helton didn't fool him for a moment: he knew exactly what would happen when he sent Paul to escort her in. He'd set her up to provoke his brother then conveniently stepped in before things got out of hand. Tessa surely recognized that. It all pointed to the fact that Nathaniel didn't trust her and may suspect she is something more than she appeared to be.

He began to pace while she and Helton made small talk. The whole situation made him uncomfortable. Something wasn't Kosher about it all.

"What are you thinking?" Bruce asked.

"This doesn't feel right. I think you're right, he is suspicious of her…let's look at it from his point of view. This beautiful, wealthy, unattached woman shows up at one of your meetings. She's hot, she stands out in a crowd so you want to meet her, then BAM! Within four days you're kissing her and she's moving in, she thinks for the night but you're sure you can convince her to stay longer…but why? Why would a beautiful, wealthy, educated young woman be interested in staying, especially after you've hinted at what goes on here and you've given her a taste of violence. Why would she stay unless she has a hidden agenda?'

Gibson regarded Shane thoughtfully for a moment. "You don't think he's arrogant enough to think she's genuinely attracted to him?"

Shane shrugged. "It's possible, sure…but I still come back to this: he knows Paul is unstable. He knew what would happen if he left Tessa alone with him. If you really cared for a woman you would never put her unprotected into a volatile situation."

"What do you suggest then?" Gibson asked. "We could pull her out now."

"I honestly don't know," he admitted. "The part of me that loves her says yes, I want to go in, guns blazing and pop that miserable SOB out of existence…but the cop in me isn't sure. We don't have any real evidence to take them down yet."

"This is a tough one for me as well," Gibson admitted. "Tessa was one of those soldiers under my command that I could always rely on. She's solid."

Bruce spoke up. "Let's give her a little more time. She's surely got the same suspicions we all have. Let's give her a chance to work through it."

Shane took a deep breath. He knew Bruce was right; they needed to give Tessa a chance to build her case. Didn't mean he had to like it.

He turned his attention back to the monitor. Helton was leading her out of his office and up the main staircase, he assumed to her room.

"So, what's the history of these buildings?" she asked

Nathaniel as they headed up the stairs. "This house is beautiful."

"Thank you. My great grandparents built it."

"Really?" she asked, surprised. Why hadn't she known this was family land?

"Just our own little piece of Texas history. That's Paul's wing to the right. I suggest you don't venture down his way."

"Duly noted," she said, smiling up at him.

He stopped and looked down into her upturned face, caressing her cheek with such tenderness it surprised her.

"What is it?" she asked, trying to interpret the look on his face.

"I'm just amazed how you can smile after that run-in with Paul."

"Why not? It's over and he's not here with us now."

"God's in His Heaven, all's right with the world?"

She laughed. "Something like that."

"I wish I could be as forgiving. I didn't like seeing him touch you, hurt you. How is it I could feel this way for someone I just met?"

"Maybe you should get out more," she teased.

He laughed. "You may be right. Let's go check out your rooms, shall we?" he said, taking her hand.

Tessa told herself to stay in the moment and not think of Shane to help her focus. She hated to think of what seeing her flirt with another man was doing to him.

"Here you are," he said, opening the door.

"Oh, Nathaniel, this room is stunning," she said, and she meant it. The room was huge. A luxurious canopied bed was against the far wall, draped in white and soft rose hues, extremely soft and feminine décor. There was an enormous bay window with a window seat the size of a full bed, a fireplace and conversation area. It was beautiful.

"Through this door is the bathroom," he said, ushering her inside. It was like something out of a magazine. The bathtub was the size of a small pool. The shower was a large walk-in with multiple shower heads. There was a long vanity and sink along one wall and another sink along the other wall, that held notably men's accessories. "The door at the end of the room connects to my bedroom," he told her.

Shane closed his eyes. Sharing a bathroom with him would severely limit her privacy, not to mention the threat to her safety.

"Oh, wow, Nathaniel, I..." she began but he stopped her.

"Not to worry, I will respect your privacy," he said, taking her shoulders into his hands. "I want you to be happy here, Madelyn."

"OK, but..."

"Trust me," he said, kissing her brow.

"All right, but Nathaniel, I don't give my trust freely.

Don't abuse it."

His smile was bright. "I won't."

Tessa allowed him to continue the tour of his living quarters and did her best not to let him know that she was worried about the joint bathroom. Privacy was going to be hard to come by, she knew, but what really concerned her was her tattoo. If he were to walk into the bathroom while she was in that huge shower she wouldn't be able to hide it.

"She's wigging out," Pete said, pulling Shane's attention to him, "he's called her name several times and she hasn't replied."

Shane watched the monitor a moment, seeing Helton touch Tessa's hair. He wished she had the earpiece in so he could calm her down. She wasn't 'wigging out' as Pete put it, but her concentration was definitely not where it should be.

"She'll pull it together," he said, praying he was right.

Tessa looked up into Nathaniel's golden eyes, forcing a smile and telling herself to calm down.

"I'm sorry, Nathaniel, what were you saying?"

"Are we going too fast?" he asked, stroking a finger down her cheek.

"No...well...maybe...it's just..."

"It's OK, you can tell me."

She took a deep breath. "The shared bathroom thing has me a little concerned, I won't lie to you."

He nodded. "I understand. What can I do to ease your mind?"

"Is there a different bathroom I can use?"

"I want you to be comfortable here, Madelyn, but I also want you to trust me...and I want the others to know you trust me...appearances are very important here. Especially with Paul on your bad side. You don't want to give him any reason to doubt you, do you understand?"

"Don't have to tell me twice about him."

He smoothed a hand over her hair. "You don't know how happy I am that you are here. I hadn't realized how lonely my life has been...and while I understand your concern for privacy, I'm really hoping you'll choose to become closer to me and that won't be an issue.

Her eyes widened briefly and she took a deep breath, praying for the strength to do what she needed to.

"I'd like that too, Nathaniel, but you have to give me time. I'm not one to just fall into bed with someone after a few meetings."

"You are no longer virgin, though, correct?" he pressed.

"We need her to have that damn earpiece in," Crownover growled.

Shane wanted to agree but he had to trust Tessa to take care of herself and he had to present a show of confidence in her to the team so as not to undermine her. It was hard, though, when he was listening to her discuss her sexual status with Helton. She dodged for a bit, then by admitting a partial truth, she helped to diffuse the situation.

"I have only ever slept with one man. I was going to marry him," she admitted.

"What happened?" Nathaniel asked, still toying with her fingers.

"He had his career. I had...my goals. We realized along the way that our goals were taking us to different places. Neither of us wanted to bend."

"And so he let you go?"

"We let each other go," she replied. They were standing on the balcony off her bedroom that she now could see connected her rooms to his; yet another security threat. She made sure to look at every corner and angle, giving Shane and the team a full view of it all.

Nathaniel raised her fingers to his lips, drawing her gaze back to him.

"His loss is my gain," he said softly.

"Perhaps," she said with a smile, "if you're lucky."

He stepped closer to her, his hand sliding into her hair dangerously close to the implanted mike.

"Ah, but then, my dear, Madelyn, you're here with me and not with him."

As he leaned in to kiss her, Shane got to his feet and turned away from the monitor to pace. He tried not to let his blood pressure soar but it was hard. He hated the thought of another man touching her. He began pacing even more as the kiss was drawn out; the small sounds coming from her as she played the part were killing him.

"This is such bullshit!" Crownover growled.

"It's undercover work," Shane said, his voice raw with emotion.

Joe and Pete were watching Shane, looks of sympathy on their faces. Shane acknowledged them with a chin lift but continued his pacing.

"Nathaniel," Tessa said, her voice breathless, drawing Shane's attention back to the monitor.

"Forgive me," he said low, "you drive me to distraction. Why don't you take some time to settle into your rooms and unwind? I have a few meetings to attend then I'll be up to escort you to dinner."

"That sounds good. Thank you."

He kissed her once more then left. She stood gazing out across the grounds for several long moments before going back inside. She took the earpiece from her pocket and discreetly inserted it then tapped her mike three times, her signal for Shane.

"Hey, baby," his voice poured over her like warm honey, "you're doing great."

From her bag, she pulled a small dry erase board then sat on the bed.

I'm so sorry, she wrote.

"Nothing to be sorry about, babe," he dismissed, "we're good."

Privacy is going to be a problem.

"I know. Do the best you can."

They discussed strategy for a while then she had to get ready for dinner. She wasn't looking forward to another run-in with Paul but she was hoping to be able to see more of how the compound worked. She dressed carefully, wanting to appear worthy of being the focus of Nathaniel's attention, yet approachable by the other women. She settled on a semi-formal black cocktail dress with an empire waist and a skirt that flowed gracefully to her knees. She chose simple silver jewelry, nothing overpowering and kept her make-up light and sophisticated.

"You look beautiful, Tess," Shane told her when she put the glasses back on and stood before the mirror. She gave him a quick wink before turning to answer the door when a knock sounded.

Nathaniel stood there wearing a cream colored suit and matching shirt, collar open, a single yellow rose in his hand.

"For you, my rose," he said, offering it to her.

Tessa ignored the comments from Pete and Joe and smiled as she accepted the rose.

"Nathaniel," she breathed, "thank you."

He stroked the backs of his fingers over her cheek.

"Just a small token; a glimpse of what I could give you."

"It's lovely."

He leaned down and gently kissed her. "Not nearly as lovely as you, Madelyn. Shall we?"

She took his offered arm and together they walked down the main staircase and into the dining hall. Whatever she'd been expecting, what she found was not it. There were several long tables arranged in columns and a head table raised on a dais, reminding her very much of medieval days. Nathaniel walked her down the main aisle, smiling and greeting men and women alike as they passed on their way to the head table.

The seating at the tables was arranged with women on one side and men on the other. All the women were again wearing long white shift dresses. The men wore black slacks and black shirts. It was all very monochromatic and it was not lost on Tessa that she and Nathaniel were dressed in the same colors but opposite of the rest of the room.

As they stepped up onto the dais, everyone stood. Nathaniel walked to the center of the head table, seating Tessa to his left and then gesturing for everyone else to sit while he remained standing.

"Good evening, my children," he greeted the room.

"Good evening, Sir," was the unison reply.

"As you know, we have a Very Special Visitor among us," he said, turning to smile down at Tessa. "Madelyn?" he asked, gesturing for her to stand and take his hand. Tessa placed her hand in his and allowed him to help her to her feet. "This is Madelyn Parker. She has agreed to stay with us at first as my Very Special Guest, but now, before all of you, my children, I proclaim that Madelyn is to be my Beloved, Cherished above all others,"

"What the hell?!" Crownover exploded.

"Sarge, did he just -?" Joe began but Shane raised his hand to quiet him.

"Nathaniel, I don't know what to say," Tessa said softly so that only he could hear.

He leaned down and placed his lips to her ear. "Quiet now. A single woman in our midst is fair game unless claimed. By my proclamation, I am offering you my protection."

She pulled back and looked into his golden eyes for a moment, unsure of what her next move should be. If she allowed him to claim her, keeping him out of her bedroom was going to prove even that much more difficult.

"I only just arrived here, Nathaniel," she began.

"Relax, love, it is only a formality," he assured her, lifting her fingers to his lips, then placing her hand over his heart. "Kiss me and confirm to all present your acceptance of me," he said louder.

"Holy shit," Joe ground out.

"It's OK, Tess. Go with it," Shane told her. "We'll figure out what to do next. Just go with it for now."

On Shane's advice, she stepped closer to Nathaniel and placed her lips against his. A resounding masculine cheer sounded from the tables below while the women quietly clapped. Nathaniel's smile beamed down upon her as he turned back toward the audience.

"Eat, my children. Rejoice this day."

When Tessa turned back to take her seat she caught Paul's eye as he glared darkly at her. There was pure evil emanating from his gaze. She would have to be on high alert for sure around him.

Her eyes swept the length of the hall, looking for Stephanie Quinn amongst the women seated at the tables. She estimated there were at least sixty women and perhaps thirty men. All the women were in their early twenties and beautiful, all white or of mixed race, no full African-American, Hispanic, Asian or otherwise. In contrast, the men were all white, all appearing to be in their thirties or forties, and other than the men seated with Nathaniel and Paul at the head table, none of the men were shining examples of the male species. They were men that most of these women would never give the time of day to; either overweight or frames reminiscent of the awkward teens they no doubt once were. So, what was the appeal to these girls, she wondered. What made them sit there looking star-struck and enraptured of every man in the room?

"I don't see Stephanie Quinn," Gib said, having just arrived at the command house.

"She's not there," Joe commented. He had taken a screen shot of the whole room and was running each face through facial recognition software. "There are a few who have shown up in Missing Persons reports, and a few of these men are registered sex offenders, surprise, surprise. Nothing violent. Most were busted in prostitution stings."

"A toast, Madelyn," Nathaniel said, turning her gaze to him, "To new beginnings."

She took the glass of red wine he offered and touched it to his, again ignoring the Captain Obvious remarks when Gib cautioned her to eat and drink lightly. She could tell from her first sip that her wine had been doctored.

"So, tell me, Nathaniel, what just happened here?" she asked.

He stroked his index finger lightly down her cheek. It seemed he enjoyed touching her.

"Our society has few formalities but to keep the peace, we do encourage our men to formally claim the woman he would consider off-limits to anyone else's attentions. Not all women are claimed and not all men have claimed a mate. Before witnesses, I claimed that you are mine and mine alone, therefore untouchable by anyone else. It is a measure of respect and protection for you...a betrothal, if you will."

"I see...and have you claimed any others as your own?"

A smile touched his lips. "As Supreme Leader, all women, even claimed ones, are available to me. I admit that in my youth I readily exercised that privilege, but I have, shall we say, mellowed in recent years. I found that I wanted someone I could actually have an intelligent conversation with. Someone strong enough to lead alongside me. I knew the moment I saw you walk into my tent that you would be that special someone for me."

"Someone call Hallmark, I think he just wrote their next sappy card for them," Pete spat out, giving Tessa a genuine reason to smile when she really wanted to throw up.

"That's so sweet," she breathed, leaning in to kiss him, "but I'm still not sure of all this."

"Tell me. Perhaps I can put away your doubts."

Her gaze swept the room. "These women...they are all very young and very beautiful."

"All are over eighteen and all here by invitation, yes based on their beauty, but also with full disclosure and consent for our lifestyle."

"A lifestyle that involves actual whippings? The girl I saw, Stephanie, her back was bleeding. Will she scar? What could she have possible done, Nathaniel?" she asked for the third time since discovering the girl.

"Careful, Tess," Shane cautioned, having noticed the two men over Nathaniel's shoulder tense at her questioning. "Don't force his hand before witnesses."

"A whipping of that severity could only mean she violated a direct command from Paul or one of the Elders you see at the table with us."

"Violated a direct command?" she repeated and could not keep the disgust from her tone.

"Tessa," Shane again warned.

"Again, my rose, each woman present has agreed to our lifestyle."

"Not every woman, Nathaniel," she pressed, "as much as I am intrigued by you, I will never consent to allow anyone to beat me in such a way, and that includes you."

"Nor would I allow it," he said, raising her knuckles to his lips. "For myself, I do not choose a woman such as that. I would have a woman who is above all others."

She leaned in closer to him, until their faces were mere inches apart. "That, I certainly am, Nathaniel." A hush fell over the hall when she placed her hand on his cheek and kissed him soundly for all to see.

"You are a diamond among rubies, Madelyn," he whispered to her.

"And don't you ever forget it," she said with a laugh and a wink.

"Not likely," he breathed, then in a lower voice, "I can't wait to have you in my bed."

She traced her thumb along his lower lip. "I'm afraid you will have to wait a while for that," she said, smiling at his raised brow expression. "Yes, I know you aren't used to waiting, which is exactly why you will for me."

"My people expect a bedding ceremony," he informed her. "Tonight."

"Oh, well, I'm afraid they will be sorely disappointed. You are Supreme Leader, Nathaniel. Tell them we demand and expect the privacy your position is due. But know this, Nathaniel Helton, what I do is for your benefit and your benefit alone. I am to be yours, then I will be solely yours, for your eyes only. That is solid and non-negotiable."

His eyes glinted, clearly intoxicated by all she said. Tessa wondered if anyone like her had ever been in his life or if he'd always been surrounded by subservience.

"I do believe I shall enjoy my pursuit of you, my fiery one. It will make your ultimate surrender that much sweeter."

"Count on it," she tossed back at him.

"Know this, though, Miss Parker. I will indulge you only so long. You will be mine, in every way."

The pencil Shane had been holding snapped in half. He prayed for patience for himself and divine protection for Tessa. How she was ever going to continue to dodge Helton he just didn't know.

Chapter Twelve

Over the next days, Tessa settled into learning how she was intended to fit into Nathaniel's life and organization. She spent several hours each day in the classroom with the children. She told Nathaniel she would like to spend time with the single women in the dormitories, something he resisted at first but she managed to manipulate him into agreeing to during a romantic interlude in the gardens. Against her initial instincts, she began to develop a grudging admiration for Nathaniel. The image he presented to her was one of actual caring for his "people". It was Paul who had begun the practice of subjecting the women to rigorous rules designed to result in them being sent to the Arena for "adjustment" at least once a week. Tessa resisted this and questioned Nathaniel on it to which he once again insisted that the women chose this lifestyle. It wasn't an outright S&M outfit, Tessa decided. It was some crazy in between. Indeed, the women were given full disclosure of the society's expectations and tenets and she did see at least three new recruits who decided it wasn't for them and were given leave to go.

After the end of her first month in the compound, she began to wonder if she would ever gain enough info on the group to shut them down. If it was truly a lifestyle choice made by each woman, then how could they put a stop to it? By passing themselves off as a religious group, it wasn't as if the women were paying the Heltons for this service or that the men were paying to have sex with the women thus making it a prostitution ring.

It was during one of the times she did not have her earpiece in, that Shane got a call that changed everything. He'd been monitoring her with Nathaniel just before bedtime with Crownover being the only other team member present when his cell rang.

"McCanton," he answered, not looking at his caller ID.

"Shane!" he heard his sister's shaky voice.

He sat up, his heart beat accelerating. "Cordy? What is it? What's happened?"

"Shane...you need to come home. There's been...an accident," she said, through her sobs.

"What kind of accident?"

"Daddy...he had someone stopped. It was raining. A truck rounded the corner and hydroplaned and hit him. It doesn't look good. You need to come home."

He was already scrambling to his feet. "I'll be there as soon as I can."

"Hurry, Shane," she cried.

He ended the call and immediately began dialing Bruce's number. His eyes locked on Tessa on the monitor.

"Shane? It's almost midnight, what..."

"I have to go home. My dad was in an accident. Cordy says it's bad and that I need to hurry. You need to send someone here with Crownover."

"Of course, son, you go. Be careful. Keep me updated."

He turned to Crownover. "Tell Tessa I'm sorry. I don't know when I'll be back."

Crownover nodded. "Yeah, sure, man, I'll take care of her, don't worry."

Shane sent him a pointed look. "I'm trusting you with her. Don't let me down."

He hurried out to his truck and began the three hour drive back to Indian Springs. Once he was safely away from the area of the compound, he put his light in the dash and flipped on his siren and floored it, determined to make it home as fast as he could.

He called his sister when he arrived at the hospital and she ran out to greet him, leaping into his arms and sobbing. He held her tight and listened as she cried. From what he could tell, his dad was still in surgery. They rushed in and he embraced his mother and his other sister Gracie. Practically the whole town of Indian Springs was in the waiting room with them. The McCanton family had been involved in law enforcement in Indian Springs for as long as anyone could remember.

Luke McCanton was strong. He came out of surgery and survived the night, but his condition was critical and touch and go for days. He was placed into a medically induced coma to aid in healing. Shane stayed at the hospital with his family, and at the town council's request, helped the Sheriff's department with the investigation into the accident and filled in for his dad, all while keeping tabs on Tessa's investigation, which was crawling at a snail's pace.

Three weeks after the accident, Luke woke. Shane was in the room with his mother when his father opened his eyes, lifted his hand and touched his mother's cheek. After a few hours of tests, Luke was alert and talking and everyone breathed a sigh of relief to know that it looked like he was indeed going to be OK. It was Luke's sharp eye that was the first to notice that something wasn't right with his son.

That morning, Shane had received a call from Bruce that contact with Tessa hadn't been made for several hours. It wasn't unusual except that she had never gone quite this long with the mike turned off.

"Has anything changed in her investigation? Any behavior toward her changed?" he asked Bruce.

"Not that has been reported. Gib and I were getting ready to pull the plug on the whole thing. She hasn't really come up with anything to show that any women are being held against their will. Stephanie Quinn seems perfectly happy to be there. Not much we can do with that."

"But Tessa hasn't turned the mike back on?"

"She turned it off for her shower and they have not gotten her back online since. That was three hours ago."

Shane cursed under his breath, an uneasy feeling washing over him. "OK, look...my dad is awake and doing better now. I'm gonna see if a friend who has a helicopter here can fly me in. I don't like this."

"I'm sure it's nothing...but yeah, I'd like you to be here."

When Shane came back into his father's room after that, Luke's sharp eyes zeroed in on him.

"Son? What is it?"

Shane raked his hand through his hair. "Maybe nothing. An investigation I was running hit a snag. I'm gonna have to go back. I'll see if Bob can fly me over, I need to get back fast."

"Is it Tessa?"

For a moment, Shane froze then he remembered that Bruce had briefed his dad on what was going on, and that his dad likely knew much more than he realized he did.

"Yeah, it's Tessa. I'm hoping it's nothing, but it doesn't look good right now."

Luke nodded. "You go take care of things, boy. I'm fine."

Shane stepped to his dad and embraced him. "Love

you, Pop. I'll be back as soon as I can."

During his short flight back to the command house, Shane couldn't fight off the uneasy feeling in the pit of his stomach. Something was wrong. He knew it. Tessa wouldn't cut off communication for that long.

When he exited the chopper and he saw Bruce's face as he emerged from the house, he knew his fears were justified. Something bad had happened.

"Tell me," Shane said, following Bruce into the house.

"She came back online as you were en route. It's bad, son. Somehow they found out. They know she's not who she said she was...I think the mike came back on when her head struck something...we've got to get in now. They're killing her."

Shane rushed in, ashen. Crownover met him at the entrance to the control room, flak jacket in his hand. Gibson was there and gearing up as well, his eyes piercing Shane as he took the vest from Crownover.

"I need to know if you can handle this," Gibson said.

"I'm going in and bringing her out. You won't stop me. I..."

He fell silent when he heard Tessa scream. It was an ear-piercing, pain-filled scream like he'd never heard before. Cold sweat broke out over his entire body. They heard another chopper land and knew that SWAT had arrived.

"Do we know what room she is in?"

"GPS has her in the Arena," Pete replied.

They hesitated only long enough to form a takedown plan and then loaded up for the compound. They were greeted with light resistance at the gate, which was surprising. They barreled through and drove through the grounds to the gymnasium referred to as the Arena and blasted their way inside. Screams of the other women scattering greeted them as the smoke cleared from the door. The entire population of the compound was gathered in the arena. Tessa was in the center of the room, arms suspended above her while Paul and Nathaniel took turns beating her. When Shane led the way into the room, Nathaniel grabbed her around the waist and held her before him as a shield, a knife to her throat. The SWAT backup quickly evacuated the others from the room, leaving a small contingent to confront the Helton Brothers. Paul held a gun on them, just to the right of Nathaniel and Tessa.

"Let her go, Helton," Shane demanded. "This ends now."

Sweat beaded on his brow and ran down the small of his back. Shane couldn't remember ever being this scared in his entire life. He aimed his gun at Nathaniel, trusting the others to have Paul covered. He dared not look too closely at Tessa, not wanting anything to break his concentration. He knew she was nude and severely beaten already, but she was on her feet and that had to be a good sign. Even without looking directly at her, though, he could see she was losing blood fast.

"It's over, Helton," he said, "the place is surrounded. You can't win. Let her go and have your day in court."

"I don't recognize your courts. My word is Law."

"That's fine. You can recognize that I've got a gun on your head and if you don't cooperate, I will shoot."

"You won't chance hitting your colleague here," Nathaniel countered.

"I won't hit her."

"Terribly sure of yourself," Helton said, tightening his grip on Tessa's hair and pulling her head back, further exposing her throat to his blade.

Beside him, Paul began to move but Gib and Crownover advanced on him. Tessa didn't make a sound, not that Shane expected her to. Tessa was the strongest person he knew.

"Let her go," Shane repeated, taking a small step forward.

"Take one more step and I'll slice her open," Helton warned.

"I'll put a bullet in you first."

Helton laughed then, pushing the point of the blade into Tessa's throat so that blood began trickling down.

"If you were going to shoot me, you'd have already done it. Now, you get me a car and let me out of here or I'll cut her damn head off."

"Not going to happen, Helton, you know that. Only way you're getting out of here is in custody, on a stretcher, or in a body bag. Now what's it going to be?"

"I'm not afraid to die, but if I go, she goes with me."

"Shane!" Bruce yelled from the doorway behind him.

Shane saw something flicker across Helton's face, knew the situation was about to elevate. He watched Helton's grip on the knife change slightly.

"Shane, huh? This Shane?" Helton asked, indicating with the blade the tattoo on Tessa's abdomen. "This is the man you whored yourself for?" he breathed into Tessa's ear.

Tessa grit her teeth, staring intently at Shane and doing her best to ignore Nathaniel altogether. Shane's gaze was trained on Nathaniel; he had yet to look her in the eye. Blood loss was beginning to make her dizzy and she feared she would pass out at any moment. Her vision was already blurred due to repeated blows to the head. She studied Shane's face as best as she could, trying to memorize every detail. It had been so long since she'd last seen him, she was glad she got to see him one last time.

She listened to the two men tap dance around each other, each trying to make the other back down. Twice Nathaniel inflicted more pain on her but she kept her jaw clenched, refusing to cry out.

Bruce called from the other side of the door, calling

Shane's name. Now Nathaniel knew who he was; knew that he was the man whose name she'd marked her body with. Things were escalating now. She could feel it in Nathaniel's body...that tightening of muscles, the dampening of skin. It had to end now.

Steeling herself, she swallowed hard and licked her lips, happy she at least got to see Shane one last time.

"Shane," she said, her voice hoarse and weak, but she knew he heard her even though his eyes never left Nathaniel. "Shane. Wildcat." She saw recognition flash in Shane's eyes and then there was nothing.

Chapter Thirteen

"McCanton! What the hell?" Gibson cried. "What did you just do?"

Shane's eyes shifted to Crownover cuffing Paul Helton's wrists behind his back as he and Gibson rushed over to Tessa and Nathaniel who were now in a tangled heap on the ground. Shane pulled Tessa away from Nathaniel, allowing Gibson to slap cuffs on him. He cradled Tessa's head and shoulders in his lap, gently stroking her face.

"Shane?" she whispered when he shifted to apply pressure to her bleeding shoulder. "You came."

"Shh, yeah, I'm here, baby," he said, taking a blanket from Bruce to cover her.

"You remembered...about Wildcat."

"Yeah, I did. Don't talk now, OK? Just rest. What's the ETA on an ambulance?" he asked the room at large.

"Five minutes," Crownover replied.

Shane nodded, his eyes locked on Tessa's swollen face. She'd been severely beaten. Before covering her, he noted every inch of her body was bloodied and bruised, including a large amount of blood between her thighs. He also noted that the Helton brothers were both wearing some sort of ceremonial robes and when Nathaniel went down, his opened to reveal he was nude beneath it. Shane prayed all of that didn't add up to what it looked like had happened.

Tessa had passed out but her pulse was strong. The gunshot had done exactly as he'd hoped, gone clean thru the muscle of her shoulder and lodged in Helton's body, minimal damage to Tessa. He stepped back when the medics came and surrounded her, letting them do their jobs.

"You wanna tell me what the hell just happened?" Gibson growled at him.

"Ever seen the movie Speed? Shoot the hostage? Dennis Hopper's character called Sandra Bullock's character "Wildcat". Tessa was telling me to shoot her to get to him."

Gibson swore viciously under his breath. "You meant to shoot her," he stated flatly. "What if you'd seriously injured her? What if..."

"The boy is the best shot in our division, likely in the whole state," Bruce cut in. "He would hit what he aimed for and she knew it."

Bruce and Gibson continued talking; Shane shut them out, listening to the medics assess her wounds; there were several, too numerous to count. She was covered in blood and Shane hoped that more of it was Helton's than just from the gunshot wound. He hadn't been able to see if there were any scrapes or scratches on him, but he prayed that Tessa had wounded him.

He saw her beginning to move and pushed his way thru the medics to her, taking her hand in his. Her eyes opened and locked on him, a tear falling down her cheek.

"Hey, baby, there you are," he said, wiping her tears away with his thumb.

"We need to load her up," one of the medics said.

Shane nodded and leaned down to kiss her brow.

"I love you, Tess," he told her, then stepped back so they could roll her thru the building to the waiting ambulance.

"Do you have her mother's contact information?" Gibson asked from behind him, "I need to call her."

"Let me," Shane replied, "I know her. She should hear this from me."

"I'm Tessa's supervisor, I should-"

Shane put his hand on Gibson's shoulder. "I've known Mrs. Kelly all my life. Let me call."

Gibson nodded. "All right, perhaps it should be you."

Shane took his cell from his pocket and dialed Mary's number.

"Mrs. Kelly, it's Shane."

He heard her laugh. "Honey, after all these years, you can call me Mary, it's OK."

"Yes, ma'am...listen, you need to come to Austin, and you need to hurry. Tessa's been...injured...on the job. She's en route to the hospital. I'm going to call Bob Potter. He can fly you here."

"Is it bad?"

"She's been shot and beaten...I think she will be OK, but you should be here. I'll have someone come pick you up and take you to Bob at the airfield."

"OK. Shane?"

"Yes, ma'am?"

"You tell her I love her."

"Yes, ma'am."

He made arrangements for Mary to be brought there, then rode with Gibson to follow the ambulance to the hospital, leaving Bruce and the team to see to the situation at the compound. Tessa was taken immediately into surgery so Shane and Gibson settled into the waiting room.

"Tessa never talked much about her family," Gibson said. "I know the basics, that her father was abusive and her mother finally tossed him out when he turned his fists on Tessa."

Shane nodded, sitting with his forearms braced on his knees. "Her mother, Mary, was afraid she couldn't make it on her own, but when he hit Tessa, she finally found the strength to throw him out and press charges. She opened a wedding and party planning service and made a real success of it."

"Is Tessa not close to her mother? I've never met her, and I've met most of my staff's parents or spouses at one point or another."

"Mary wanted Tessa to stay and help her run the shop. There was some tension there."

"She never came to visit."

"Tess probably didn't want her to. She was a little...weird about being in the Army around everyone from home. She didn't even tell anyone she was considering joining, just up and did it...then didn't tell anyone she'd left the Army for the FBI."

"Didn't tell anyone, or didn't tell you?" Gibson asked pointedly. "She mentioned you, when she got that tattoo."

Shane let his head drop, feeling the weight of the world had settled on his shoulders.

"We hadn't been together for years when she got that. I left for college. She went into the Army. We talked some. Texts. Emails. Video chats. She told me she got it to keep the guys at bay."

Gibson nodded, a faint smile touching his lips. "It was a problem for a while, Tessa being...well, Tessa. The guys hit on her all the time. After the tat, they backed off some. We were working late one night, just the two of us. So I asked her, all the years she worked for me, why had she never dated...and she proceeds to tell me this long story about a little boy back home whom she made life a living hell daily for years, then ended up falling head over heels for."

"Dammit," Shane muttered, raking his hands through his hair.

"Shane?" Mary asked, coming into the waiting room. He stood and she gasped, seeing the blood on his jeans. He'd forgotten he was covered in Tessa's blood. "Oh my God!" she cried.

He embraced her, assuring her once again that Tessa would be all right.

"Why didn't you call me? I would have met you..." he began but she cut him off.

"I didn't want you to leave in case anything happened. Any updates?"

"None yet. Mary, this is Tessa's supervisor, Glen Gibson," he said, gesturing to Gibson.

"The infamous Gib," Mary said, extending her hand to him. "Tessa has spoken of you often."

"She is an amazing young woman, Mrs. Kelly."

"Mary," she corrected, "and thank you." She looked back to Shane. "What happened? I thought you were home with your dad."

They gave her an edited overview of events, as much as they could without jeopardizing crucial case information. Mary grabbed onto Shane's hand while they spoke, leaning on his strength.

"Tessa Kelly," a doctor said, walking into the room.

"I'm her mother," Mary spoke up.

"Tessa's in recovery right now. Damage to her shoulder was minimal. She has four broken ribs. Her right cheekbone and orbital bone are fractured. She's lost two teeth. Her back where the whip cut into her may need a skin graft or two to repair damage. We just don't know at this point how bad the scarring will be. We performed a DNC and..."

The temperature in the room dropped as Shane's head snapped up.

"I'm sorry...a DNC?" Mary asked.

"The sexual assaults resulted in miscarriage."

"Sexual...she was raped?" Mary cried.

"She was pregnant?" Shane asked hoarsely.

"Less than six weeks. I doubt she even knew, possibly was just beginning to suspect. The biggest concern at this time is the tearing to the uterus. The brutality of the assaults combined with scarring from a previous injury resulted in severe damage to the uterine wall. At this point, it is uncertain whether she will ever be able to carry a child."

"Oh no!" Mary gasped.

Shane was trembling and finding it hard to breathe. Pregnant. Tessa had been pregnant...so, not only had the Helton's assaulted his woman...they'd killed his child. His...Tessa had been carrying his child.

"Doctor...if Tessa doesn't ask about...about a baby, please, don't tell her," Mary said, her hand on Shane's shoulder. "She will have enough to deal with. Please. She doesn't need to know that."

"Agreed...we will be keeping her drugged for the next two days at least. Her pain will be off the charts and she needs several hours of uninterrupted sleep. At this time, I would ask that visits be kept to a minimum."

Gibson cleared his throat, speaking for the first time since the doctor's arrival. "You said sexual assaults...with an S?"

"We are running a rape kit...but there were at least four different sperm samples so far."

An anguished cry roared through the room as Shane exploded, turning and grabbing Gibson by the shirt with one hand, the other drawn back as if to pummel him.

"How the hell could you let this happen?!?!?!?! I trusted you!! You were supposed to keep her safe!!"

"I wasn't there this morning, Shane. Things had fallen into such a routine, we left Joe and Pete on watch."

"They lost contact for over three hours!"

"What would you have done? Stormed in within the first hour? She was taking a shower. They didn't want to invade her privacy and they didn't want to overreact."

"I would have-"

"Gentlemen!" Mary snapped, cutting Shane off, "Second guessing yourselves won't change anything."

"She...our baby...my...Tessa." Shane lost it then. He released Gibson and then his legs just gave out from under him and he slid to his knees. Mary went down with him, holding his head to her shoulder while they both cried, clinging to one another for support. In the background, Gibson spoke quietly to the doctor, finding out room information and thanking him for his care of Tessa. After several long moments, Shane felt Gibson's hand on his shoulder. He took several deep, shuddering breaths to help pull himself together. He knew he had to be strong for Tessa. The days and weeks ahead were going to be difficult for her; she'd need his strength now more than ever.

Mary stroked her hand over his cheek when he pulled back from her shoulder. "My Tessa is lucky to have you," she told him, her voice soft. "I'm so sorry about your baby."

He drew a deep, cleansing breath and another, then scrubbed the tears from his face.

"Have they moved her to a room yet?" he asked Gibson, his voice raw.

"They were preparing to. Let's go check."

Shane stood and helped Mary to her feet and together followed Gibson to a nurses' station. The nurse gave them directions to Tessa's room and they arrived just as Tessa was being wheeled in. When they were cleared to enter, all three stood around her bed, taking in her damaged form. She was placed on her stomach in concession to the injuries to her back. Bandages and tubes were everywhere. What little could be seen of her face was swollen.

Shane's whole body was tight. He wished he'd have

killed that son-of-a-bitch...both of them...all of them! What they did to Tessa! And he couldn't wait to get his hands on Joe and Pete and rip them a new one. Three hours before he was notified. An hour for him to get there. God, what she went through. Just the thought of it all...

"Shane, honey, sit down," Mary's voice broke through the red haze he was in. "You can't change what's done. You can't torture yourself playing What If...and you know she would tell you the same. You got them all in custody. They'll stand trial for what they did and they'll never hurt another girl ever again. My Tessa did that; you did that. Now you need to focus on what's important right here and now in this room. Do you hear me?" He didn't speak, concentrating on forcing air through his lungs. With everything else, he didn't notice before, but he did now. Tessa's beautiful, long golden hair had been butchered. There were some long strands here and there but most of it had been hacked away. "Shane Gabriel, did you hear me?" Mary's sharp tone cut through his thoughts.

His eyes shifted from Tessa to her mother, who Tessa looked very much like. Mary wore her hair in a shoulder-length cut and it was just a tad darker than Tessa's but their faces were nearly the same.

"I want my hands on them," he confessed darkly, "All of them. Every single one whose DNA they confirm on her. Every. Single. One."

"Look at me, McCanton," Gibson snapped, "I want that, too. I would love nothing better than to lock you in a room with each one of them and let you beat them to a bloody pulp...but that won't help her. Tessa is strong. She can survive anything...and she's going to need your support, not your anger."

He closed his eyes and breathed sharply through his nose. "I know that, Gib. Doesn't change how I feel."

"I know...but, if Tessa were to open her eyes right now and see you like this...it wouldn't be a good thing. I've seen the changes you made in her these past weeks. You are what was missing from her life all these years. She's going to need you now more than ever."

He knew what they were telling him was true; didn't help, though. Not when he took in Tessa's battered body.

The door opened and Bruce and Crownover stepped in. Crownover took one look at her and swore viciously, then immediately apologized when he saw Mary. Gibson made quick introductions but Shane ignored them, his eyes on Tessa's closed ones, willing them to open. He silently begged her to wake up. He needed to know that in spite of everything, she was going to be OK.

"Shane, a word with you?" Bruce asked, breaking his thoughts.

"I'm not leaving her," he said low.

"It'll only be a minute. I just need-"

"I said, I'm not leaving her," he stressed.

"You need to give your statement and-"

"Get. Out."

"I know you're upset. I know how-"

Shane lunged at him, grabbing his Godfather by the throat and slamming him back against the wall. "You don't know how I feel, Bruce!" he exploded. "You want my statement? You screwed up. You left her alone and unprotected and damn near got her killed! She was gang raped! They were so brutal they tore her uterus. She miscarried my baby and she may never be able to have children now. I told you to take care of her and this is what happened. There's your statement, now get out! And tell Pete and Joe they better steer clear of me...and by the way? I quit," he growled, releasing him and turning away to take a deep breath.

"Now, don't make any rash decisions, you-"

"I'm done with this, Bruce. All my notes for all my cases are at my desk. You already have my gun. Here's my badge," he said, ripping it off his belt and throwing it at him, "I'm done."

Bruce caught the badge then wearily placed it on the bed next to Tessa's hand.

"Procedure still has to be followed and you know it. Nathaniel Helton just came out of surgery. He's expected to make a full recovery. Paul Helton and the Council of Elders are all in custody, all lawyered up, but we have one who is talking. They are going down and they are going down hard and they will stay down, thanks to Tessa. Stephanie Quinn is with her family. She says she signed membership forms but doesn't recall signing anything giving her consent to be beaten. She is afraid of Paul but adores Nathaniel. As hard as this will be for you to hear, what was done to Tessa may be our only way to take Nathaniel down."

Shane didn't speak and refused to look away from Tessa to acknowledge Bruce further. Bruce sighed loudly and spoke again.

"You need to give your statement. Joe and Pete-"

"You keep them away from me. I'll give a statement to you or to Crownover but that's it and it won't be now."

"Dammit, Shane," Bruce growled.

"Please," Mary finally spoke up, "Tessa doesn't need all this tension around her."

"You're right, she doesn't," Shane agreed, "You need to go, Bruce."

"Come on, Captain," Gibson said, opening the door, "I'll walk you out."

Bruce shook his head but wisely followed Gibson out into the hall.

"I get that he's upset but-"

Gibson held his hand up to stop him. "I don't think you do get that he's upset, not like I saw him. It's never easy to witness someone fall apart but what I saw earlier...you've got to give him time."

"We have an investigation to run."

"You think I don't know that? Tessa is mine, remember? How do you think you would feel if a doctor came out and told you your wife was brutally gang raped? You're his Godfather. You need to back off."

Tessa's door opened and Mary and Crownover stepped out. Both men looked to them, then with a nod to her, Bruce and Crownover left. Gib's eyes turned to Mary, struck by how beautiful she was.

"Tessa still out?"

She nodded. "I just thought I'd give Shane a moment to be with her. He is barely hanging on by a thread."

"I know. It's tough to watch. Buy you a cup of coffee?" he offered.

"That would be wonderful," she said smiling and taking his arm when offered.

Inside the room, Shane held Tessa's hand and raised her fingers to his lips. So much had happened since they met that day in Kindergarten. She made his life miserable for longer than he could stand, then for a short time, she'd made him happier than he'd ever been...and then she left. He'd understood; she had to get out of Indian Springs and on with her life and he was away at college. But it hurt, her leaving. And he'd missed her. He'd had a few relationships between then and now but no one ever measured up to her.

He rested his forehead on the bed next to her hip, her hand held tightly in between his. He let his mind drift over every moment of their lives together up until now. Every moment of the last few months. Seeing her when she stood in front of the meeting room, when they walked into her hotel room, their time in San Antonio.

"Come on, Tess...come back to me," he said softly, kissing her hand.

"Shane, honey," he heard Mary say, jerking him awake.

"Tess?" he asked, looking down at her still sleeping form.

"No, there's no change," Mary assured him, her voice soft. "Your friend Crownover brought some clothes for you."

He took the bag she offered then looked back down at Tessa.

"I keep expecting her to open her eyes and start ordering me around and arguing with me."

Mary stroked her hand over his hair to soothe him.

"She will before you know it. I didn't know she was working with you," she confided. "She told me she would be out-of-touch for a while, and a little bit about her investigation, but not who she was working with. It never occurred to me that she could be working with you...how long have you been back together with her?"

"Little over two months," he said, "we're engaged."

A smile spread across her face. "Oh, Shane! That's wonderful!"

"After this, how can she get past what they did to her?"

"She will...with you by her side. You are her rock, Shane. You always have been, even all these years you were apart; she always spoke of your conversations and texts and emails."

He shook his head, eyes on Tessa. "As a rape victim, she has a long road ahead of her. I couldn't stand it if my touch made her relive what they did to her."

"We have a lot to learn about how to handle her, you more than me. I'm certainly no expert on rape, but I know about violence. What was done to her was done with hatred and fear. When you are with her, there will be love in your touch; I have to believe that will make a difference. And you can't forget, Shane, my Tessa, she's a lot stronger than we give her credit for."

He brushed his hand over Tessa's hair. "God, I hope so," he breathed. "You think we could get someone to come shape her hair up? I don't want her to wake up and see it like this."

Mary offered him a sad smile. "What a wonderful idea. I'll go talk to the nurses. I bet they would know someone willing to come fix her up."

A couple of hours later, Shane held Tessa against him while a very sweet and compassionate stylist cut Tessa's hair into what she described as a short, choppy pageboy. He didn't care what the cut was called, he just knew it looked a thousand times better once it was done. He also took her engagement ring off her dog-tags around his neck and slid it in place on her finger. He wanted her to know beyond a shadow of a doubt, as soon as she woke up, that he still wanted her.

"Visiting hours are almost up," the night shift nurse, who introduced herself as Linda, announced.

"I'm not leaving her," Shane insisted.

"You won't do her any good if you push yourself to exhaustion," Linda told him.

"I wasn't there when she needed me the most," he said, "I won't let that happen again."

"Shane," Mary began but the look he shot her silenced what she would have said. "Typical McCanton, stubborn to a fault."

"Damn straight."

"Like I said before, my Tessa is lucky to have you."

"I can take you to a hotel, Mary," Gibson offered.

"Just go to my place," Shane said, pulling his keys from his pocket.

Mary nodded. "OK, honey, we'll go there. I'll bring

you a change of clothes in the morning."

"Thanks."

"Try to rest," she said, kissing his cheek.

The nurse left with Mary and Gibson but came back ten minutes later pushing a roll-away bed.

"I know you're going to be stubborn and not use this, but it's here, just in case," she said after she made it up.

"Thank you," he replied softly.

She checked Tessa's vitals, then turned to face Shane. He guessed her to be slightly younger than his parents and Mary. She had dark hair with a sprinkling of grey here and there; just enough to make her look authoritative.

"Your girl has been all over the news," she announced. At his alarmed look, she held a cautionary hand up, "they haven't released her name, but they are all over the story of how an undercover agent took down the Naturalists. Media ever gets a good look at the two of you and Hollywood types will be falling all over themselves to tell your story."

"Everyone should know what she did to take them down. What she sacrificed," he said hoarsely.

"She's not the type to want that kind of attention, though, is she?"

"No, ma'am. She's not."

She studied Tessa a moment. "It's a fine thing she

did. The daughter of one of my co-workers got mixed up with that bunch a few years ago. No one's heard from her since. We're all hoping she's among the girls recovered."

"Get me her name and the most recent picture her family has and I'll find out for you."

"I'll do that. Her mother would certainly appreciate it."

"Would be my pleasure. Something good needs to come of all this."

She smiled and gave his shoulder a pat. "Try to get some rest. I mean it."

"I'll try," he promised as she left.

Alone with Tessa, he took her hand and kissed her fingers then leaned forward to rest his head on the side of her bed. He must have fallen asleep, but his eyes flew open when he felt a gentle touch to the crown of his head. It was dark in the room save for a small night light near the head of her bed but he could just barely see the shine of her eyes.

"Hey," he said softly, slowly lifting his head. She didn't speak, just locked her gaze on his and again brushed her fingers through his hair. "Do you need anything?" She shook her head slightly. "OK...you're going to be all right, baby," he assured her. "Are you hurting?" She again shook her head but a tear rolled down her cheek and even in the darkened room he could see it. He raised her hand again to his lips. "It's going to be all right, Tess. You're safe now." Her hand tightened in his hair and then she closed her eyes;

it wasn't long before she was asleep again.

He got up and paced over to the window, looking out over the parking lot and fountains on the front grounds of the hospital. His thoughts drifted back to that night by the waterfall. They lay spent on the blanket and began to daydream about the house they would build there. He still had the list they made and decided that when she was released, he would get the ball rolling on building that house.

The door opened and Nurse Linda came in to check her vitals and IV.

"You aren't resting," she said to him.

"I was. She woke up briefly a few minutes ago."

"Ah, that explains the blip we got on our monitors. Did she say if she was in pain?"

"She shook her head when I asked."

"It's almost time to give her another dose," she said, "Doctor Roberts wants to give her time to heal a bit before we start scaling back the meds."

He nodded. "I agree, but I know she hates feeling doped up. She rarely even takes Tylenol."

"Likes to keep her wits about her, huh?"

"She rarely even drinks much. Hazards of the job."

"All the more reason for you to get in that bed and get some rest of your own."

"Yes, ma'am," he chuckled lightly.

When she left, he crossed over to the bed and leaned

down to place a soft kiss to Tessa's brow.

"I love you, Tess. Come back to me."

Chapter Fourteen

The road back from Hell was never as easy as the one that led you there in the first place. Tessa knew that truth better than most. She'd been to Hell and back several times in her life. The first time was when she and her mother pulled their lives together after years of abuse from her father. The second time was when she crawled out of the nightmare that was her life in Iraq. She supposed now was the third time, and though she'd already been through enough to try the patience of a saint, this time seemed insurmountable.

She felt completely drained and empty. Shell-shocked. She'd woken last night in a drugged haze to see Shane sitting by her bed side, asleep with his head resting on her bed. When she touched his hair and he lifted his head, she could see the silvery tracks of tears on his cheeks and it nearly killed her. Shane McCanton was not a crier.

It was early morning now and she knew Shane was still beside her though she had yet to open her eyes. She could feel the warmth and energy his presence created in the room. A nurse had come in not too long ago and announced that the doctor would be in shortly on his rounds.

She wanted to be awake for that meeting and she didn't want Shane in the room when she spoke to the doctor. The pain was so intense, however, she was afraid she'd pass out before the doctor came. To try to keep herself awake, she opened her eyes and reached out to Shane.

"Shane," she whispered, surprised at the weakness of her voice.

"Hey," he said immediately, leaning forward and gently stroking her hair, "there's my girl."

"What time is it?" she asked.

"Little after six. Do you need anything?"

"Are Nathaniel and Paul in custody?"

"Paul is. Nathaniel is in protective custody here at the hospital."

A sharp jolt of fear shot through her before she could stop it. "He's here? In the same hospital with me?" she asked and watched alarm spread across his face when her machines registered her elevated heartbeat.

"He's cuffed to the bed, there are two cops on his door, two cops outside your door and I'm here. You are safe, baby. He can't get to you."

The door opened and the doctor and a nurse rushed in.

"Tessa? What's going on?" the doctor asked, pressing his stethoscope to her chest.

Her eyes left Shane and met the doctor's gaze. "I

need to speak with you...privately."

"Of course," he replied.

"Sergeant McCanton, could you step outside a moment?" the nurse asked.

"Yeah, OK," he said, standing. "I'll be right outside, Tess, OK?"

She nodded but didn't speak. He leaned down to kiss her brow but stopped when she couldn't stop the cringe his nearness produced. He flinched but offered her a sad smile as he pulled away from her and walked out. Tessa waited for the door to close, then met the doctor's direct gaze.

"What are my injuries?" She listened quietly as he listed them out matter-of-factly. "I know I was raped and I certainly know it was brutal. Prior to that, I was just beginning to suspect that I might be pregnant."

The doctor was quiet a moment and she felt a squeeze to her heart. This was the elephant in the room. The thing no one wanted to tell her.

"The assaults caused tears in the uterine wall, which, unfortunately, led to a miscarriage," he said directly.

She sucked in a deep breath, released it slowly. "So I was pregnant." It was a statement rather than a question.

"Approximately six weeks."

She closed her eyes and fought the tears that were gathering. "Does anyone else know of this?"

"Your mother, your supervisor and your fiancé."

"Oh, God," she cried softly.

"I'm sorry, Tessa. Even if I hadn't told him, being law enforcement, he would have discovered this in the reports."

"I know," she whispered, then shook herself. "Anything else?"

"There was significant damage to your uterus. We repaired two large tears that, combined with previous scarring, I'm afraid may make carrying a pregnancy to term impossible."

She looked up at him through her tears. "Are you saying I won't ever be able to have children?"

"I'm not a specialist, but what I am saying is that carrying a child to term may prove difficult."

She was unable to stop her tears from falling and reached up to swipe at them angrily. She'd lost Shane's baby. How could he ever forgive her?

"I'm going to have Linda give you more pain medication."

"Can we hold off for an hour or so? I need to talk to a few people and I need my wits about me to make it through these conversations."

"Are you sure? I know your pain must be off the charts."

"It is...but I need to do this."

"OK. Linda will come back in an hour, all right?"

"Sure thing, doc. Thank you."

When they left, she had just a moment to collect her thoughts and take a deep breath before Shane, her mother and Gib walked in.

"Hi, Sweetie," her mother said, kissing her brow.

"Hi, Mama, Gib," she replied, her voice sounding tired even to her own ears.

Shane leaned down to kiss her but she again shied away from him. She watched the alarm spread across his face from the corner of her eye. She hated what she was about to do but for his own good, she knew she needed to let him go; he deserved a chance to have children of his own.

"Are you hurting?" her mother asked.

"All over. There's nowhere that doesn't hurt."

"You should have more pain medication," Gib said.

"The nurse is coming back in a bit," she offered.

"I'll go see what's taking so long," Shane said, turning to the door.

"That's fine. And go on home once you do," she said coolly.

"What?" he asked over his shoulder.

"Go home, Shane. I don't want you here."

"Tessa!" her mother gasped.

Shane turned back to her, confusion marring his brow. "What's going on, Tess?"

"You left me," she bit out. "You left me alone with

those monsters when I needed you."

"Tess, I...my dad..."

"You left me!" she yelled. "You were gone for weeks and they raped me!"

"Tessa Nicole!" Mary gasped. "That was not Shane's fault and you know it!"

"He said he would never leave me but he did and they hurt me."

"Tessa, I..."

"Go!!! Get away from me! You make me sick! It's your fault! It's all your fault, Shane McCanton!!!"

He stumbled back a step as if she'd struck him, his face pale, and as she regarded him, she felt a huge part of her die inside. Tears stung her eyes but she knew she had to finish this. She loved him and knew he deserved better than to be stuck with her.

"Get out and don't come back. Ever!!"

"Tessa!" Mary cried.

"GO!!!!!" she screamed.

Shane walked backward to the door then with one final, shell-shocked look to her, he was gone. She grabbed her stomach and tried to breathe through her tears but it was like all the air in the room left with Shane. Nurses came running in and cleared her mother and a stunned Gib from the room. Tessa caught sight of Shane sitting on the floor across from her door just before the sedative the nurse injected into her IV knocked her out.

Over the next days and weeks, Tessa refused any contact from Shane. She refused his calls. She returned his engagement ring via Gib. She stuck to her story of blaming him to her mother, but in a moment of weakness, confessed the real reason to Gib.

"Don't you think that was Shane's decision to make?" he asked her. She hadn't wanted to go back to Indian Springs upon her release, so Gib offered to let her stay at his beach house in Cabo San Lucas for as long as she needed, where they were now, along with her mother. One good thing had come from her ordeal - Gib and her mother had fallen for each other. They were inseparable now. Tessa was thrilled. Her mother deserved to be happy and it was obvious that Gib was head over heels for Mary Kelly.

"He would have stayed with me, Gib, I know that...but it wouldn't have been fair to him. The McCanton's are one of the ruling families of our hometown. He's his father's only son and he has no male cousins. The McCanton line could end with him. How could I let him risk that?"

"You could be perfectly healthy and only have girls. You aren't being fair to him, Tess," he said bluntly, "and you aren't being fair to yourself."

She looked out over the bright blue water and shook her head.

"I didn't want to take that chance. You've been

around me. I can't stand to have anyone touch me other than you and Mama."

"It's only been three months. You can't expect to come out of a trauma like that without some adverse effects. You have to give yourself time."

"I know. I'm so screwed up, I just don't think it would be fair to ask anyone to deal with that."

He fell silent for a while and they sat listening to the waves. They could hear Mary in the kitchen preparing dinner, and Tessa knew her time to talk freely with Gib was running out.

"Please don't say anything to Mama about this. She loves Shane and she would be all over me to go back to him."

"He's back in Indian Springs now, you know. The town council wants him to take over for his dad permanently. He's considering it."

Tessa sighed and shook her head. "That would be a waste of his talents."

"And what you're doing now isn't a waste of yours?" he asked pointedly.

"Maybe...but I can't go back to that life, Gib. You know. You retired because of all this."

He offered a soft smile. "Well, that was part of the reason...not all."

At that, Tessa smiled, too. "Have I told you how

happy I am for you both?"

"A few times," he chuckled.

"Well, I am. You both deserve to be happy."

"As do you, kid. Don't forget that."

"I'm happy that the two people I love the most are happy. That is enough for me."

"For now," he supplied.

Her eyes turned back to the ocean and she let out a deep sigh.

"For now," she confirmed.

Her mother and Gib soon went back to Indian Springs. Tessa stayed. She took a job as a bartender on day shifts at a beach bar. It was mindless work that kept her busy and prevented her from thinking too much about anything else but the next drink order. She'd resorted back to her Army days of evading men's attention, and other than the hours she was at work, she kept primarily to herself.

Months went by, each one melting into the next. Tessa barely even noticed. Her mother and Gib came to spend Thanksgiving and Christmas with her. Every time, Mary would mention Shane, and every time, Tessa would change the subject or walk away.

Nightmares plagued her and it was when they were visiting at Christmas that Mary and Gib learned how bad they'd become. On Christmas Eve, Mary and Gib were jolted awake by a blood chilling scream. They flew to

Tessa's room to find her writhing on the bed, sobbing and calling for Shane. Mary climbed onto the bed and pulled her sobbing daughter into her arms, desperate to calm her.

"This has got to stop," Mary told Gib while she rocked Tessa in her arms. "Tessa has always been strong. This isn't her."

"Don't talk about me like I'm not here," Tessa said, her voice raw from her screams.

"Then stop acting like you aren't part of the world," Mary snapped back at her.

"Mama, please, I don't need a lecture right now."

"Well, too bad, because the "Oh Poor Tessa Party" has gone on long enough. It's time you came home and joined the rest of the world again."

"I am home. I have a job. My life is here. Not in Indian Springs."

"You have an existence here, not a life, and you only have that because Glen has let rentals pass. This was meant to be temporary, Tessa. It's time to come home."

"I'll pay rent to Gib. I won't go back to Indian Springs."

"Do you think you are the only one suffering? All those horrors were done to you but it affected someone else, too, Tessa. And he is just as lost without you as you are without him."

"I don't want to hear about him, Mama."

"Too bad because it's time you should. Shane is just

as much a walking corpse right now as you. He has lost a lot of weight. He rarely smiles. He's all about his job now...Sinclair County Sheriff now that Luke has retired. You did that to him, Tessa. He loved you so much and you just threw it in his face."

"Mary," Gib cautioned but she ignored him.

"He begged you not to take that assignment. You just had to prove you had bigger balls than the boys, didn't you?"

"Stop it, Mama," Tessa snapped.

"No, I won't stop! You made that boy's life miserable from the day you met him and then when you finally got him, you used him up and broke him. His father almost died! Luke...well, it was bad for a while. How could he leave? Everything was running slow on your end. He isn't psychic. He couldn't know things would go the way they did for you. No one could. How could you blame him? When that doctor came out of the operating room and told us what had been done to you, what had happened to you, Shane was devastated. I know. I held him in my arms when his legs gave out and he cried on the floor of the waiting room. He loves you so much and you just threw it away."

"I had to let him go, Mama, don't you see? They broke me. I'm so messed up; he doesn't deserve to be stuck picking up my pieces, his chance for a family of his own down the drain. He deserves to see his own eyes reflected in a child of his own. I can't give him that."

Mary cupped Tessa's face in her hands, shaking her head. "Oh, honey...what a messed up mind you have. You think by giving him up you've done either one of you any favors? You're both miserable. You need to come home. You need to face him."

"I can't, Mama," Tessa whispered. "I can't. I can't see what he's become because of me. I can't."

Mary let it drop then, but not all together. She knew that Tessa and Shane belonged together and she knew she had to figure out a way to make that happen. It wasn't until the spring hit that something drastic enough happened that spurred her into action. Three somethings, really. First, Gib asked her to marry him. Second, the trial of Nathaniel and Paul Helton was approaching. Third, and most important, Shane McCanton began dating again.

Part Three

Chapter Fifteen

Shane knew he shouldn't have been surprised at how fast he was sucked back into the routine of his hometown. He came home lost. Reeling. He fell into the work of his dad's job, tying up loose ends for him. His dad's recovery hadn't gone as well as they hoped and Luke McCanton made the difficult decision to retire. Once his retirement was accepted, it took the town council all of two seconds to ask Shane to step in to his father's position, and, seeing as how he had no reason to return to Austin, it took Shane all of two seconds more to say yes. It also didn't take him long to realize that as much as he loved his folks, he was not going to be staying with them longer than he had to. He quickly found an apartment to rent and began construction on his new home...by the waterfall on his family land, just as he always planned.

He tried not to think too much of the fact that many of the features he was adding to his home were from the Dream List he and Tessa made that night on the blanket. He tried not to think much about Tessa at all, though that was pretty much a moot point; he thought about her all the time.

The first few days after she threw him out of her room, he kept going to the hospital, hoping she would relent. When she didn't, he went home, picked up a bottle of Jack Daniels and for the first time in his life, drank himself into oblivion. He wasn't proud of it, and really hated that Crownover had come and picked his sorry butt off the floor where he'd collapsed. He swore that was the last time he'd ever turn to the bottle to ease his pain. It had helped, but only temporarily, and then he'd felt worse.

After Tessa was released from the hospital, Gib came to see him and updated him on her condition, and told him they were flying her to his beach house in Cabo San Lucas for her recovery...and then with a look of apology, Gib handed him Tessa's engagement ring.

Shane packed up that night and went home to Indian Springs. Aside from his father, his family had no idea he and Tessa had begun dating again, much less that they'd been engaged. So, as devastated as he was, there was no one at home he could share why with, because he wasn't going to unload on his dad or do anything to risk his recovery. Of course, they knew something was up with him. He was a shell of his former self. He had very little appetite so he was losing weight, but at the same time toning up because he found a long, vigorous run numbed his mind better than alcohol and a strenuous workout was even better, so when he wasn't working or running or working on his new house, he was in the gym.

The only relief he found was when his childhood best friend, Steve Sinclair's younger sister, Ivy, moved back to town. Ivy was four years younger than him and Steve and madly in love with Steve's college best friend, who was a football player for the Dallas Cowboys. The first Sunday she was back in town, she followed him out of church, offering him a smile.

"Hey, Shane."

He stopped and regarded her, smiling as he noted that his friend's sister had grown up.

"Hey, Baby Girl," he greeted, embracing her. "When did you get into town?"

"Wednesday. Home to stay," she told him, kissing his cheek before she pulled back. "What's wrong, honey? You look so sad. What's happened?"

He took a deep breath and looked over her head, watching everyone file out and into the parking lot.

"It's...a really long story."

"Well...I've got time. Wanna tell me about it?"

For a moment he hesitated, then decided he needed to talk to someone about it.

"Wanna come check out my new place? Just moved in last weekend."

"Love to," she smiled.

Over beer and pizza, Shane spilled the whole agonizing tale.

"So that's it. She couldn't even stand for me to touch her, not that I blame her. I stay in touch with her mother. Tess is in Cabo San Lucas staying at her former boss' house and working as a bartender."

"She staying there with him?"

"No, he's dating her mother now. It kills me to think of her all alone down there, but what can I do?"

Ivy took a sip of her beer. "Know why I came back? I had to get away from Reese," she said, referring to her brother's friend.

"Away? But I thought -"

"Yeah, me, too. Reese is too wrapped up in his career for a relationship, and as much as I want him, I couldn't keep putting my life on hold. I was offered the job as the assistant band director at the high school here, so I took it."

"He'll come around," Shane assured her.

Ivy laid her hand on his shoulder. "I hope so...Tessa will, too."

Shane kissed the side of Ivy's head when she leaned into him. "I won't hold my breath on that one. I just hope she can overcome what was done to her."

Ivy sighed. "Why couldn't we be attracted to each other?"

He chuckled. "Life would be so much less complicated, huh?"

"It really would. I've been in love with Reese my whole life it seems. I thought when I was living there close to him that we'd finally get together."

"Didn't quite work out that way, did it?"

"No. Well, it did, but not like I wanted. He's not ready."

"So, what, you're just going to sit around and wait for him to come to his senses?"

"I love him," she said simply, "like you love Tessa."

"Pretty pathetic, aren't we?" he snorted, finishing off his beer.

"Pretty much. So, how long do we wait?"

"Damned if I know," he replied, resting his cheek on the top of her head. For a while they sat in silence, just enjoying each other's company. Like she said, it really would simplify things if they could feel something more than just friendly brother/sister affection toward one another. His mother had always wanted him to end up with Ivy. Her mother was his mother's best friend.

"Are you really going to be happy being Sheriff here, Shane? After all the action and excitement of the big city?"

"I couldn't stay there. Too many memories at my place and at the office...and too much resentment toward my team members who were on watch when she was...when all that happened to her."

"That's perfectly understandable."

"God, I love her, Ivy," he said, his voice cracking. "I miss her so much. I want to help her, but she blames me for what happened."

"She doesn't blame you, honey. That was just her self-preservation talking. You always hurt the ones you love? That kind of thing."

"I promised her once that no one would ever hurt her again...but someone did hurt her, on my watch."

Ivy sat up and faced him. "Stop that. What happened to Tessa was not your fault. You had to come home to be with your dad. Tessa knew the risks involved when she took the assignment, right? You can't beat yourself up over this."

He shook his head, eyes brimming. "I can't stop. They broke her, Ivy. They...and I wasn't there to stop it. I couldn't-"

He broke then. Months of holding back, of pushing everything down came to the surface. Ivy gathered him into her arms and held him tight, stroking his hair and back to soothe him and just let him ride it all out.

"It's OK, honey, just let it all go. It's all right," she whispered.

After several minutes, he took a deep breath and pulled back, scrubbing his hands over his face.

"God, I'm sorry," he breathed.

"Oh, please. Don't apologize. I understand...and you're human. I won't tell a soul. Promise."

He reached out to stroke a hand over her brunette hair.

"Reese is an idiot," he said softly.

"Oh, yeah, he's a huge idiot," she laughed, turning her head to kiss his palm when he touched her cheek. "But Tessa's not. She'll come around, Shane. She just has to heal."

He and Ivy began to spend a lot of their free time together. The town thought they were an item and neither of them did or said anything to set the record straight. They enjoyed each other's company and it helped them both to not be alone all the time. He was grateful for the time he got to spend with Ivy until the day her man retired from the Cowboys, took the job of Indian Springs' new high school football coach and moved to town. While Shane was happy things were beginning to work out for her, it made him acutely aware of how much he missed Tessa. It had been months since he'd last seen her and lately he'd been fighting the urge to hop on a plane to go to Cabo and try to talk some sense into her.

He still loved Tessa in spite of it all, which was why he'd been surprised when one night while making the rounds on patrol he came across a woman stranded on the side of the road and he felt a stirring of interest when he looked into her clear blue eyes. She was Wendy Shapland, and she was moving to town to be the new public librarian. She'd run out of gas 20 miles outside of town. He'd taken her to a gas station to fill a gas can, brought her back to her car then followed her back to the gas station to make sure she arrived safely. They chatted while he filled the car up for her and he learned she'd rented his old apartment in town, and when she was about to leave, he surprised them both by asking her to a Welcome to Town dinner at Miss Nettie's Restaurant.

    Wendy was as different from Tessa as night and day. Tessa was tall and athletically built. Wendy was shorter and a bit curvier, more Girl-Next-Door than Tessa. She had a calming effect on him and he found he liked being around her. On their third date, he kissed her outside her door. She was the first woman he'd kissed since Tessa and while he didn't feel the overwhelming, all-consuming passion Tessa's kisses ignited, there was a definite spark between them. For the first time, he considered that just maybe there was life after Tessa Kelly.

Chapter Sixteen

Ivy went into Shelmerdine's with the intention of buying new tennis shoes in preparation for the start of Summer Band. As she browsed the selection, she saw Mary Kelly talking to Mrs. Shelmerdine. She didn't intend to eavesdrop but when Mrs. Shelmerdine asked about Tessa she couldn't help it.

"Tessa is coming home in a few days," Mary Kelly announced.

"Oh, Mary, how exciting! It's been years since Tessa was last here. Is she coming home to stay?"

"Glen and I are hoping we can talk her into it."

Tennis shoes forgotten, Ivy dug her phone out of her purse and rushed out of the store to call Shane.

"Hey, Baby Girl, what's up?"

"Are you at the office?" she asked.

Her abrupt tone alerted him. "No, I'm making the rounds. What's up?"

"I can't get into it on the phone. How soon can you meet me at your house?"

"Fifteen minutes. What's this about?"

"Just be there, Shane."

She ended the call and rushed to her truck. She'd

been praying for this day to come ever since he told her about what happened with Tessa. Nothing would be right in Shane's world until he dealt with his feelings for Tessa.

Shane was on his front porch waiting for her when she pulled up. He stood as she got out and met her half way.

"What is it?" he asked, "Did Reese-"

"No, no, this isn't about him. Look, I was just in Shelmerdine's and heard Mary Kelly say that Tessa is coming home in a few days. I just didn't want you to hear it from someone else."

A muscle ticked in his jaw, the only outward reaction to the news.

"Well, we knew she would come home sooner or later. The Heltons' trial is approaching."

"Yes, but that's in Austin. She's coming here and Mary wants to try to convince her to stay."

"She won't," he dismissed.

"What makes you so sure?"

"She hates it here," he said simply. He walked back to the porch and sank down to the steps.

"Will you talk to her while she's here?"

He shrugged. "It's been a year since I last saw her. I've respected her privacy and left her alone as she asked. My number hasn't changed; she's known how to contact me."

"You can't avoid her forever."

"I know. She's ripped my heart out twice now. I barely survived this last time. I can't go another round with her. I wouldn't survive."

"But what if this time she sticks?"

He drew a deep, ragged breath.

"I don't think I can afford to find out. I'm just now getting back on my feet. Wendy-"

"Is not Tessa and she never will be."

"No. She's not. Wendy would never hurt me."

Ivy sighed. "But you don't love Wendy."

"I could," he said defiantly.

Ivy looked directly into his eyes. "No. You couldn't. Not when your heart still belongs to Tessa."

"Ivy-"

She cut him off. "You can lie to everyone else but not to me. You love Tessa. You always have and you always will. I gotta go, I just didn't want you to be blindsided by this. I love you."

He stood and kissed her brow. "Love you, too. Thanks for letting me know."

He watched Ivy leave and then slowly climbed the steps to go inside. One year and just the mention of her name had his guts churning. What would he do when they were face-to-face for the first time, because, in a town this small it, was going to happen.

He checked in with his deputies to make sure there wasn't anything that required his immediate attention, then let dispatch know he was taking the rest of the day off. Going to the fridge, he took out a beer then went into his home office.

Images of those last few days with her flooded him. From seeing her bloodied and broken body in Helton's clutches to that morning when her eyes finally opened and she accused him of abandoning her. He'd known she really hadn't meant it all but she'd been so upset he'd been forced to leave. He wondered if time and distance had changed her views, or if she still blamed him.

Beating himself up all over again, he pulled the chain with her dog-tags and ring from around his neck and held them tight in his fist. If he'd never left, if his dad had never had the accident, would things have happened differently? Would they have pulled her out as planned? Would she have pulled herself out knowing that she was pregnant?

He opened his hand and studied the tags and ring he'd bought her. He needed to face the facts. A year without a word from her pretty much told him all he needed to know. He opened a drawer in his desk and let the chain fall inside. With a sigh, he realized he needed to call Wendy; she needed to be prepared for what was coming.

Tessa rented a car to drive to Indian Springs from the

airport rather than having her mother and Gib come pick her up. She thought it would be better to be by herself as she drove into her hometown for the first time in nearly ten years. She kept her mind as calm and empty as possible but it wasn't easy. With every mile closer to town, memories came flooding back: some bad, of her father, some good, too, but painful because they revolved around Shane. So much of her memories of her hometown were tied to him, so much of her life.

    She forced the memories back. No use dwelling on them. She'd pushed Shane away and refused to contact him for over a year. Whatever chance they may have had was gone now. Besides, she was still messed up; she wouldn't want to burden anyone with trying to figure her out.

    Keeping her eyes straight ahead as she drove through town, she still couldn't keep memories from flooding her. By the time she pulled up to her mother's house she was exhausted and emotionally drained.

    Mary was sitting on her front porch swing waiting for her. She didn't see Gib, but she was sure he was there somewhere. It was still a little weird to think of him with her mother; that he was going to marry her mother and be her stepfather, but she was glad that it was working out for them. God knew someone in her life deserved to be happy.

    "There's my girl," Mary said, coming to embrace her.

    "Hi, Mama," she replied, her voice sounding tired,

even to her.

Mary cupped Tessa's face in her hands and studied her. She was sporting a terrific tan thanks to her months on the beach, but she knew how tired she looked and knew that her mother saw it too.

"I've missed you," Mary said simply. Tessa was grateful that she didn't start lecturing her.

"Tessa," Gib greeted her, stepping out onto the porch. "Bags in the trunk?"

"Yes, thank you," she said as he went to get them.

"Come on, sweetie, let's get you settled. Dinner will be ready in just a bit."

Tessa nodded and followed her mother inside to her old bedroom. She pointedly avoided looking at the porch swing as she passed, but not looking didn't erase the memory of it. Shane had hung it for them when they moved in to this house when they were in high school. Her head began to pound. How would she survive being back here?

"Honey, are you OK?" Mary asked when they got into her room.

"I'm just tired," she dismissed.

"Tessa," she began.

"I'll be fine, Mama, really. It was time for me to come home and stop running from my life. And I wanted to be here to see you and Gib get married. You deserve to be happy."

"As do you."

Tessa shrugged as she sat on her bed. "Some things just aren't meant to be."

Mary shook her head. "I don't believe that. Not one bit. Not for you and Shane. He loves you so much. It killed him to leave you at the hospital. He stayed for days after you threw him out. Being without you has devastated him. He lost weight. A lot of weight. He threw himself into two things when he came back, his job and the building of his new house. He's better now but still not himself. He's polite and courteous as always, but his eyes are troubled."

"I really don't want to talk about Shane, Mama," Tessa said wearily.

"Honey, I'm just preparing you for what you'll see and hear in town."

"Didn't you say he's dating again? Two women?"

"Well, one was Ivy Sinclair, but they weren't really dating. They are just good friends. Her football player boyfriend just moved to town so he doesn't see as much of her anymore. The other one, though, is the new librarian. He's been seeing her for about a month now."

"Well, there you go. He's moved on. End of story."

Mary shook her head at her daughter. "What is wrong with you? Do not tell me you still blame him for what happened."

Tessa closed her eyes and drew a long, deep breath.

"He's better off without me, Mama. Trust me."

"I don't believe that."

"I do."

"Tessa, honey -"

"What's up with the pity party, Soldier?" Gib asked, bringing her bags in.

"Glen," Mary admonished.

"What? We've left her alone long enough. It's time to get on with things, don't you think?"

"Gee, Gib, love you, too," Tessa said, dryly.

He winked at her. "There's the Tessa I know."

She took a deep breath and reached out her hand to him. "I'm gettin' there, Gib," she said, squeezing his hand.

"I know you are," he returned.

"Come on, dinner's just about ready," Mary said, standing.

Tessa had been home for nearly two weeks when she finally decided she needed to stop being a coward and venture out of her mother's house. For those two weeks, she stayed home, reconnecting with her mother and Gib, catching up on reports and paperwork she'd been neglecting regarding her upcoming testimony, and just adjusting to being back in Indian Springs. Her mother and Gib were planning to marry soon and take a honeymoon to England, so that they would be home in time for the start of the Helton's trial. She wanted to be able to run the shop for her mother while they were gone. Therefore, when she came down to breakfast on the second Friday she was home, dressed and ready to go, conversation halted and they both stared openly at her.

"Good morning," she greeted them. "Mama, I thought I'd come into the shop with you today, see where everything is so you and Gib can go on your Honeymoon worry-free."

She caught the quick glance her mother sent to Gib before she smiled big and bright at her.

"That would be wonderful, Sweetie. I don't have any weddings scheduled for that time frame but it would be nice to be able to have those times available should someone want them."

"We've got a few weeks until then. I haven't forgotten how to do all the stuff for weddings. If anyone wants to book while you're gone, I can do it."

Mary couldn't hide the joy those words filled her with. Gib winked at Tessa and squeezed Mary's hand.

"So, what are you doing these days, Gib? I just realized I never really asked you that. I guess I haven't been paying much attention to what's been happening around me since I've been home."

He smiled. "I'm working at the Army recruiting offices some, helping new recruits get into shape. I'm also doing some consulting work for Mike Casiano, remember him?"

Tessa nodded. "He was the head of that joint forces

Task Force that some of the guys joined. Coop and Whit and Colt. He is a SEAL, right?"

"Yes. He and several members of that Task Force are out now and running a private securities firm. I've been helping them out with a few things here and there. Coop and Whit and Colt are part of the group. Keeps me busy but still gives me plenty of free time to be with Mary."

"Good all around, then. I'm glad you're happy."

"Mike could probably use you on a few things. I could ask him, if you-"

She shook her head. "No, that's OK. My days of that kind of work are over."

"Tessa...you're good at what you do. You shouldn't..."

"Gib, please, let's not go there, all right?"

"Are you ready to head into town?" Mary asked, pulling them away from the subject.

"Sure. Let's go."

Tessa grabbed the breakfast dishes from the table to rinse out in the sink and was surprised when Gib lightly touched her hand. She jumped and the mug she'd been holding slipped from her fingers and shattered on the tile floor.

"Oh, Mama, I'm sorry," she said, squatting down to pick up the pieces.

"I'm sorry, Tess, I shouldn't have startled you," Gib said, squatting down to help her.

"It's OK, both of you," Mary said, approaching with a broom and dustpan. "I've got this. You two just back away before you cut yourselves."

Gib stood and then held a hand out to Tessa. She stared at him a moment, then took a deep breath and put her hand in his and allowed him to help her up.

"Baby steps, Tess," he said, giving her hand a reassuring squeeze. "You'll get there."

"Why don't you meet us for lunch at Miss Nettie's, Glen?" Mary suggested when she'd finished the clean up.

"I'll be with a recruit class at lunch but I can meet you there for dinner."

"Perfect. Five-thirty?"

"I'll be there," he confirmed.

The day at the shop was busy and pretty much old hat for Tessa. She was amazed at how easily she slipped right back into the swing of it all, like she never even left. She'd taken over all her mother's special requests pile, finding all the wild, off-the-wall and exotic things that various brides wanted for their special day.

"How the heck does she think we will find a hundred bats to release at the end of her ceremony?" Tessa cried. "That isn't even safe."

Mary looked up from the bouquet she was making. "Let me guess...Becca Radley?"

"Yeah. Goth girl extraordinaire I'm guessing. She's

just going to have to get over wanting bats. Does Simon still handle all your animal requests?"

"Yes."

"I'll see if he can get ravens and I'll convince her that those will be more Goth than bats."

"Works for me, but call him tomorrow. It's time to shut down and meet Glen at Miss Nettie's."

Tessa's eyes widened. "Really? It's five-thirty already?"

"Time flies," Mary confirmed.

"I guess so...though I'm not really sure I'm ready to take on going to Miss Nettie's," she admitted.

"Honey...you can't avoid the town forever."

"I know...but Miss Nettie's on a Friday night...that's a bit of a trial by fire, don't you think?"

"Well, maybe a little...but you may as well jump right in."

Tessa hesitated before finally agreeing, "Yeah, sure, why not?" she said, her voice dripping with sarcasm.

Mary gave her a hug. "Come on. Sink or swim time."

Tessa followed her mother out and together they walked the two blocks from the shop to Miss Nettie's Restaurant. She kept her eyes straight and avoided looking at the end of the street where the Sheriff's Office was. Avoiding Shane wasn't practical in a town this size but she intended to put off seeing him again for as long as possible.

They walked into Miss Nettie's and before the door even shut behind them, a loud squeal sounded and Tessa found herself wrapped in the warm, enthusiastic embrace of Miss Nettie herself. She braced herself and forced the feeling of panic down to awkwardly return the embrace, but she kept her eyes locked on her mother.

"Tessa Kelly, look at you!" Miss Nettie cried, cupping Tessa's face in her hands. "You are just as beautiful as ever. I can't believe it's been ten years since you were last here."

"I've been busy," Tessa hedged.

"I know you have! Our own G.I. Jane! Come on, Glen is already seated," she told Mary. She led them through the restaurant slowly, letting people stop them along the way to greet Tessa. By the time they made it to the booth where Gib was waiting, Tessa was trembling and barely holding it together.

"You're doing great, kid," Gib encouraged her when she sat down.

"You did wonderful, honey," her mother agreed.

Tessa shakily lifted the glass of water in front of her and desperately wished it was something stronger, but unfortunately, Miss Nettie didn't serve alcohol. This was the first time she'd been around a large group of people without the safety of the bar to shield her like she'd had on the beach...and this was home; these were people that, for the most part, she'd known all her life. She really didn't want to have a melt-down in front of them.

"Deep breaths, kid," Gib encouraged, his gravelly Sam Elliott voice a soothing balm to her.

She nodded then reached across the table and for the second time that day, took his hand in hers, surprising all three of them.

"I love you, Gib," she said, further adding to the evening's surprises. "Thank you for being there for me, and for loving Mama. You are the father of my heart and you have been since I met you ten years ago. I just...well, life's too short for you not to know that."

He gave her a smile and squeezed her hand. "I love you, too, kid."

Tessa smiled then pulled back and brushed her hand over the menu in front of her. "Why does she even bother giving us these? She's going to bring us whatever it is she thinks we want anyway," she said, in effort to lighten the mood.

Mary wiped a tear from her cheek and smiled, too. "You're right, she will."

While her mother and Gib exchanged talk of how their day went, Tessa settled back in her seat and for the first time, glanced around the room at some of the faces she'd known all her life. She took note of the couples who had been together even in high school and pondered over all those she'd grown up with who now had miniature versions of themselves seated around them.

It was about mid-way through their meal when she felt the atmosphere of the room change. She couldn't quite place what it was until the doors to Miss Nettie's private dining area at the rear of the room (which she was facing) opened and a group of kids ran out and one adorable little dark haired girl cried: Uncle Shane! Uncle Shane!

Her eyes shifted to her mother, whose expression confirmed that the little girl's uncle was indeed Shane McCanton, and he was currently walking toward the back room.

"Hey, Kitty Kat," she heard him say, and she heard the little girl squeal in delight. Two seconds later, he was walking past their table, the little girl holding tight to his neck, the other kids surrounding him.

She thought she'd be prepared to see him again but she wasn't. If he had looked the same, maybe she could have dealt better, but the man who walked past her wearing a blue button down shirt, faded jeans and scarred boots was just as her mother had described him: a shell of his former self. He had lost a lot of weight...she'd guess fifty pounds at least. His dark hair, which he'd always worn in a neat, military-style razor cut, had grown out so that it curled slightly, but gave him a softer more vulnerable appearance by calling to attention how much his face had thinned.

As she watched, he approached the table where his family sat then he leaned down to place a kiss to the lips of a pretty brunette who was looking up at him like he was every movie star rolled into one. He sat, settled the little girl in his lap, and draped an arm over the back of the woman's chair. She knew the woman had to be the librarian he was seeing, and she saw that this woman was welcomed as part of his family in a way she never had been. It hurt, seeing him, seeing him with someone else. She thought she was prepared but she'd been sorely mistaken.

"I've got to go," she said low, her eyes still locked on Shane.

"Honey, I tried to tell you..."

"It's OK, I just...I need to go. Finish your dinner. I'll walk home."

"Tessa," Gib began but stopped at the look she gave him as she stood.

"I"m fine, Gib, just...let me walk. I need it."

With obvious reluctance, Gib nodded. Tessa's gaze shifted again to Shane who had now noticed her and his face had gone ashen. Their gazes held for a moment, then she forced herself to turn her back on him and walk away. Several people called out to her; she ignored them all and kept walking. Her mind was blank but for one thought: she'd really and truly lost him.

She made it out to the gazebo at the town's center

before her feet just wouldn't go forward any more. It felt like a fifty pound weight was sitting on her chest. She desperately tried to suck air into her lungs but it was difficult.

"Tessa," her mother called cautiously, coming slowly to her.

"Knew this could happen," she rasped, "Knew...knew it was happening, I just...I didn't expect it to hurt so much."

Mary rubbed her hand in soothing circles over Tessa's back. "I know, baby."

"He really is seeing someone else. He's moved on," Tessa breathed.

Gib pulled up beside them and rolled the window down.

"Your chariot awaits, my ladies," he called.

Tessa locked gazes with Gib and focused on him. He had seen her safely through the desert in Iraq, he'd come back and stayed with her when shrapnel from an IED pierced her and killed two of their unit members, and as she'd said, he was the father she never really had. It was in that moment that she realized that while Shane had been the rock of her youth, she wasn't totally without support. The weight lifted from her chest, not completely, but enough for her to be able to breathe again.

She stepped out of the gazebo and to Gib's truck. As she was getting in, she caught sight of Shane standing across the street, hands stuffed in his pockets, shoulders hunched. It hurt, seeing him; seeing what she'd done to him, but she knew at least now that, although it did hurt, she knew she could face going on without him.

Chapter Seventeen

Shane finished the last of his paperwork for the day and shut his computer down. His family was meeting at Miss Nettie's for dinner since his sister Cordy was in town. He hadn't seen her in a few weeks so he should have been looking forward to it, but instead, he'd been dreading it all day.

Could be because his mother was on a tear lately about him settling down. Of course, he knew why; it was because Tessa had come home. Susie McCanton didn't know of his recent history with Tessa, but she knew of their past and now that he'd begun seeing Wendy, she was determined to see them together. Shane liked Wendy well enough, but ever since Tessa had come back to town, his budding relationship with Wendy stalled out. He'd yet to see Tessa but knew it was only a matter of time.

He left the office and walked over to Miss Nettie's, greeting town folk as he went. A lot of guys wouldn't have been able to transition from big city investigator to small town sheriff but because he'd grown up here, he slipped into the role with ease. After all that had happened with the Naturalists, he found that the simplicity of his small hometown suited him.

"Hey, Sheriff," Holly, Miss Nettie's hostess, greeted him when he walked in. "Miss Nettie set y'all up in the private dining room this time. Just go on back."

"Thanks," he said, doing just that.

As soon as he stepped into the main dining room, Cordy and Gracie's kids came running out of the private area toward him.

"Uncle Shane! Uncle Shane!" Cordy's youngest girl cried, beating the others to him.

He scooped her up and tossed her high in the air, causing her to squeal in excitement.

"Hey, Kitty Kat," he said to her as he made his way to his family.

"Well, it's about time," his mother admonished lightly.

"Sorry. Busy day...Hi," he said to Wendy, leaning down to briefly kiss her. Wendy smiled up at him and placed her palm on his cheek in a light caress. He turned his head to kiss her palm then sat with his niece in his lap and draped an arm over the back of Wendy's chair. He called out greetings to Cordy and her husband and was turning his head to greet Miss Nettie when a movement in the main dining room caught his eye. He felt all the blood drain from his face when he saw it was Tessa who had caught his attention by standing. She looked up and their gazes collided, then she turned her back and walked out.

"Uncle Shane, too tight," Kat protested and he

realized his fingers had tightened on her waist.

"Sorry, sugar, go on over to your mom, OK? I gotta go check on something."

Kat scurried off his lap and he stood, watching Mary and Gib leave.

"Shane?" Wendy asked, turning his attention, "what is it?"

He leaned down and kissed her cheek. "I'll be right back."

"Shane Gabriel, where are you going?" his mother asked.

"Be back," he tossed over his shoulder. He made his way out of the restaurant and saw Tessa stop by the gazebo, her mother not far behind her. He crossed to the other side of the street and stayed back a clip, not wanting either woman to spot him. He stuck to the shadows and got close enough to hear Tessa's strained voice say, "Knew it was happening, I just...I didn't expect it to hurt so much."

He felt his gut flip. Obviously, seeing him with Wendy upset her, but he wasn't sure how he felt about that. Gib pulled up to take the women home. Shane stepped up onto the sidewalk and shoved his hands in his pockets in frustration. Tessa turned and looked across the street to once again meet his gaze. What he saw in her eyes then he knew would be etched on his memory forever. While at the restaurant, her eyes had been bright with unshed tears, now they were tear-free and flat...dead...very un-Tessa-like.

He stood for several moments after they drove away trying to collect his scattered thoughts. When he found himself hoping a call would come in so he wouldn't have to go back and face his family, he knew he had to get moving. Taking a deep breath, he turned...and found Wendy standing a few feet away. He hadn't even heard her approach.

"Hey," he greeted, stepping up to her.

"That was Tessa?" she asked softly. He hadn't told her the full story, but she knew more than his family did about Tessa.

He glanced back in the direction Tessa disappeared off to, then again to Wendy.

"Yeah, that was her."

"She's beautiful."

"Wendy-"

She smiled softly but cut him off. "It's OK, you haven't seen her in a long time. Does her being here change things with us?"

He took a deep breath, released it slowly. "I don't know," he admitted. "I'd be lying if I said it didn't."

She nodded. "I understand...do you want to be with her again?"

He closed his eyes. "Right now? My heart can't take another round with her."

"But?" she prompted.

"But...when she stood up back there and I saw her, it was like everything else in the world disappeared."

"I see," she replied in a small voice. "Even though she hurt you?"

He wiped a tear from her cheek with his thumb. "I'm not saying I want to take her back. I'm just saying that at some point, she and I will need to talk. If for no other reason than to just formally say good-bye."

More tears fell down her cheeks. "OK...then just know that I'll be waiting for you, on the other side, but I won't wait forever." He nodded. She stood on her toes to kiss him then she walked away, leaving him again alone on the street.

He rubbed the back of his neck. What the heck was he doing? One look at Tessa and here he was, turning his life upside down for her...again. God, would he ever learn? He watched Wendy walk safely to the library where she was parked, then headed back to the restaurant.

"That was Tessa you followed out, wasn't it?" Luke asked when Shane returned. He was sitting on a bench just outside the entrance.

"Yes, sir."

"And Wendy just walked back to the library alone."

Shane nodded, meeting his dad's direct gaze. "Yes, sir."

They were quiet a minute, Luke staring down at his

walking cane while Shane did his best to just keep his mind calm.

"You have been broken ever since you returned. Your mom and sisters have been worried sick about you. I didn't tell them what I know."

"Appreciate it," he murmured.

"I saw her when she stood up. She's changed a lot since I last saw her. Not a little girl anymore. She looks haunted. Like a lot of the guys did coming home from 'Nam."

"She went through Hell, Dad. The kind no woman ever should have to...and she blames me for it."

"You know that's not true, Son."

"Maybe. Hell. I don't know. We were engaged. She threw me out and I haven't seen her again until tonight."

"Trauma changes people...but bottom line? She's here now and from the look on her face tonight, I don't think she liked seeing you with Wendy."

Shane actually chuckled. "No, sir, I don't think she did. I hurt Wendy tonight and I hated that...but I've got to deal with these feelings I have for Tessa."

Luke nodded. "Your mother won't be happy. She really likes Wendy."

"And she's never liked Tessa, I know. I'm not saying I'm gonna go running back to her exactly. Her shutting me out this last time just about killed me."

"I know it did, Son. It's been hard to see you hurting and know there was nothing I could do to help you."

"Am I crazy, Dad? To even think of starting anything with Tessa again? A relationship, a friendship, whatever? She was brutally gang raped and beaten within an inch of her life. You saw her. Do you think she's even capable of getting close to a man again?"

"All you can do is try. One way or another, you need to resolve what's between you for either of you to be able to move forward in your lives."

That Monday, Tessa found herself walking into Miss Nettie's alone. It was three o'clock in the afternoon. Her mother and Gib had gone into Sorghum Mills to a matinee movie. Things at the shop were slow, so she'd shut down and decided after skipping lunch, to grab some of Miss Nettie's pie at a time she knew the diner wouldn't be that crowded.

She walked in and wasn't surprised in the least when Miss Nettie herself greeted her with open arms.

"Hello, sweet girl," Miss Nettie said, "I have missed you so much."

Tessa smiled, returning the elderly woman's embrace. "I've missed you, too. Mama and Gib are at the movies so I thought I'd come by for some of your World Famous pie. I've missed it."

"Well, you just come right over here and I will serve you up the best slice of chocolate creme pie you've ever had. I know that's your favorite."

"Yes, ma'am, it is," she replied, following her over to the booth by the main window, the same booth she always used to sit in when she came in for pie. When she sat down, though, her eyes were drawn down the street, to the Sheriff's office, where Shane's truck was parked out front.

"Here you go, honey," Miss Nettie said, then sat in the seat opposite her. "So, tell me, how was the Army? Mary said you were in the Middle East and that you'd been wounded at one point in the war."

Tessa took her first bite of pie and closed her eyes, savoring it. "Oh, my gosh, Miss Nettie, this is so good," she said. Then, knowing she couldn't avoid the question, she took a deep breath. "My convoy was ambushed in an IED attack. Shrapnel pierced my lower abdomen. The medics got to me immediately so it wasn't as bad as it could have been. I resigned my commission after that and went to work for Gib at the FBI. He'd been my Commanding Officer for all but the last six months of my service."

"I hadn't realized you'd joined the FBI."

Tessa raked her hand through her hair. "Yes...there's...quite a bit that's happened that very few know about."

"I saw you leave and Shane follow you out Friday

night. Gracie told me that he ended things with Wendy."

"Did he?" she asked, her eyes again drawn toward the Sheriff's office.

"Honey, why did you stay away all these years? I thought you and Shane...well, I thought you two were perfectly matched."

"We were just kids. His life moved him one way, and mine took me in another."

"You were a good match. When you two were together, there was joy in both your faces. Shane hasn't had that look in a long time; and it's been worse since he's been back here to stay. Something happened to him, Tessa. He's hollow."

A tear rolled down Tessa's cheek and Miss Nettie reached out to capture her hand.

"I hurt him," she admitted softly. "I sent him away."

"I suspected as much. You had found each other again?"

Tessa nodded. "We were engaged...but, I'm not good for him, Miss Nettie. I'm a wreck. He deserves so much better."

"Better than you? Better than the one who has always been meant for him?"

"I'm not..."

"Honey, I've been around much longer than you. I've seen much more than you and trust me when I say that I've never seen two people more right for each other than you and my great-nephew."

"I wish I could believe that. I know he is the one for me, but I just don't think I am the one for him. He may have been happy for a time when we were together, but trust me, for the most part, I've caused him nothing but grief."

Miss Nettie squeezed her hand. "No one said that life and love has to be perfect. There are going to be hard times and heartache on your road. That's an inevitable part of life. But the good times far outnumber the bad, and if you look back at your history with Shane, the bad times were just bumps in the road. You have to have faith that the good will stamp out the bad. You have to believe that."

Tessa sighed. "That's the problem. I've lost the ability to believe that."

Chapter Eighteen

Nearly two weeks after her first sighting of Shane at Miss Nettie's, and her conversation with Miss Nettie, Tessa found herself at the town square gazebo once again, entwining elaborate sunflower garlands along its columns. Her mother had taken over the town's seasonal decorations a couple of years back. Today they were decorating for the late summer season. Sunflowers were going everywhere along the town's two main streets. It was a lot of work but Tessa had to admit the results were phenomenal; no one else who'd been the town decorator prior to her mother ever put this much into it all. Tessa thought it was wonderful and added to the town's charm.

"Mary never ceases to amaze me with the things she comes up with," Tessa heard from behind her. She looked over her shoulder to see Mrs. Shelmerdine standing at the gaze of the gazebo.

"Hey, there, Mrs. Shelmerdine," Tessa greeted her, offering a soft smile.

"Hello, Tessa, I was just on my way to the Post Office and thought I'd come take a look. Your mother does such beautiful work."

"Yes, ma'am, she surely does."

"I heard your mother say that you were in Afghanistan when you were in the Army."

"Yes, ma'am, I was for a while, but I spent most of my time in Iraq."

"How exciting! I'm sure you have lots of fascinating stories."

"I was basically a glorified secretary. Not much to tell."

"Really? A secretary?"

"Yes, to Mama's fiancé, Glen."

"Is that right? I guess I didn't realize you'd known him for that long."

"I met him right after I completed basics and was assigned to my first duty station. He was the Captain of the base at the time. I worked in his office and when his secretary retired, I took over. Been with him ever since."

"He's been so good for your mother. I've just seen her blossom over the last few months with him around. Did you ever imagine one day he would end up with your mother?"

Tessa laughed. "I never imagined a scenario where they would ever meet...but Gib was always a father-figure to me, so I suppose it's only natural that now it will be official."

"And what about you, Miss Tessa? Will you be settling down here? Staying?"

"Hey, Tessa, Miz Shelmerdine," Ivy Sinclair greeted them enthusiastically, stepping up to the gazebo. "Tessa, this looks amazing."

"I was just telling her that," Mrs. Shelmerdine agreed.

"Thanks. Mama worked hard on them."

"Last Christmas was my first year back...her decorations blew me away," Ivy continued. "Oh, Miz Shelmerdine, Miss Nettie was looking for you. She said she had something for you."

"Oh, that's right! I got so distracted by these beautiful sunflowers I forgot. Tessa, you give your mother my compliments on all of this, OK?"

"I will."

"And you come by my store. Shopping is good for you."

"I'll do that, too."

Tessa and Ivy watched Mrs. Shelmerdine rush off toward Miss Nettie's. Ivy began laughing and Tessa shook her head, smiling.

"Your timing is impeccable," Tessa told her. "You saved me from having to discuss my future plans and possibly my love life with her. I owe you one."

"Good, because I actually had another reason for coming here, other than delivering Miss Nettie's message."

Tessa hung the last of the garlands and began packing up her box of supplies.

"Oh yeah? What would that be?"

"I was wondering if you would want to get together some time, drinks and girl talk."

Tessa paused in packing her box. Of all the things she could have possibly imagined Ivy Sinclair coming to talk to her about, that certainly wasn't one of them.

"I'm sorry?"

"Well, you know how it is...aren't many single women our age around here. Just thought it would be nice to have someone to shop with and drink and talk about men with." Both women's heads turned when Shane's Sheriff's truck drove past them and parked at the Sheriff's Office. "Would be a great way to take your mind off of things."

Tessa regarded Ivy for a moment. Although four years her junior, Ivy was usually around her group of friends when she was in high school. Tessa's senior year, Ivy worked as an equipment manager for the Flag Corps, laying out flags during changes for their halftime shows. Her older brother, Steve, was Shane's best friend growing up and usually Ivy was tagging along behind them. She didn't recall that Ivy ever acted as if she had a crush on Shane, but then again, her mother said that Ivy and Shane had grown really close after he returned to Indian Springs.

"There are those around town who have said that you and Shane had something going for a while," she hedged.

Ivy smiled. "Shane is a sweetheart. He's always

been good to me. When he came back, he and I were in a similar state. He was reeling from you. I was the same over Reese. We leaned heavily on each other...as friends. I love Shane, but only as a brother. Believe me, it would have simplified both our lives if we could have been attracted to each other. We had a good laugh about that over pizza and beer...but my heart has always belonged to Reese...and his...well, you know."

"I appreciate your honesty," Tessa said.

"Look...it's been a while for you, but you remember what life is like here. Any budding romance becomes the center of attention for the likes of Mrs. Shelmerdine and Miss Nettie and their crew. We live in a fish bowl here. So, I figure right now, with Reese and I butting heads and you and Shane dancing around each other, we're in that fish bowl together. Might be better if we stuck together, don't you think?"

Tessa smiled and shook her head. "Princess Ivy and Tornado Tess...is this town ready for us?"

Ivy again returned her smile. "Why not?"

At that, Tessa laughed. "OK, sure,

"Awesome. Oh, my brother is having a cookout tonight. Wanna come?"

"Oh...wow...um...yeah, I'm not so sure I'm quite that ready to jump back in the whole social -"

Ivy cut her off. "Why not? Best way to get a bandage

off is to just rip it off fast. Don't over-analyze, just close your eyes and jump."

"Easier said than done."

Ivy nodded in understanding. "I know. You'll never know until you try, though, right?"

Tessa sighed and closed her eyes a moment. Coming home to Indian Springs meant that she was trying to pick up the pieces of her life, and part of that was getting involved with people again, rather than shutting them out. In that sense, she knew Ivy was right.

She took a deep breath. "OK, sure."

"Great. Be there at 6:00."

Tessa watched Ivy walk off, not sure exactly what she'd just gotten herself into. Ivy was the town darling; she definitely was not...and if word got out that she was the reason behind Shane's obvious weight loss and other issues, she'd be even less of a favorite.

She sighed as she headed back to the shop. A cookout at Steve Sinclair's house was a guarantee to run into Shane. Avoiding him wasn't an option and she figured it was time to try to find out if there was anything left between them...and if she could handle having a close relationship again.

Ivy took a roundabout way to loop around town and go back toward Shane's office so Tessa wouldn't see her heading directly there after leaving her. She wasn't sure how he would react to her interfering but at this point, she didn't really care; she was tired of seeing him suffer.

He was standing at the office door when she walked up, a look of wariness on his face.

"Hey, how's it going?" she asked as she walked in.

"Save it," he snapped, taking her upper arm and walking her back to his office. "You wanna tell me what you were doing out there with Tessa?"

"I asked her if she'd like to meet me for drinks and girl talk sometime."

"Really?"

"Yes, really. Most women my age in town are married. Would be nice to have someone single to hang out with."

He nodded but she could tell he wasn't convinced.

"What? You don't agree?"

"No...I mean, it's not that...it's..." His voice trailed off and he began to pace. "Tessa has been through so much in the last year or so. I mean...a lot. Traumatic stuff."

"OK...well, even more reason to get her involved in something, get her mind off things."

"Maybe," he said absently.

"She's coming to Steve's tonight."

He cursed under his breath and shook his head. "You just couldn't resist, could you?"

She flashed a huge smile at him. "Misery loves

company. If I have to suffer with all the agony Reese is putting me through then you have to suffer through all your crap with Tessa."

He scowled at her. "I used to think you were smart. Now I just think you're yet another meddling female in my life."

"Yes, but you love me."

"That's up for debate right now."

"Shane...you sent Wendy on her way. You need to have a conversation with Tessa and you know it."

He rubbed the back of his neck. "Yeah, I do...but..."

"But nothing. Just be there tonight, OK?"

"You women are going to be the death of me," he swore.

Ivy laughed and quickly kissed his cheek. "See you in a bit."

Tessa tried to push out of her mind the surprised and pleased looks on her mother and Gib's faces when she told them she was going to attend Steve Sinclair's cookout. She knew getting back into the swing of things socially was a big step and that they were proud and happy for her. As she pulled up into Steve's drive, she knew they were right. This was a big step. She just hoped she wouldn't blow it.

She saw Ivy approach as she got out and returned her welcoming smile. She heard music and voices coming from the back of the house, as well as plenty of laughter and it warmed her heart.

"You made it!" Ivy greeted her.

"Said I would."

"Yeah, I know, but I wasn't sure. Fair warning...Wendy is here. She and Shane have cooled things off since you've been back but she's become good friends with Steve and his wife Carrie."

Tessa nodded. She didn't have to ask if Shane was there; she'd seen his truck parked toward the back and side of the drive where he could get out easily should he be called to duty. She followed Ivy around the side of the house and accepted welcoming hugs from people she'd grown up with. It wasn't easy for her and by the time the fourth guy embraced her she was extremely on edge. That was when she looked up and made eye contact with Shane from across the deck. As always, he seemed to know what she was feeling and the calm and steady look on his face helped her make it through the rest of the greetings.

She saw Wendy approach him and by speaking, turned his attention to her. She watched him turn to face her fully, his head dropping as she spoke to him. He looked so tired, she thought. Looking at them from a distance, though, she had to admit they made an attractive couple.

"Ivy?"

"Yeah?"

"Shane and Wendy...how serious were they?"

Ivy shrugged. "More on her end than on his, but neither of them were 100% in it. She's recently divorced."

"Whatever she's saying to him, it's not going well for him."

Ivy nodded. "You know Shane. Carries the weight of the world on his shoulders."

"Mmm, that he does," she mused.

"Ivy, could you give me a hand here," Steve called.

"Yeah, yeah, keep your shirt on!" she called back to him. "Make yourself comfortable, Tess. Drinks in the coolers, food everywhere, take your pick."

"Yeah, sure," she murmured to Ivy's retreating back. She settled into a chair at the far corner of the deck and unashamedly watched Shane and Wendy. She spoke with him for several more moments, embraced him and placed a lingering kiss on his cheek and then walked away. Shane stood for a moment, head down, shoulders hunched. He turned back toward the party, made eye contact with Tessa, and then walked down the steps of the deck toward the lake. She watched him a few more minutes as he stood staring out at the sunset. Unable to stand it any longer, she grabbed two bottles of beer from the nearest cooler and made her way down to him.

"You look like you could use this," she said, holding one of the bottles out to him.

Shane glanced over his shoulder at her. For several

minutes, they stood in silence, neither moving, just looking into each other's eyes. Finally, Shane sighed and turned to face her, taking the beer from her.

"Thanks."

She watched him take a long pull from the bottle and took a small drink from her own. An awkward silence settled between them. They had been many things with each other over the years but awkward had never been one of them. She stood for a few more moments, her gaze shifting between him and the lake, unsure of what to say. Finally, when it became apparent that he wasn't going to speak, she nodded and decided to go.

"Well, I just thought you could use a drink. I'll be going now," she said, turning to go.

"What did you expect?" he asked, eyes still focused on some unknown point out at the lake.

"Excuse me?"

"Did you think all you had to do was come back to town and I'd just fall at your feet again?"

She stared at him a moment in disbelief then shook her head. "Look, now's obviously not a good time. I brought you a drink, we spoke. I'll go now."

She made it maybe five or so feet before she heard a vicious curse and then the shatter of glass as the beer bottle she'd handed him was smashed against a nearby tree.

"I believe that's called littering, Sheriff, and carries a

fine."

"Just stop, Tess."

"Stop what? Talking to you? No problem, I'll just leave you to your glass clean-up."

"Yeah, there you go again, just walk away. Typical Tessa. Going gets tough and you just leave rather than face up to it."

She glared at him, fists clenching. "Screw you, McCanton."

A bitter laugh escaped him. She turned on her heel to leave but he grabbed her arm to stop her, causing her to whirl and lash out on instinct, her fist connecting with his jaw.

"Son of a bitch!" he growled, releasing her as he stumbled back.

"Don't. Grab. Me like that," she panted.

"Dammit, Tessa! Do you think I would ever hurt you?"

"I went through...hell in that compound. Having men's hands all over me and not being able to do anything about it almost destroyed me. I will never be in that position again. Not ever again."

His eyes closed briefly and when he looked back at her, she saw a bit of his anger slip away.

"I'm sorry, Tess...I know this hasn't been easy for you."

"No. It hasn't. These last few months have been...let's just say I needed that time on the beach. And I hated that I hurt you when I threw you out of my hospital room. I look at you now and I hate myself even more. It makes me sick to think that I hurt you...but I needed that time, Shane."

"Do you think I wouldn't have given it to you? I would have done anything for you." His voice was raw and whisper soft, driving yet another nail into her heart.

She felt a twinge in the scar over her lower belly, a reminder of why she had really thrown him aside. Asking him to give up his chance at a child of his own was too much; it was why she'd said all those horrible things to him.

"I didn't want you to," she said softly.

He shook his head. "Then, you do blame me. For what happened. For not being there to stop them."

"No, Shane, I don't blame you."

"Then why did you send me away? God, Tess, I would have helped you in any way I could. I would have..."

"I wouldn't have let you. I couldn't stand to have anyone touch me after all of that. I barely tolerated the doctors and nurses touching me. The only person I allowed to touch me was my mother and occasionally Gib. What they did to me was horrendous. I had to deal with the emotional scars as well as the physical ones. I couldn't...I wasn't in the best frame of mind in the hospital."

"I noticed," he said wryly.

"That day I threw you out...you came in right after the

doctors had just delivered some pretty devastating news; news that would have an impact on you...that still would impact you, actually, so I did what I felt needed to be done."

He shook his head. "Just like when we were kids. You decided. You made a decision that impacted us both without even consulting me. You joined the Army but didn't tell me until after the fact. You joined the FBI and again didn't tell me until after. You say you love me and then throw me aside again and again. What kind of weak minded fool am I to keep coming back to you?"

"Shane..."

"I had finally decided to wise up and stop waiting around for you like some sick puppy dog. Wendy came along and for the first time since we were kids, I felt something for someone other than you. And I let her go two weeks ago that night I saw you in Miss Nettie's, proving just what an idiot I really am. Tessa Kelly's Own Private Whipping Boy, at your service," he said with a bow.

"Stop it, Shane."

"Then tell me why you sent me away. I think after all these years, I deserve at least that."

"Because you are the last of your line!" she snapped.

Shane blinked at her, not expecting to hear anything like that.

"Come again?"

"Your father's brothers all had girls."

"Yeah? So?"

"So, you are the last male McCanton. You are the only one who can carry on the family name."

"What does that have to do with anything?"

A tear slipped down her cheek. "What was done to me...was so brutal, it tore my uterus. Severely. With the scarring I already had from the IED attack, the doctors said I most likely won't ever be able to carry a child to term. I couldn't let you risk a chance to have a child of your own."

"God, Tessa. We've been down this road before, when I asked you to marry me in San Antonio. Do you think I care about that? You could be perfectly healthy and we could have nothing but girls like my uncles did. There are no guarantees in this life."

She wiped at the tears that were falling on her cheeks. "See? I told you...I wasn't in the best frame of mind at the time...and then after I left the hospital, I just couldn't...I thought I could let you go. I thought I could give you the future you deserved...but when Mama told me that you were dating someone...I realized I couldn't handle it after all. Imagining you with someone else and knowing you were with someone else were two totally different things...and when I saw you with her at Miss Nettie's a couple of weeks ago...it just hurt so much."

"You've walked away from me twice now. I barely survived this last time. I don't know if I can chance going through that again, Tess."

She nodded. "I understand...I'm sorry I hit you." She began walking away again, and this time, he didn't stop her.

When she reached the deck, Ivy was sitting on the rail, waiting for her. As Tessa met her gaze, the smile that had been on her face faded. Ivy hopped down and crossed over to her.

"I take it things didn't go well?"

"Not so much, no," she replied, sinking down onto a step. "He's understandably upset with me. I don't blame him."

"I know a bit about what happened," Ivy told her, "but not all. I know that when he came home, he was shredded. You don't get that way over someone unless you have serious feelings for them...and those type of feelings just don't go away."

Tessa was quiet a moment, staring out at Shane who still stood facing the lake, hands shoved in his pockets, shoulders hunched. She wasn't quite sure how she felt about the fact that he had confided in Ivy about what had happened between them, but glad in a way that he had someone to talk to.

"I said some harsh things to him. I didn't mean them, but at the time, I thought I was doing what was best for him. After things got bad, after what was done to me...I just wanted to see Shane. I knew everything would be OK if I could just see him...and when I did see him...no one should have to live up to what I put on him...but Shane has always been my rock. He's always been the one I leaned on; he was my strength and my courage, and after what was done to me, I didn't think it was fair to ask him to bear my burdens any more. Shane doesn't deserve to be saddled with someone like me."

Ivy shook her head, a small laugh escaping her, a bitter laugh. "No offense, Tess...but how messed up is that? Don't you think that was his decision to make?"

"He wouldn't have chosen to leave me. You know what kind of person Shane McCanton is. He would have been right by my side every step of the way. I know that. And because I loved him, I didn't want him to have to do that for me. I wanted to give him the chance to have a normal life with a nice, normal woman who wasn't as screwed up as me."

"That is the dumbest thing I have ever heard," Ivy said bluntly.

Tessa tore her gaze from Shane to look at Ivy. "Maybe so. Can't say that my mind was in a good place at the time. Can't say it is now, either."

"If you wait around for everything to be perfect, you'll be waiting around forever. Nothing is ever perfect."

"I know that. I do. But Shane...he is perfect. And he deserves to have a perfect life."

"Nobody is perfect, Tessa. You can't place Shane in a glass house. He'll die."

With that, Ivy got up and walked off. Tessa watched her go, then turned her gaze back to Shane and was surprised to see him walking toward her, an intense, determined look on his face. She braced herself for another confrontation with him.

"You didn't leave," he stated flatly, stopping a few feet from the bottom of the steps she sat on. Slowly, still holding his gaze, she shook her head. "Why not?"

"Did you want me to?" she asked quietly, studying him for his reaction.

"No. Yes. Hell. I don't know. I don't want to analyze everything to death. Why did you come back?"

"Mama and Gib are getting married."

He nodded. "That the only reason?" She shrugged. "Are you leaving as soon as they are back from their honeymoon?"

"I haven't decided. Mama would like me to be here to stay. I've stepped back in at the shop. It's been nice. I'd forgotten how much I enjoyed it. Not exactly as exciting as investigative work, but then, I think I've had enough excitement to last me a lifetime."

"Hey, Tessa!" Lara Grant, one of their school friends greeted her, embracing her. "I'd heard you were back in town. How are you?"

Tessa fought to keep control of the immediate panic that overtook her while Lara embraced her, keeping her eyes locked on Shane.

"I'm good, Lara, how are you?"

"I'm good, I'm good. I can't believe you are finally back after all these years. No one thought you'd ever step foot back in Indian Springs."

Tessa offered her a smile as she stepped back. "Yeah, well, after years of rambling, it's nice to come back home. Somewhere solid, ya know?"

"Can't get more solid than here," Lara said, then looked over her shoulder at Shane. "Even have the next generation McCanton in charge. The more things change the more they stay the same."

"Yeah, well, consistency and dependability are good. It's what makes this place home."

"Very true. Well, I just wanted to drop by and say hi. Steve said the food is ready if ya'll are ready to eat."

"Thanks, Lara, we'll be along in a bit," Shane told her.

She smiled and left them, no doubt to go tell everyone that she and Shane were facing off with one another just like in the old days. Tessa loved Lara but she did tend to have a bit of a big mouth.

"To listen to you talk to her, someone would think you were here to stay, defending the town like that," he said.

She again shrugged. "This is home...and where you

are."

She watched as those words rocked him back on his heels.

"What do you want from me, Tessa?" he asked, his voice low.

Tessa stood. "Nothing, Shane...except what you want to give. I know I hurt you and I have no right to ask, but...you've been in my life for as long as I can remember. This last year without you...sucked. I just want you back in my life, in whatever capacity you will allow."

He nodded. "Anything else?"

She studied him a moment, trying to ascertain his thoughts from his stance. His hands were still shoved in his pockets, but his shoulders were no longer hunched as if expecting a blow.

"Yeah...I could really, really use a hug right about now. I just...yeah, I just need to feel your arms around me. I know I've no right to ask and..."

He stepped to her and folded her into his embrace. "Shut up, Tess," he murmured against her ear.

She stiffened for just a moment, and then it was as if a switch was flipped and she found herself melting against him, her arms wrapping around his powerful back, hands fisting in his shirt. He shifted his hold, one hand cupping the back of her head and holding her against his chest, his other arm around her waist.

"Oh, God...Shane," she breathed.

"Shh," he soothed, kissing her temple. "It's OK. You're safe now."

"I was so scared I wouldn't be able to handle your touch," she whispered, her voice thick with emotion.

"What are we saying here, Tess? I'm back to my earlier question: what do you want from me?"

She took a deep breath and pulled back enough to look up into his blue eyes. She wasn't sure what he was offering or what he was feeling, but after months of being apart and realizing what a mistake that had been, she decided now was the time to lay it all out on the line.

"All I know is that I miss you. You've been my best friend for so long, it hurt not to be able to talk to you these last few months."

He nodded and kissed her brow. "I've missed you, too. But I meant what I said earlier. My heart can't handle another round with you," she stiffened in his arms and tried to pull back, "let me finish...if you want me back in your life, then you're going to have to come into this with the attitude that we're in this together. You can't get spooked and decide on your own to walk away. You start feeling that way, you talk to me. No making decisions because you think it's for my own good."

"I'm so messed up, Shane. I have...so many issues...I don't know if I can be what you need me to be, I don't know if I can handle being intimate, or..."

"We'll figure it out, Tess. You cut my heart out but you didn't give it back. It's still yours. Always has been yours."

She pulled back giving him a skeptical look. "And the librarian?"

"I thought you weren't coming back. I tried to move on with my life. I have feelings for her, I won't lie. If you hadn't come back, I don't know where things would have gone with her, if at all. Like I said, you still had my heart."

She had more questions but let them go for now. There were other things they needed to address now. Seeing the party begin to surge closer to where they stood, she took his hand and led him away from the deck, going again down to the shore of the lake.

"How much do you know, about what happened to me that day?"

He looked down at their joined hands and smoothed his other hand over the back of the one he held.

"Just what was in the reports. You were raped. There were 6 different sperm samples recovered in the rape kit. Multiple broken bones. You've a plate in your cheek now. Shoulder has two pins in it, your back had several skin graft surgeries...they messed you up...bad."

She noted that he didn't list the miscarriage. Did he still think she didn't know?

"Yes...as I said, my uterus was heavily damaged. And I lost..." her voice cracked.

"I know," he replied softly. "What happened that day?"

She shook her head. "I can't talk about it."

"Tess..."

"No...I mean, I will, but I can't talk about it now. Not here, and not...not while we're finally talking and together again for the first time. I don't want that ugliness here now."

"The trial is coming up, babe. I gotta know what happened before then. Don't make me hear it for the first time in the court room."

She took a deep breath and released it slowly. "OK, but not here. We need to be somewhere private."

He nodded. "Let's go."

Chapter Nineteen

Shane held tight to Tessa's hand and led her past the gathering on Steve's back deck and around to the front of the house. He knew she'd driven her mother's vehicle there but no way was he letting her out of his grasp now. He'd call Gib and let them come pick it up...later. For now, he led her to his truck and opened the door for her. He saw Tessa's eyes stray over to her mother's car but she didn't say anything as she climbed inside his truck. He shut her door then crossed over to the driver's side and got in.

"Good thing you're the Sheriff and everyone knows not to block you in," she said, noting that her mother's car was nicely caged in.

"Oh, yeah, has its advantages," he said dryly.

The corner of her lips rose slightly and he took that as a small victory. He felt a small knot form in his gut as he drove her the three miles around the bend of the lake to his house. It was important to bring her here; important that she like it...he'd done it all for her.

When they approached the gate, he saw her sit up a bit straighter as recognition dawned on her as to where they were. He hit the remote and as he drove through and rounded the bend, couldn't help but sneak a glance over at her. The gasp that escaped her when she saw his house was priceless. It told him all he needed to know.

"Shane!" she cried softly, leaning forward as he approached the house. "Stop. Let me out now," she demanded, not wanting to wait for him to park in the garage.

He indulged her, letting her scramble out while he pulled into the garage. When he walked out, he found her standing right where he'd let her out, staring up at the house, visibly trembling.

"It's just like I pictured it!" she exclaimed. He doubted she was even aware of the tears that were spilling down her cheeks, but he was. He looked up at the house, seeing it through her eyes.

"Well...I had a pretty specific list," he said, referring to the list they made up when they were kids, sitting on a blanket on the site where the house was now. "I tried to incorporate as much of it as I could."

"Really?" she asked, looking up at him, her eyes bright.

For Shane, the world stopped moving in that moment. He looked down into the face of the only girl he'd ever loved and knew he was on the verge of finally, finally getting everything he'd ever wanted and wished and prayed for. He lifted his hand and brushed the backs of his fingers along her cheek, wiping her tears away.

"It was our dream house...how could I not build it?"

"Shane," she gasped.

He gently kissed her brow. "Come on...let me show it to you."

Tessa froze, shaking her head. Shane turned to face her and gently cupped her face in his hands.

"What is it?"

"I can't believe you did this," she whispered.

"I guess I always hoped, in the back of my mind, that you'd be back. Come on," he let his hands trail from her face and captured one of her hands in his to lead her up the steps to the huge wrap-around porch. There were porch swings and rockers spaced comfortably about, just as she'd envisioned. They followed the porch around to the back where she froze once again. The natural waterfalls where they'd first made love were enhanced by a swimming pool that looked more like an extension of the lake rather than a swimming pool.

"It's breathtaking," she whispered to him.

"Is it how you saw it when we talked about it?"

"It's better."

She followed him inside and again saw several of the features they'd put on their list. The kitchen was warm and inviting and had the fireplace that she'd wanted, along with the marble countertops and butcher-block island. The dining room was formal but inviting with a large rustic pine table.

Everything about the house was rustic, masculine, but welcoming and warm. She loved every inch of it already.

The master suite was the only deviation from their teenage list. It had the fireplace that was shared by the bedroom and bathroom but her teenage mind could never have conjured the decadence of a multi-head steam shower and enormous two-person Jacuzzi bathtub.

"This place is more than I could have ever dreamed, Shane. You did great," she said, accepting a glass of wine from him when they'd worked their way back down to the family room.

"Thanks."

She crossed back to the window to gaze out at the waterfall that he'd had enhanced with landscape lighting. She felt him move closer to her but knew he was keeping his distance, giving her space.

"I'd been worried about you and your dad," she began, eyes still out on the waterfall. "No one had an update for me. I got careless in my worry. Paul walked in when I was asking Gib for an update. I tried to play it off, but his suspicions were already raised. He tipped Nathaniel off. They began monitoring me more closely, and then that day, Nathaniel walked into the bathroom when I was in the shower..."

...Fourteen months earlier...

Tessa froze when she heard the bathroom door open

and saw Nathaniel step in. Cursing under her breath, she did her best to cover herself, but in a completely open glass shower, it was difficult.

"Nathaniel? I thought we agreed that you wouldn't come in while I was showering."

"Turn the water off, Madelyn," he ordered, his voice harsh.

"What is..."

"NOW!" he roared, causing her to jump.

She turned the water off and reached for her towel, but he viciously yanked it away.

"Nathaniel? What has happened?" she asked, cursing the fact that the mike would not work while her hair was wet so she couldn't clue the guys in to what was happening.

He ripped the shower door open and reached in and grabbed a handful of her hair, roughly yanking her out.

"Who are you?" he growled.

"You're hurting me!" she cried, trying to escape his grasp. He tightened his hold on her hair and let the back of his hand fly across her cheek, knocking her further off balance.

"You aren't who you've portrayed yourself to be," he growled, his face inches from hers. "Who are you?"

"I'm Madelyn," she insisted, trying to regain control of the situation.

"Stop lying!!" he screamed, hitting her once again.

"What is this?" he demanded, his hand over her belly where Shane's name was tattooed, proclaiming her as his. "Who is Shane?"

"A mistake from my youth," she told him, "Nathaniel, I am here with you now."

"You've denied me at every turn yet you have another man's name marked on your body like a whore!" He hit her again. Her cheek felt like it was on fire and she was having a hard time seeing out of her right eye. "I'll ask you once again, Who. Are. You?"

"Madelyn. Maddie. Madelyn Parker!" she screamed, trying to block yet another blow to her face. Her wet feet slipped on the tile as he jerked her around, earning a kick to her ribs. She heard a crack and knew a rib or two had just broken.

The door opened and Paul and two other of the Elders came in, each dressed in long black robes. She was grabbed and her wrists bound, but not before she managed to kick and hit and scratch as many of them as she could. She pleaded with Nathaniel and was rewarded with a blow to the head so fierce it knocked her out.

She woke up when cold water was thrown on her and a sharp slap landed on her face. She was now standing in a gymnasium of sorts, in the middle of the room on a platform, arms raised above her head, ankles shackled and spread by a bar between them, surrounded by men in black robes and

Nathaniel in a papal white robe. He was standing before her, his hand on her throat, painfully squeezing her air supply.

"Nathaniel," she whimpered, "please." She screamed when the sting of a whip cracked across her back. It was then she saw Paul standing just within the line of her peripheral vision, whip in hand.

"You don't speak unless we give you permission," Paul spat out.

She turned toward his voice and spit at him, causing him to deliver three more vicious lashes. Nathaniel stepped up then, grabbing her hair and crushing his mouth down on hers in a brutal kiss. She fought the wave of nausea that assailed her and bit down on his lip. He backhanded her again then yanked her hair to pull her head back.

"You will pay. For every night you denied me, for making me think you were more than the whore you are...and when I'm done with you, Paul will have you and when he's done with you, each of the Elders will have you. That's how we treat whores here."

She fought, but with her hands and ankles restrained, there wasn't much she could do. Nathaniel came closer behind her and she felt his robes shift as he roughly forced himself in her. His possession was brutal, one hand in her hair and the other on her hip, cutting into her. All the while, he hurled insults at her, repeatedly calling her a whore.

Tessa held herself together as best she could and when he climaxed, she regarded him over her shoulder, and in the most derisive tone possible she taunted him.

"Really? Is that all you got? No wonder you have to resort to rape. No one would ask for that little stick you keep in your pants."

Of course she knew that wasn't the brightest thing to say and it earned her another vicious beating, but her pride wouldn't allow his pathetically short session to go unremarked.

Once Paul got his hands on her, her mind checked out on her. She began thinking back over her time with Shane, from the first day of Kindergarten to the last day she saw him. She clung to each and every memory, even as she was beaten for not responding to the men. She prayed she would have the strength to not disgrace herself and not reveal who she really was.

It wasn't until a loud boom sounded and the door at the far end of the arena burst open did she allow her thoughts to return to the present. Armed men came storming in but all she cared about was the one in the center. Shane was there! He'd come in, rifle at the ready like her own Avenging Angel and now he was in a confrontation with Nathaniel. She felt Nathaniel grab her hair again and felt the blade he held press into her throat. One of the others called Shane's name, sending Nathaniel off on a tangent. Now he knew he was looking at the man who, prior to tonight, had been the only man to ever have her. She felt the point of the blade slide into her throat and knew her time was running out. Gathering what little strength she had left, she focused her blurry gaze on Shane and called out to him.

"Shane...Wildcat."

...Present Day...

"God, baby, I'm so sorry," Shane managed when she stopped talking.

"It wasn't your fault, Shane. Looking back, I should have pulled the plug on it all myself, a couple of weeks before. I wasn't really getting anything. The girls who were there were being abused but they were like those in the BDSM scene...they were so enraptured by Nathaniel and Paul that they were buying into it hook line and sinker. Those I was able to form a relationship with seemed genuinely happy."

He raked his fingers through his hair. "If I hadn't have been so distracted with my dad's situation I probably would have pushed for the end of it. I could tell from the updates Bruce was giving me that the investigation had stalled. I just...it was a bad time for my dad. We almost lost him and I couldn't think beyond that."

She turned to face him and caught his hand in hers. "We can't sit here and second guess ourselves. What's done is done."

He was quiet a moment, his thumb stroking over her hand, then he looked into her eyes and asked what he'd been needing to know for a while.

"Did you know that you were pregnant?"

Her eyes closed briefly. "I didn't know for sure. I'd begun to suspect that I was, though. I hadn't had morning sickness, but I'd missed my period and I had a few other physical signs."

"After you were released from the hospital, I knew I couldn't stay in Austin. I couldn't stand being in my condo without you; I couldn't face being at the office. I couldn't even be around Pete and Joe without wanting to kill them. I still haven't seen them to this day. My dad was out of the hospital but still out of commission as far as his job went. The Council asked if I would step in as a temporary fill-in. Gib told me he was taking you to his place in Cabo. I packed up that night and came back here."

"But, Shane, it's...you were on the path to make Ranger."

He shrugged. "I stopped caring the day you left. I couldn't go back and work with Pete and Joe. Right or wrong, I knew I couldn't work with them every day and not think about what had happened to you. I don't know what I would have done if I had been in the control room that day and lost contact with you. I'd like to think that I'd have pulled the plug on it all weeks before, but I just don't know."

"I've talked to Pete and Joe since it all ended. I even talked to Crownover, who is not my biggest fan right now, let me tell you."

A dimple appeared in his cheek. "Crownover is very protective of me."

"Obviously. Do you know his first name?"

He laughed. "Yeah, actually, I do."

She smiled. "So do I...now."

He looked stunned. "What? How do you know?"

"He told me."

"He did not," he countered.

She nodded. "Really, he did. He came to see me in the hospital. He didn't know I was awake and he leaned down and said, 'if it will help you get better any faster, my first name is Bartholomew.' It took everything I had not to open my eyes and gape at him."

Shane busted out laughing. She narrowed her eyes at him.

"What?"

"His name is Harry."

"What?!"

He wiped a tear from his eye. "He must have known you were awake and was yanking your chain. His name is

Harry Crownover, Jr."

"Is his middle name Bartholomew?"

"Nope. Edward."

"That jerk! I'm gonna get him next time I see him. Why would he do that?"

"He has always hated his name. He didn't get along with his father at all."

"Yeah, but why tell me...oh well, doesn't matter. I'll get him."

Shane laughed and reached out tucked a lock of her hair behind her ear, watching her closely to make sure she didn't flinch or move from his touch. To his surprise, she reached up and captured his hand, turning her head to press a kiss to his palm. His eyes closed briefly, then he stepped closer to her.

"Tessa?"

"Yes?"

"May I kiss you?"

She smiled and his heart soared.

"Please do," she said.

He leaned down and kissed her brow, then her left cheek, then a lingering kiss on her right cheek where she now had a metal plate inserted, then placed a kiss to the corner of her mouth before gently pressing his lips to hers. It was sweet, gentle contact, but when he moved to pull away, she slid her hand to the back of his neck and licked at his lips until he deepened the kiss and folded her fully into his arms.

A tear slipped down her cheek and she tightened her hold on him. All these months, this was where she wanted to be but was terrified to find out if she could ever handle it again. She should have known, though, that she would never have cause to fear this; this was Shane, her rock, her home.

"Don't cry, Tess," he said against her lips.

"These are happy tears," she told him, stroking her hand over his face in a light caress.

He kissed each cheek, kissing her tears away.

"No more tears, Tess. Promise me. Not one more tear. I can't handle your tears."

A little half laugh escaped her. "I'll do my best, but no guarantees. I'm a girl, after all."

He kissed her once more, then took a step back.

"How about we order a pizza and see if the Rangers are playing, or watch a movie."

She looked up into his bright blue eyes and smiled. "Sounds like Heaven to me."

Opportunities presented themselves to those who knew where to look. Nathaniel Helton had made a successful career out of spotting prime opportunities and exploiting them for all they were worth. Upon arriving at the incarceration facilities, he quickly learned he could charm the guards and learned which ones would be most susceptible to bribery. It wasn't long before he was moved to a cell adjoining Paul's and not long after, they were able to hatch a good escape plan. All it took was charming the right people, bribing the others and one day, when attention was conveniently turned away from them, they were able to slip right out the door and right out the front gate.

    Madelyn Parker, aka Special Agent Tessa Kelly. She was his focus now, along with her lover, Sheriff Shane McCanton. They would pay and pay dearly, he and Paul would ensure that.

    Just as requested, a loyal follower picked him and Paul up just a mile past the woods outside the penitentiary. It wouldn't be long before that whore got what was coming to her now. All he had to do was wait...

Chapter Twenty

It had been a week since the night Shane and Tessa worked out their differences. They'd stayed quiet during that time, choosing to keep their relationship private for as long as they could manage it, which they both knew wouldn't be long. Tessa's mother and Gib knew, and Shane's father but that was it, as far as they knew. Keeping their relationship a secret in this town, though, wasn't going to work and they both knew it was only a matter of time before folks began to put two and two together. As much as Tessa really didn't want to, she knew it was time for them to let his mother in on what was going on before she heard about it from someone else.

"You're right," Shane admitted when she told him as much when they sat together on his back porch, listening to the sounds of the waterfall.

"Do you think your mother will be upset again?"

He was idly stroking her hair, her head resting on his shoulder. "I honestly don't know. Her attitude about your mother has changed a lot since Gib is in the picture. She may not care so much now."

"One of the times Mama and Gib came to Cabo, I asked her about your dad, about how she really felt about him all those years. She said what I pretty much always knew, that he was her first love and she always held a special place for him and when things went bad with Harrison, she knew she could always count on Luke to keep her safe but she said at that point, what she felt for him was just friendship. She'd loved Harrison until that accident when we were kids changed him. She said, though, that having met Gib, she knew that what she felt for both Luke and Harrison was never the real thing like she has with Gib. Gib was married before, but his wife died of cancer. He buried himself in his work, never remarried and never really had a relationship until now. He didn't have kids of his own, either, which is kinda sad, because I think he would make a great father."

Shane kissed her brow. "What are you talking about? He's been your father essentially for the last ten years."

She smiled. "I know. I really lucked out, drawing the assignment to his office when I was fresh out of Basics. He looked out for me and taught me a lot. I'm really not surprised he and Mama hit it off. I talked about them both to each other all the time...So, what are you thinking about your mom and sisters?"

He drew in a deep breath and released it slowly. "I'm not worried about my sisters. Once I tell Mom, she'll give them an earful so by the time I talk to them, the shock will have worn off. And besides, they both have always liked you so there really isn't anything to worry about there."

Tessa laced her fingers with his and stroked her other hand over the back of the one she held, trying to calm her racing heart.

"Do you think your mother will be OK? Was it just the fact that I was Mary's daughter she didn't like, or did she really not like me?"

"It had nothing to do with you, baby. She may be a little frosty at first, but she'll come around."

"I hope so," Tessa sighed.

The next day, Shane asked his parents if he could come over for lunch. Susie had immediately agreed and so he found himself pulling into their drive, his heart hammering.

"I'm so glad you called," she said to him after they'd eaten, "I wanted to talk to you. I saw Wendy yesterday. She looked just plain awful and she said y'all were no longer seeing each other. What happened? I thought things were going well for you two."

He sighed, rubbing the back of his neck. "It was. Wendy is the first person I've had any interest in dating in a long time...since Tessa."

He watched her be taken back by Tessa's name. "Tessa? But you dated a few women since high school."

"Yeah, but, see...Tessa came back into my life nearly two years ago. We worked a case together. An investigation that nearly got her killed. That did get her severely beaten...and during that time, we got engaged."

Susie gasped. "Engaged? And you're just now telling me?!"

"I didn't tell anyone. Things were...well, we only had a short amount of time to be together before she was sent in undercover...deep undercover for months. And then Dad's accident happened and I left and the investigation took a nasty turn. That was why I had to leave as abruptly as I did when Dad was still in the hospital and why I was so wrecked when I came back. Tessa was...they broke her...and trying to protect me, she cut me loose, and so when I came back here, I was just..."

"I know how you were," she replied softly.

"Yeah, well...when I met Wendy, I thought I could move on with her. And she did help me...but, she wasn't Tessa."

Susie sighed. "And now Tessa is back."

He nodded. "And now Tessa is back."

She stood and began clearing the table. Shane met his dad's gaze and shook his head. Neither of them was quite sure how she was taking it, but neither wanted to be the one to push her on it.

"How is Tessa doing?" Luke asked, his voice low. "How bad were her injuries?"

Shane knew his dad already knew the answers but

was asking for his mom's benefit.

"She has a metal plate in her face, pins in her shoulder; she's got whip scars on her back, surgical scars on her lower abdomen and a gunshot scar...that she got because I shot her."

Susie froze in clearing the table and looked at him, alarm on her face. "You shot Tessa?"

"She was being held as a shield. Was the only way to get her free."

Her eyes widened, horrified. "So you shot her?!? Shane Gabriel!"

"I knew what I was doing. Dad taught me to shoot well, and I'm pretty good at it. I knew I wouldn't hit anything vital on her."

She was quiet a moment, sinking back down into her chair.

"Are you back together with her now?"

He met her direct gaze. "I'm hoping to be. We talked some things out at Steve's last weekend, and I brought her to see the house. Look, Ma, I know you haven't ever really approved of Tessa..."

She cut him off. "It wasn't Tessa. It was that she was Mary Kelly's daughter, you know that. Right or wrong, it was how I felt."

"I gotta know if you still feel that way, because...I want Tessa in my life."

She closed her eyes a moment, then looked back into his. "And Wendy?"

"I talked to her that night we had dinner at Miss Nettie's when Cordy was in town. Of course, she isn't happy, but she said she understands."

Susie sighed. "Yes, she would. Wendy is a very nice girl."

"So is Tessa," he countered. "You just never gave her a chance."

Susie wiped a tear from her cheek. "It saddens me to know you had a whole relationship going with her, long enough that you were engaged, and you couldn't tell me. That hurts, and I know it is because of how I treated you when you were kids."

"I didn't want to keep it from you...things were...intense. We only had a couple of months together before the investigation heated up and she was sent in undercover. Then she was under for three months, in the hospital for six weeks, and then she spent the last year in Cabo San Lucas at Gib's condo on the beach, healing, as much as she could. She was tortured, and she was raped." Susie gasped, more tears falling down her cheeks. "She'd had an injury when she was in the Army, shrapnel from an IED attack pierced her uterus. The rapes further injured her uterus and now the doctors think she will never be able to carry a pregnancy to term. That is why she sent me away.

She didn't want me to give up my chance at a family."

Susie looked to Luke, reaching for his hand. Luke cupped her neck in his hand and placed a gentle kiss to her brow.

"I don't want you to miss your chance at a family of your own, either," she admitted, "but if you love her, if you truly love her, I don't see how you could walk away from her because of that."

Shane sighed and swallowed hard at the lump that had formed in his throat. "I do love her. And I can't just walk away. It almost killed me to not be with her this last year. She's back and she's willing to take me back and try to make a go of it. And I want it to work, Mom...I love her so damn much."

Susie nodded, reaching out to lay her hand on her son's cheek. "I can see that you do. Why don't you bring her over for dinner Friday night? She and I need to talk."

He closed his eyes briefly, and then pulled his mother into a tight embrace. "Thank you, Mom...that means...everything to me."

She returned his embrace, holding him just as tight. "I'm sorry you felt you couldn't talk to me about it, baby. I love you. I only want what will make you happy."

That Friday night, Shane picked Tessa up and drove her, Mary and Gib out to his parents' house. Tessa and Mary were both nervous. The approval of Susie McCanton was something they both had sought at one time or another. Mary had only ever wanted her friendship, but had always done her best to steer clear of her because of her past relationship with Luke. Tessa had never really cared much about Susie's lack of approval, until that night she'd seen Wendy sitting at the table at Miss Nettie's as an accepted member of the family. She had to admit, that bothered her.

Now, she only cared for her approval in so far as she knew it was what Shane wanted and needed. For herself, she only needed Shane, and whatever would make him happy.

"So, Shane's father was your first boyfriend, huh?" Gib teased Mary as they turned down the road toward the McCanton's ranch. "Should I be worried, here?"

Mary laughed. "Of course not. Luke and I have only been good friends ever since he came back to town after he and Susie married. I've told you that."

"Just trying to lighten the mood here," he teased, "relax, ladies. It will all be all right."

"I just want it all to go smooth for Tessa," Mary confessed.

Tessa turned slightly in her seat and offered her mother a smile. "I took on the entire Naturalists' hierarchy, I think I can handle Susie McCanton."

Shane glanced at her. "She's my mother, not Attila the Hun," he teased. "And besides, she feels bad for how she treated you before."

Tessa shrugged. "She really didn't treat me any way at all...she just ignored me. It was how she treated you about me that was upsetting. But that was a long time ago."

"What about Cordy and Gracie?" she asked.

"Cordy and Gracie have always liked you. No worries there."

"But they liked Wendy, too," she offered.

He took her hand and kissed her knuckles when he turned into his parents drive. "Cordy and Gracie like everyone. Relax."

Tessa smiled and leaned over to kiss his cheek when they parked. "I'm fine, Shane, don't worry about me."

When they got out, Susie and Luke were waiting for them on the front porch. Susie watched Shane slide his arm around Tessa's waist as they walked up the steps. She took in Tessa's smile at her son and noted that they looked right together, and that for the first time in a long time, Shane's eyes looked settled. Tessa was the piece that had been missing from his life ever since he'd come home, and as much as she still felt a little pang of jealousy that it was Mary Kelly's daughter who made her son happy, she decided in that moment that his happiness was all that mattered.

"Tessa," Susie said, stepping up to her and holding both hands out to take Tessa's in hers. "You have grown up to be absolutely beautiful," she complimented her, squeezing

Tessa's hands when she placed them in hers. "I'm so glad you're home."

Tessa shot a surprised look over her shoulder to Shane and her mother before returning Susie's greeting.

"Thank you, Mrs. McCanton. It's good to be home."

"Please, call me Susie. Mary, Mr. Gibson, thank you for coming out."

"Call me Gib," he said, shaking her hand and then Luke's. "Thanks for inviting us."

Mary smiled at Susie and the women embraced, and just like that, Tessa and Mary were welcomed into the McCanton fold. Tessa smiled at Gib, knowing that whether he wanted to admit it or not, he had a big part in this, just by virtue of loving her mother.

In the coming days, Tessa and Shane spent all their free time together, just getting to know each other again. Tessa found the more time she spent in Shane's house, the more she loved it and the more she loved him for having built it with her in mind. They had yet to take their relationship any farther than just kissing at this point. At first, Tessa wasn't sure she was ready to move on to the next phase and Shane didn't seem to be in a hurry about it, either, but she'd begun to feel something was missing, and it was becoming harder and harder each night to leave him.

Shane had been wonderfully kind and patient with her and she knew he was afraid to take things beyond kissing, afraid of triggering unpleasant memories for her, and while she loved him for it, she knew they needed to try to take things to the next level if they were ever going to have a future together. On Friday she decided to go about planning his seduction.

They didn't have a wedding that weekend, so that afternoon, she told her mother and Gib that she wouldn't be home that night and that it would be better not to expect her for the entire weekend. She could tell they were both happy and alarmed, but out of love for her, neither voiced these opinions.

She decided to go into Shelmerdine's and shop for lingerie for the weekend, something to entice Shane out of his chivalry and into her bed. It was while she was on her way to the lingerie section that she noticed two figurines in the collectibles section. They were about 12 inches tall, of a fierce male warrior angel. In one, he was facing off against a large black dragon and in the other, he stood guard over two children, his wings curled to protect them. She knew the minute she saw them that she had to have them. They were her Shane; her Dragon Slayer and her Protector. His middle name, Gabriel, was after the Archangel Gabriel, after all. She turned one over and blinked at the high price but decided it really didn't matter; she'd already made up her mind.

"Aren't those beautiful?" Mrs. Shelmerdine asked,

coming to stand beside her.

"They really are," Tessa replied, holding the one with the dragon.

"Harold bought those from an artist out of Tyler. We've had them for months. No one ever seems interested enough to buy them, though."

"I want them both," Tessa told her.

Mrs. Shelmerdine smiled. "Really?"

"Yes, ma'am. They are perfect."

"Well, all right, let's get you checked out. I have boxes for them. Are they gifts?"

"This one is. I'm keeping the other one."

"Who is the lucky recipient?"

Tessa smiled. Gotta love small towns.

"Actually, I'm going to give this one to Shane. It fits him, don't you think?"

"It surely does."

They chatted a bit more and then Tessa took her purchases and headed toward Shane's office. Becky greeted her with a warm smile when she walked in.

"Tessa Kelly. I haven't seen you in years! Everyone was talking about how you were back in town and how beautiful you've become. They certainly weren't lying."

Tessa smiled. "Thanks, Becky. How have you been?"

"Oh, can't complain. I get to come to work with six of

the hottest men in town every day," she said with a grin and a wink.

"You are one very lucky girl," Tessa laughed.

Tessa looked up when Shane rounded the corner, her smile brightening when she saw him. He wore his usual work attire of boots, jeans and black henley and her heart accelerated at the sheer masculine sexuality rolling off of him.

"Very lucky indeed," Becky said.

"I thought I heard your voice out here," Shane said, eyes only for Tessa. "What brings you here?"

Tessa raised her shopping bags slightly. "Brought something for you."

"Oh, yeah? Come back to my office, you can show it to me. Hey, Becky, could you fax this over to Sheriff Braswell for me?" he asked, handing Becky the papers that were in his hand.

"Sure thing, Sheriff."

He placed his hand on the small of Tessa's back to lead her down the hall to his office. It was the first time Tessa had been in there since he took over from his dad, and when she stepped in, she was surprised at the changes she saw from Luke McCanton's office to now Shane's. For one, computers covered the credenza behind his desk and one with two monitors sat on his desk. She remembered from when she used to volunteer in the file room that his father had resisted having a computer brought in for as long as he could, and how he would curse at his so loud the whole office could hear him.

"Close the door, please," she told Shane when he stepped inside. One dark brow lifted in surprise but he obediently shut it behind him. Tessa stepped to him and also closed the blinds on the window that let him see out into the squad room.

"Is something wrong?" he asked warily, watching her turn toward him.

"Oh, no, Sheriff, everything is right. I just didn't think you would want an audience when I did this," she said, sliding her arms around his neck and pulling him down for an intense, passionate kiss. After a few moments, he groaned and tried to pull back but she caught his lower lip between her teeth and began to suck on it, not letting him pull away.

"Tess," he groaned when her hands slid down his back to cup his muscular butt.

She smiled up at him while she squeezed her second favorite part of his body.

"Yes?" she asked innocently.

"What are you doing?"

"Saying hello to you."

"You're killing me," he groaned.

Giving him a final kiss and squeeze, she stepped back and lifted the shopping bag to his desk.

"I'll give you a reprieve...for now. I bought something for you. I was in Shelmerdine's and saw these and I immediately thought of you. Let's see, which one is yours...oh, this one," she said, handing him a box. He took it and leaned on the edge of his desk to open it. When he pulled the figure out of the box, she loved the way it looked in his big hands, and the way he studied it, his thumbs tracing over the angel's wings.

"Tess...this is...wow."

"You like it? He makes me think of you, my own personal Dragon Slayer, and you know, since you're named for an angel..."

His head came up. "What?"

"The Archangel, Gabriel. Shane Gabriel. I mean, I know it's a family name, that you're named after him," she said, gesturing toward the picture on his wall of the first McCanton to be named Sheriff of Indian Springs, Gabriel Shane McCanton, "but Gabriel is also the most powerful of all the Angels in Heaven. The Protector of women and children. And anyway, I saw that and I knew you had to have it. I got this one for me," she said, unwrapping the one of the Guardian Angel.

He looked at it then looked into her eyes and her breath caught at the look in his, just before he leaned down and placed a tender, lingering kiss on her lips.

"Thank you," he whispered against her lips.

She smiled softly at him. "Do you like it?"

"I do, yes. It's perfect." He stepped away from her and placed it on the shelves over his credenza, so that it would be seen right when someone walked into his office.

She couldn't stop smiling as he walked back to her and folded her into his embrace. They stood for several moments, just holding on to each other, taking comfort from each other's presence. Then, feeling that it needed to be said now, when they were in the midst of a moment of sweetness, Tessa tilted her head back and looked him square in the eye.

"I love you, Shane McCanton."

His hold tightened on her and he captured her mouth in a kiss that left her clinging to him.

"I love you, too, Tessa Kelly."

She smiled. "Good. Now, give me your house key. I'm going to go start dinner. When will you be home?" He blinked at her rapid change of subject, but dug his keys out of his pocket.

"I've got a conference call in about thirty minutes that will probably last an hour or so. Should be able to leave after that."

"Perfect. Call or text when you are leaving."

He cupped her face in his hands and kissed her until she was once again clinging to him for support, then pulled back.

"Thanks for coming by and for the statue."

She winked as she reached for the door. "Anytime, Sheriff."

Shane watched her leave and felt his heart swell in his chest when she winked at him over her shoulder before closing the door. Was he really being given this second chance with her? He felt like the luckiest man in the world in that moment...and it scared him.

"Sheriff," Becky said, leaning into his office. "You have a call on line 2. He says it's urgent."

"OK, thanks, Becky," he crossed to his desk and absently picked up the receiver. "McCanton."

"Shane," he heard Bruce's voice and he was immediately alerted by the tone of his voice that something was wrong.

"Bruce...what is it?"

"The Heltons escaped."

"Both of them?" he asked incredulously.

"Afraid so. And they know who Tessa is, since they are working as their own attorneys...you need to be prepared."

"Son of a bitch! How could this happen?"

"They underestimated the brothers' appeal. They charmed and bribed their way out. I've called the state guys in your area but you need to be ready."

"Yeah, I hear ya. Damn it."

"I'll keep you updated on any information I find."

"Thanks."

He slammed the receiver down and stormed out of his office to call his guys together and brief them on the situation. Then he picked up the phone and called his dad and asked him to be on alert and to call any of his friends to do the same. He then alerted the Sheriffs and Police Chiefs of neighboring towns and counties. If the Heltons were in the area, he wanted as many eyes as possible looking for them.

"Becky, I'm heading out. Forward any urgent calls regarding the Heltons to my cell, OK?"

"Will do."

He went out to his truck and headed out of town to his house, trying to tamp down the feelings of anxiety over this most recent development. Tessa was on her way to becoming some semblance of her old self; she didn't need the threat of the Heltons hanging over her head.

A smile touched his lips seeing her car in his drive as he pulled in to the garage. When he opened the door, his smile widened when he smelled the delicious aroma coming from the kitchen.

"Hey, Tess!" he called, dropping his keys on the counter. He stepped out of the kitchen and then froze when he saw a trail of rose petals on the floor and noticed candles lit on every surface along the path of roses, leading to his bedroom. His heart immediately began beating faster as he slowly followed the path. God, was he ready for this? Tessa had been through so much at the hands of those monsters, was she really ready for this?

He opened the door to his room and heard soft music playing, and what looked like thousands of candles flickering in his room and in the open door of the bathroom. He stepped in and found Tessa neck deep in the tub, two flutes of champagne sitting on the side of the tub and an open bottle chilling in a bucket of ice next to the tub. Her golden hair was piled on top of her head, a few tendrils clinging to her face and neck in the steam.

"Welcome home, Sheriff," she said low, her eyes locked on his.

"Hey," he said coming to sit on the side of the tub. "What's all this?"

"This, is me, welcoming you home. Champagne?" she asked, handing him a flute.

"Tess, this is…"

"Shh," she said, slowly standing. He kept his eyes locked on hers, doing his best not to admire the way her wet body glistened in the candle light. She smiled and stepped out of the tub, accepting the towel he held out for her. "Come on, Shane, don't play shy now."

"Tess…are you sure about this?"

"I love you. We've wasted enough time being apart. I

want your hands on me."

He kissed her but held back. "I don't want to hurt you, Tess...and I couldn't stand it if my touch caused you even a moment's fear."

"And we'll never know unless we try. Touch me, Shane. Make me not afraid," she whispered against his lips, fisting her hands in his shirt to bring him closer.

"Baby," he breathed, still trying to hang on to his composure. "Are you absolutely sure?"

She let the towel fall at their feet and used both hands to cup his face.

"You are the only man I've ever chosen to give myself to. You, Shane Gabriel McCanton, are the only man I ever wanted to touch me. I know who I am standing here with. I know who I am inviting to touch me...and it's you. It's only you, now and always. We'd be married now if not for the Heltons. They kept me from you long enough."

"Fine...but you are going to drive this. You take me at your pace."

She yanked his shirt out of his jeans and whipped it over his head, then jumped up and wrapped her legs around his waist.

"Take me to bed, Shane," she said, kissing him. He walked with her into the bedroom and then let her slither down his body to her feet. She pulled on his belt and opened his jeans, pushing them and his underwear down, then pushed him to sit on the bed, straddling him.

"Look at me, Tessa. Who am I?"

"Shane. My Shane," she replied, smoothing her hands over his face as she kissed him. She held his gaze as she slowly settled over him, taking him in. A tear slid down her cheek and he quickly kissed it away.

"There you are," he breathed, "My Tessa...are you OK?"

She licked at his lips as she began to move against him. "I'm better than OK," she answered, pushing on his shoulders to have him lie down.

Shane looked up at her riding him and knew he'd never seen a more beautiful sight ever in his life, and he knew in that moment, he would do whatever it took to keep her safe.

Chapter Twenty-One

Tessa had a moment of panic in the night when she woke and found a heavy arm around her waist, pinning her to the bed, but then she realized it was just Shane and she was safe in his bed, wrapped in his arms. Her Shane. Her rock. She'd almost lost him forever out of fear and wanting to spare him from dealing with all the fallout from her experience. She turned in his arms and placed her hand on his cheek, brushing her thumb over his lower lip.

"Hey," he murmured sleepily, smiling softly at her.

"Hey," she echoed.

"You OK?"

She snuggled closer to him, nuzzling his neck. "I'm good. I panicked a bit when I woke up with your arm over me, but it didn't take me long to remember where I was. I've missed you so much. I'd forgotten what it was like to wake up in bed with you."

He smoothed his hand over her hair. "We haven't really had a chance to just be a couple. To lay in bed like this and not be rushed back to the office, knowing our days were numbered."

"No, we haven't. This is nice...and such a relief to know that I can be with you without being afraid."

"We'll work through whatever we can of your fears as they come up."

She kissed the underside of his jaw and worked her way around to his lips. "I don't know that I will have any fears, because it's you. You are my first and my only choice. My rock."

"You seriously never slept with anyone else when you were in the Army?"

She frowned at him. "We've had this conversation before."

"I know...you're just so damn beautiful, I always wonder why you waited around for me."

She blinked at him. "Because I've loved you since the day you walked into that kindergarten classroom when we were five. Because you have been my whole world ever since you finally lifted your ban on talking to me our senior year."

He gathered her closer and kissed her, then laying on their sides, facing each other, he took her with all the love and tenderness he felt for her. Tessa wrapped her arms around him and held on tight as he took them to the edge and trusted him to take care of her on the way back down.

"You good, babe?" he asked, forehead pressed to hers.

"Mm," she purred, snuggling closer to him, "I'm better than good."

"I love you so much, Tess...this last year without you...it's been a walking nightmare. Knowing you were out there hurting and wanting to be with you to help you. It was hell. Pure hell."

She combed her fingers through his hair. "For me, too. Wanting you with me. Wanting to feel your arms around me but afraid of how I'd react. When Mama told me that you'd begun dating again, I just...I had to come back. I had to see if there was anything left. I haven't felt safe again until I looked up across Gib's truck and saw you standing outside the gazebo."

He kissed her fingertips. "I haven't felt complete again until I looked up in Miss Nettie's and saw you...Tess, If you walk away from me again..."

She sat up and slid on top of him, pinning him beneath her. "I'm not ever leaving, Shane. Not ever again, do you hear me? You're stuck with me."

"Then marry me. Tomorrow...later today, whatever the hell time it is...just marry me."

She got up from him and turned the light on, standing nude before him.

"Look at me, Shane. Look at the scars on my body. If we marry, you may be giving up your chance to have a child of your own."

He stood and covered the scar on her abdomen with one hand and cupped the back of her neck with the other.

"And we've had this conversation before, too. Do you think I care about that? We can adopt. We can try in vitro. A surrogate. Or just be happy with the two of us. I don't care. Whatever will make you happy, babe, that's all I care about."

"Shane..."

"Don't try to read my mind for me. That's what got us in this mess in the first place...marry me, Tess. Say yes."

She closed her eyes and clutched his biceps.

"Yes," she whispered.

"What was that?" he prodded. "I don't think I heard you."

Her eyes flew open and she melted into him. "Yes, Shane. I will marry you."

"Tomorrow?"

She laughed. "Tomorrow. Later today. A soon as we can get it set up."

He picked her up and twirled her around, then sat her on her feet and kissed her breathless.

"We just have one more issue to deal with, baby," he said reluctantly.

She nodded. "The trial."

"Make that two...look, right after you left my office, Bruce called...Nathaniel and Paul escaped."

She stiffened and stepped away from him. "And you're just telling me this now?"

"I'd planned on telling you when I got home, but..."

"What's been done?" she asked, reaching for the shirt he'd discarded and pulling it on.

He walked into his closet and pulled on a pair of loose fitting warm-ups. When he came out, he followed her into the kitchen. She cut them both a piece of chocolate cream pie she'd made earlier and then sat at the table while he briefed her on all he knew.

She took a deep breath when he was done, and then another. Shane took her hand in his and lifted it to his lips, kissing her knuckles.

"I'll keep you safe, Tessa. They won't get near you."

"Thank you, but I can take care of myself, Shane."

"I know you can."

She nodded, then began clearing their dishes.

"We need to get some sleep. We have a big day tomorrow."

Shane stood and moved in front of her, placing his hands on her shoulders to stop her. She looked up into his eyes and then smiled when he scooped her up into his arms and carried her to his...their room.

"What are you doing?" she asked on a small laugh.

"Bringing you back to bed. You're right. We do have a big day tomorrow. And before we go to bed tomorrow, you'll be mine for good."

"As you will be mine," she echoed. "I love you."

The next morning, Shane reluctantly let Tessa go back to her mother's while he went in to the office. He checked in with Bruce for an update and checked all his bulletins, then headed out to his parents' house. He wanted to let them know his plans with Tessa, and to try to assure his mother that he was doing the right thing since he knew she would be upset that she wouldn't get to plan a big wedding.

When he turned onto the road leading toward his family's ranch, he saw a car stranded on the side of the road with its hood up. The road was strictly residential with no outlet so the only vehicles that should be on there were those of people who lived there and their visitors. He slowed to a stop behind them and got out, but made sure he had the clip off his holster.

"Hi, there," he announced, walking up to the car, "I'm Sheriff McCanton, can I help you?"

The hood lowered and Shane found himself face-to-face with Paul Helton. He had his gun out and shot at Paul in the same instant he was hit from behind.

"Mama, Gib?" Tessa called, walking into their house.

"In the kitchen," she heard her mother call.

She went in and immediately went to her mother, embracing her on a laugh.

"Tessa? What is it?"

"Shane and I are going to get married. Today."

"What?"

"As soon as he can get the paperwork cleared."

"That's wonderful news, honey," Mary cried, kissing her cheek.

"Thanks. I wanted -" She stopped when Gib walked in, his face grim.

"Glen?" Mary asked, "What is it?"

"I just got off the phone with Becky at the station. Tessa, Shane's gone missing."

"What do you mean, he's gone missing?"

"He left the station on his way to his parents' house. He never arrived there and Becky reports he hasn't checked in with her. They've been trying his radio and his cell and have gotten no answer. His dad headed out to look for him and found shell casings and a some blood on the side of the road...it's a match for Shane's and one other, and some of the casings came from his gun."

"Oh God!" Mary gasped.

Tessa locked eyes with Gib, taking comfort from his steady strength. She knew in her heart that Nathaniel and Paul had him, and she knew that they wouldn't kill him until they had her.

"I need to be at the station," she said, all business now. "Gib, I need to be involved."

He nodded, reaching out a hand to stroke her hair. "I know you do. Let's go make it happen."

Tessa took a deep breath and settled into the passenger seat of Gib's truck. Part of her wanted to panic but she ruthlessly pushed that part down and focused on her training. It helped having Gib with her, pulling from their past experiences together. She knew she had to hold it together, to keep her fears at bay.

"Hey," Gib said, squeezing her hand, "hang in there. Shane's good. He'll be OK."

She took a deep breath. "I know...if they wanted him dead, they would have already found his body. This is about drawing me out."

"I agree, but Tessa, you can't let this be personal. I know it is...but..."

She nodded. "I know what you're saying, Gib, I do....but there is no way that this isn't personal. I'm going to find them, and I'm going to finish this once and for all."

"Tessa..." he began but stopped when her phone rang.

She looked down and saw the caller ID. "It's Shane," she said flatly, raising it to her ear. She knew what she would hear before she even spoke.

"Hello, sweetheart," Nathaniel's voice poured through the phone. "Have you missed me?"

"Where are you?" she asked, knowing that her tone

had alerted Gib, who immediately pulled over to the side of the road.

"Let's not concern ourselves with that just now."

"Is he alive?"

"For now, but he killed Paul, he'll have to pay for that."

"I want to talk to him."

"You are in no position to make demands, Madelyn...or should I say, Tessa."

"If you want me to play your little game, you will put Shane on the phone right now, Nathaniel. I won't entertain any demands from you unless I hear his voice."

She heard a shuffle of the phone and a muffled groan that she recognized as Shane's voice. Her heart accelerated and she squeezed Gib's hand, her only outward sign of emotion.

"Tess," she heard him say weakly.

She closed her eyes and prayed for strength. "How badly are you hurt?" she asked steadily.

"Shot...shoulder, side, leg. Lost a lot of blood."

"Can you describe where you are?"

"Inner Space," he replied before Nathaniel took the phone away.

"All right, you've heard from him. I'm sure he just told you where we are. You come here, alone, and we finish this."

The call ended and she sat the phone down on the

console between them.

"You know where he is?"

She nodded. "He said Inner Space. That's what we called the caves around the lake. But there are dozens of them, and he's bleeding out."

"Tell me where to go," he said, putting the truck in gear. "Call it in to his office."

Tessa gave Gib directions and called in to Becky to let them mobilize backup to help search the caves. There weren't too many caves, but enough that she and Gib couldn't cover them all on their own. Gib pulled over when they got close to the turn off to get to the caves and they got out to arm up. Tessa's eyes widened when he lifted the panel over the cargo hold and she saw the arsenal he had back there, as well as Kevlar vests, one his size and one her size.

"You preparing for a war, Gib?" she asked when he handed the vest to her.

"I stocked up when Bruce called me about their escape," he explained.

"Smart man...look, there are a dozen or so caves, and they all go pretty far back under the cliffs. Shane is losing blood fast, we are going to have to split up."

"Agreed, but you listen to me...you find him, you let out the loudest whistle you can, and I'll do the same."

She nodded while strapping weapons on.   Armed,

they got back into the truck and drove the last two miles, finding Shane's truck and the Heltons abandoned sedan. Both vehicles were bloodied on the inside.

"They have to be in one of the first two caves," Gib surmised, "they can't have transported two injured men very far."

"There's a blood trail...Gib, you'll have to hold back. He told me to come alone. He's got to know I won't, but he can't see you."

"You go in, I've got your back."

Tessa took a deep breath and followed the bloody trail to the mouth of the second cave, gun drawn and ready. With each step she took, she felt her anxiety begin to lesson and an eerie calm settle over her. She was on her way to her destiny, pass or fail, whatever happened in the next few moments would change her world forever.

"Nathaniel? I'm here," she called, slowly rounding the corner toward the flickering light of a fire. She saw Nathaniel leaning against the far wall, Shane held in front of him, gun to his temple, and Paul's still body lying next to the fire. The entire right side of Shane's body was covered in blood, and what she could see of his face didn't look good. His color was gone, his skin almost grey. He was on his feet but she suspected he wouldn't last much longer.

"That's far enough," Nathaniel warned her, yanking Shane's head back by the hair. "Put that gun down or I'll blow his head off. Don't think I'm going to fall for that shoot the hostage ploy. He's lost so much blood, you give him another injury and he'll be dead before his body hits the ground." Tessa could see that Nathaniel was right but there was no way she was giving up her weapon. "I'll do it, you know I will. Put the gun down."

"I can't do that, Nathaniel," she told him.

"You better. He's not going to make it much longer. Only way to help him is to do what I say."

"Not going to happen. I put the gun down you'll just kill us both anyway. What do you want, Nathaniel? You've already lost your brother. What do you hope to gain from all this?"

"Your suffering. My end game is all about taking everything you hold dear from you. You came into my world and deceived me. You made me love you and then you took everything away from me. Now, I'm going to take everything from you. Starting with him."

"You loved me? Really, Nathaniel? You loved me so much, you beat and raped me, you allowed Paul to use a whip on me and rape me and then you let four of your Elders rape me. That's how you show your love?"

"Discipline is necessary to ensure obedience."

"You're sick, and you've wasted enough of my time. Surrender now. Shane's deputies will be here soon. It's over for you, so unless you want to join your brother, let

Shane go and have your day in court."

"I'll have my day now!" he roared.

She watched the next few moments unfold as if in slow-motion. With what had to have been a rush of adrenaline, Shane reared back and gave Nathaniel a reverse head butt, slamming the back of his head into Nathaniel's face. Nathaniel's gun fired, Shane fell to the ground, and both Tessa and Gib, who had been hiding behind her in the shadows, unloaded their guns into Nathaniel.

Tessa rushed to Shane as Gib charged Nathaniel's shredded body, kicking the gun well away. She slid to her knees and gathered Shane to her, ripping his shirt open to try to get her hands on his injuries.

"Shane! Come on, baby, stay with me! Gib! Oh God, Gib, I can't feel a pulse!"

Gib rushed to her, throwing his Kevlar off and then ripping his shirt off to press to the worst of the wounds.

"Come on, McCanton, stay with us," Gib growled. In the distance they heard sirens approaching but they knew time was running out.

"God, please," Tessa cried, caressing Shane's waxy face. "Please don't take him. Shane, please!" she sobbed.

"Tess," Gib said, low, placing his hand on her shoulder. "Tessa...he's gone."

"NO!!!!!" she screamed, her arms tightening on

Shane's shoulders, cradling him to her and rocking him with her sobs. "NO!! Shane!!! Come back! I can't do this without you! Shane!"

When the other deputies and the medics came in, Gib had to force her to release Shane's body so they could take care of him. He accepted a solar blanket from one of the deputies and wrapped her up and lifted her into his arms, carrying her out to his truck. He sat with her in his lap, rocking her as he would a child, his heart breaking for the girl he'd considered his daughter for the last ten years.

"We were going to get married today," she whispered.

"I know. I'm so sorry," Gib soothed.

She looked up when two carts bearing two body bags came out of the cave and her stomach clenched that she didn't know which was Shane. As she pushed out of Gib's lap to approach the gurneys, however, a third came out of the cave, with medics huddled around and an IV bag being held high. She took off at a sprint when she saw Shane's dark head.

"Shane?"

"We've got a pulse but it's extremely weak," a medic told her.

"Let me ride with him," she demanded and none dared deny her.

She climbed up in the ambulance with him and took his hand in hers, then leaned down to speak into his ear.

"I love you so much. My Dragon Slayer. You hang on and you fight, do you hear me, Shane McCanton? You fight and you come back to me."

His hand tightened on hers, and then his grip relaxed and lost its hold on her altogether. She didn't have to be told that time. She knew he was gone.

Epilogue

"Gib!!!! Mama!!!!" Tessa cried, pain like she'd never known ripping through her.

Lights came on and she heard two sets of footsteps on the stairs.

"Tessa? Honey?" Mary called, flipping on the light and rushing to her bedside.

"Oh, whoa," Gib said, sliding to a halt just inside her bedroom door. "I'll bring the truck around."

"Something's wrong, Mama," Tessa groaned.

"You're going to be fine. The doctor said the pain would be more intense for you because of your injuries."

"I need Shane," Tessa sobbed.

Mary rubbed the small of her daughter's back. "I know, baby."

"I can't do this alone, Mama. Shane should be here," Tessa cried, clutching her stomach.

"You can do this, baby, you can do anything."

"Truck's out front. Ready to go?" Gib said, coming to help her out of bed.

As soon as she stood, a gush of fluid covered her.

"It's coming fast," Mary said, looking anxiously up at her husband.

"We'll make it," Gib assured her.

"Mama, help me change, I can't...whoa!"

"Honey, you don't have time to change, we've got to go."

Tessa doubled over again when a strong contraction hit and found herself scooped up in Gib's arms. In spite of all the doctors had initially said, a month after the shooting, she learned she was pregnant with Shane's baby and even though there had been a few scary moments around the six month mark, she'd been able to carry almost the full 9 months. It was a bittersweet moment now, rushing to the hospital with her mother and stepfather.

She'd barely made it to the ER before the need to push was overwhelming. She kept pining for Shane, missing him more in that moment than ever before. He needed to be there. Their son was going to be born at any moment, he needed...

"Hey, hey, you didn't think you were going to do this without me, did you?" she heard, and then she saw a flash of blue eyes and Shane was there, just as an intense contraction hit and the doctor told her to push.

"How...?" she asked even as she began to push.

"Ivy sent Reese's friend with a helicopter after me when your mom said that you'd been having contractions before you went to bed. Push, baby, that's it."

She pushed as hard as she could and when she felt

her son slip free, she collapsed back against the bed, her mind drifting to that moment in the ambulance nine months ago when she thought she'd lost Shane forever...

"Shane?" she cried, leaning down to his ear. "Come back to me now. You've got to fight. You've never failed at anything ever in your life, you can't fail me now. Come back!"

The medics shocked his heart twice and then he was back. He took a deep, gasping breath and Tessa thought she'd never heard a more beautiful sound in all her life. His recovery hadn't been easy. He'd lost a lot of blood and his femur had been shattered by a bullet, but after they got his heart started that second time, he'd never had another sketchy moment.

He'd been in Austin for the last few days, testifying in the trial of the remaining Elders from the Naturalists. Tessa, being so close to her due date, had been allowed to testify via satellite, but Shane had insisted on being there in person.

"Here's our son, Tess," Shane's voice broke through to her, placing their crying, dark haired son in her arms for the first time.

She smiled, all pain forgotten. As soon as she brought him close, the baby stopped crying and looked directly into her face.

"Hello, Gabriel," she cooed at him, "I've been waiting my whole life to meet you."

Shane kissed her brow and looked down at his wife and son. Gabriel Shane McCanton, the son Tessa thought she would never be able to give him. He knew in that moment, he was the luckiest man on Earth.

Tessa kissed her son's tiny fist, then looked up and met Shane's gaze. All those years ago, when she barely even knew him and was just a baby herself, she'd had a premonition that one day she would be right here, her son in her arms, Shane by her side. She may have taken the long way home, but in that moment, she knew that Home was exactly where she was.

Six years later…

Gabriel McCanton did not want to be here. He could think of a million things he'd rather be doing than following his parents into the school. He wanted to stay home and play and even help watch over his baby sister, Jessica. Going to school was messing everything up.

His mom, carrying Jessica, walked into his classroom but Gabe stopped just outside the door. His dad noticed and squatted down so that they were eye to eye.

"Gabe? What's wrong?"

Gabe shrugged, looking down at his feet.

"Don't wanna go in."

"Scared?" his dad asked.

Gabe's head shot up and he met his dad's gaze.

"I'm not scared. I just don't see what's so great about going to school."

His dad nodded. "Kind of gets in the way of what you really want to do, doesn't it?" Gabe nodded. "But, then again, if you want to be Sheriff someday, you have to go to school so you can learn the things you need to know that will help you. Understand?"

Gabe sighed dramatically. "I guess so. But, Kindergarten is stupid. I don't want to color and do all that dumb stuff."

"It's not all about coloring. You'll learn all kinds of new stuff and all of it will help you on your way to becoming Sheriff one day."

"If you say so."

His dad stood up and ruffled his hair. "Trust me, kid. When have I ever steered you wrong?"

Gabe nodded and reluctantly followed his dad into the room. His mom introduced him to his teacher and showed him where he was supposed to sit…right next to his friend, Lily Reese.

"Hey, Gabe!" Lily greeted him, her blonde hair pulled back into a ponytail. She was entirely too happy about being there, Gabe thought.

"Hey," he mumbled, settling into his seat.

"I had the weirdest dream last night," Lily told him. "I dreamt that we were big…and that we got married!"

Behind the table, Shane and Tessa exchanged knowing glances when they overheard Lily's statement to their son. Humor danced through their eyes and each could tell the other was remembering a similar statement from another blonde haired girl to a reluctant McCanton boy. Shane reached for Tessa's hand and lifted her knuckles to his lips. Life had come full circle. He could only hope that his son would be as fortunate as he had been with his own blonde haired girl.

The End

Made in the USA
San Bernardino, CA
01 April 2014